ELEGY

TARA HUDSON lives in Oklahoma with her husband, son, and a menagerie of ill-behaved pets. After receiving her law degree, she began writing to entertain her girlfriends. They read her story about a ghost girl who awakes in a cemetery and wanted to know more. This short piece inspired the Hereafter Trilogy, which culminates in *Elegy*.

Visit her at www.tarahudson.com

ELEGY

✦TARA HUDSON✦

HarperCollins*Publishers*

First published in the USA by
HarperCollins*Publishers* Inc. in 2013
First published in paperback in Great Britain by
HarperCollins *Children's Books* in 2013
HarperCollins *Children's Books* is a division of HarperCollins*Publishers* Ltd,
77-85 Fulham Palace Road,
Hammersmith,
London, W6 8JB.

www.harpercollins.co.uk

ELEGY

ISBN 978-0-00-743729-0

Printed and bound in Great Britain by Clays Ltd, St Ives plc.
Typography by Erin Fitzsimmons

1

MIX
Paper from
responsible sources
FSC® C007454

FSC™ is a non-profit international organisation established to promote
the responsible management of the world's forests. Products carrying the
FSC label are independently certified to assure consumers that they come
from forests that are managed to meet the social, economic and
ecological needs of present and future generations,
and other controlled sources.

Find out more about HarperCollins and the environment at
www.harpercollins.co.uk/green

To Melissa Peters Allgood,
who is both beautiful and good.
And to make sure that 2013
will be so much better than 2012.

ELEGY

PROLOGUE

O nce again, I'm staring at my own death.

My heart is pounding. My breath is coming in short spurts. And I can't stop digging my fingernails into the heels of my palms, just so I can feel the little crescents of pain they create. Of course, those tiny bursts of pain can hardly match the throbbing in my dislocated shoulder. Not that any of that will matter in a few minutes, when I'm truly dead.

Dead. I can hardly comprehend the word, since it's held so many definitions for me. After all, I've done this before: readied myself for the final moment. Sometimes it's happened, and sometimes I've defied it. But tonight, I won't defy it. Tonight, I'll die.

Tonight, I want to.

For the first time in my strange existence, I want death. I need *it, in order to do what has to be done.*

Not to say that I'm not afraid; I am. Terrified, actually. But that doesn't stop me from staring down the barrel of the gun pointed directly at me. I can't figure out why it hasn't fired yet. Then I notice how badly the gun is shaking. If it fires right now, I doubt the bullet will even graze my shoulder. Which obviously won't be good enough.

Slowly, my eyes move from the gun to the person holding it.

"You okay?" I ask her.

She doesn't respond for a moment. Then, with a bitter laugh, she asks, "Are you kidding me, Amelia?"

I just smile.

Behind her, I can hear him shouting. Screaming, actually. I know that his friends are holding him back, gripping tightly to his arms as he struggles to break free and stop us. But my eyelids are so heavy, my tears so thick, I can't actually see him.

It's probably a good thing I won't be able to look into his eyes when it happens.

I turn my attention back to the gun. Not to the person holding it, this time—just to the gun itself.

"Do it," I say, my voice quiet but urgent. "Please."

She doesn't reply, but I know she's heard me. With a weird instinct, she lowers the gun until it points directly at my heart. For a split second, I think she's chickened out.

Then I see a tiny spark of light, and my entire world rips into pain.

Chapter
ONE

D eath, demons, deranged Seers—nothing I'd previously experienced terrified me as much as what I was about to do.

If I can even gather up enough courage to actually do *this.*

Steeling myself, I balled my right hand into a fist and lifted it. For a few seconds, I kept my fist suspended, letting it hover less than an inch away from my target. Then, with a frustrated groan, I dropped my hand back to my side.

My task was easy enough: all I had to do was make a

fist, rap my knuckles against wood, and repeat if necessary. So why couldn't I do it?

Why couldn't I bring myself to do something as simple as knock on an ordinary front door?

I started pacing again, my boot heels thunking across the floorboards of the porch. The sound of them spooked me a little. Even after spending a few months as one of the Risen—actually, the *only* Risen ghost left in this world, as far as I could tell—I still hadn't quite made peace with the echo of my own footsteps.

I cast a glance over my shoulder, toward the road. About fifty feet back along the curb, Joshua Mayhew leaned against the hood of his truck. He caught me staring and gave me an encouraging smile. I tried to return it, without much success.

This little project wasn't originally his idea—it was mine. But once Joshua and I had discussed the possibility, he'd latched on to it until I finally ended up here, pacing like a crazy person.

As usual, Joshua thought this would end well. But I didn't. I just couldn't imagine a scenario in which the woman on whose door I was about to knock would react positively when she saw me.

And her reaction *did* matter, more than almost anything in the world. Still, the reason I stood on this porch today—the real reason—wasn't because she needed to see me; it was because I needed to see *her*.

I flashed Joshua another tight smile and turned back to the door. I could do this. I could *do* this. I lifted my hand again, ready to knock for real this time.

But I never got the chance.

Before my knuckles could make contact with the door, it swung inward. Open.

The first time Joshua and I visited this place, the door had swung open on its own. But this time, someone had *pulled* it open. Probably because she'd finally decided to do something about the person thunking around uninvited on her front porch.

Her hand held the edge of the door, fingers gripped against the splintery, paint-peeling wood. On her ring finger, I could just make out the glint of a simple wedding band.

She still wears it.

Before I had time to process that thought, before I even had time to see her face, I felt a familiar current pass over my skin. It happened quickly—started and stopped in less than two seconds—but I immediately knew what it meant. I'd made myself invisible, intentionally vanished from the view of anyone living, including Joshua. Including the woman standing in front of me.

It was a cowardly move on my part: I'd finally worked up the nerve to knock, and now she couldn't even see me.

She frowned, squinting into the shadows of the porch and out at the daylight beyond it. Seeing the lines on her face, the streak of gray at her temples, I sucked in a tight breath and released it in one foolish word.

"Mom?"

The woman at the door immediately jerked back like she'd been slapped. Her eyes widened, but she continued to stare out at the porch without actually seeing me.

She'd heard me, though.

For a while, we both stood motionless: my mother with her fingers clawed into the door; me with my fake heartbeat hammering in my chest. Although I knew it wasn't possible, it seemed as though her brown eyes were boring into mine. Begging me to tell her why she'd just heard the voice of her long-dead daughter.

I gulped once, as quietly as possible, and leaned forward a fraction of an inch. As if in response, my mother leaned backward.

I thought she was trying to escape something that she couldn't—didn't want to—understand. But instead, another face appeared next to hers in the doorway, probably summoned by my mother's strange silence.

This new face belonged to a woman, much younger than my mother but somewhat older than me. When she peered out the doorway, the corners of her blue eyes wrinkled faintly. I froze in place, but her gaze moved smoothly across the porch, not even hesitating on the spot where I stood. As though I weren't even there.

The woman took a step forward—maybe for a closer look at the empty porch—and I got a better view of her. She was striking, with her high cheekbones and impeccable platinum-blond ponytail. Pretty and polished, like a piece of fine glass.

I knew I'd never seen her—not as a visitor to the Mayhews' house or as a teacher at Wilburton High; not even as someone I'd passed on the streets of New Orleans this past winter. But something about this woman was strangely familiar.

Before I had a chance to place her, she straightened the hem of her tailored blazer and turned to my mother with a worried frown.

"Liz? Everything okay?"

My mother's frown deepened, just for a moment, before she met her guest's gaze. "Everything's fine," she said, giving the blond woman a faint smile. "I thought I heard something out here. I guess not."

The blonde returned the smile, but it wavered on the edges, as though she thought her host might be a little unstable. It wasn't a mean look, necessarily—just a cautious one.

"The coffee, Liz," she prompted gently. "It's getting cold."

My mother nodded, looking embarrassed. "Of course. Sorry."

She hadn't removed her hand from the edge of the door, and now she began to push it shut as she and the blond woman stepped back into the house. In the seconds before the door closed completely, I caught a final glimpse of the younger woman's face. For just a second her blue eyes seemed to lock on to mine, and I felt that strange, dizzying sense of familiarity again.

The feeling only intensified when I heard the last bit of my mother's voice before the door shut.

"Sorry again, Serena. Must have been the wind."

Chapter
TWO

"Serena Taylor, the girl who *murdered* you, was having coffee with your mom?"

Joshua sounded like he still didn't quite believe me.

I lifted one shoulder and let it drop carelessly. That was the biggest shrug I could make, given the circumstances.

"That's not exactly accurate," I mumbled. "At least, not completely accurate."

In my peripheral vision, I saw Joshua raise one skeptical eyebrow. Instead of elaborating, I flopped backward into the pile of lush pillows behind us.

At the moment, Joshua and I were in his parents' gazebo. His mother, Rebecca, had recently redesigned its interior, transforming the space into something hidden and exotic. The thick curtains that enclosed its outer walls were now masked on the inside by yards of white gauzy drapes. Glittering, star-shaped lanterns hung from the ceiling, and flowering plants filled every inch not occupied by the enormous, pillow-covered daybed.

But despite the gorgeous setting, Joshua and I were tensed up on the daybed, not touching.

Not that that's *anything new*, I reminded myself. Not since New Orleans, where I lost my ability to touch the living.

After what felt like an appropriately weighted pause, I propped myself up on my elbows and turned to Joshua.

"To be fair to Serena," I said, "she didn't mean to murder me. She was under the influence of Eli and his wraiths."

When Joshua started to roll his eyes, I added, "Just like your friends when they tried to kill your little sister."

A dark look passed over his face, and I could read it perfectly. Joshua was remembering the night his sister, Jillian, nearly died, at the hands of his own friends and a malevolent ghost named Eli Rowland. Joshua shook his head, and the dark look shook away too, replaced by the thoughtful frown he'd been wearing since we left my mother's house.

"I don't know, Amelia. After what happened to you—after the part Serena played in your death—why would she still hang around your mom? I mean, shouldn't she be . . . ?"

As he searched for the right phrase, I snorted softly. "What you mean, Joshua, is shouldn't she be curled up in a corner somewhere, racked with guilt for what happened over a decade ago? Keeping in mind that she probably doesn't even *remember* what happened?"

He gave me that half grin, the one that made me ache to touch his lips, just once. "Exactly." He shifted into the pillows next to me, keeping between us the few inches that had become a permanent fixture since New Orleans—inches that represented what we could no longer do: touch.

"Besides," Joshua went on, "how do you even know this woman is *your* Serena Taylor? Just because she's blond and named Serena—"

"And about the right age for someone born in the eighties," I interrupted. "And she was having coffee with *my* mom, in one of the smallest towns on earth."

Joshua considered this, frowning again. But when his eyebrows unknitted and his mouth softened, I could see I'd won the argument.

"Fair enough," he conceded. "Maybe she's *the* Serena Taylor. But . . . what does that even mean for us?"

"Nothing, actually."

I sighed, stretching my legs across the daybed until my feet swung over the edge. "At least, it means nothing right now. It's not like I'm going to call Serena and invite her to have coffee with *me* next. And anyway . . . I think we should scrap the whole Mom idea. For the time being."

When Joshua began to protest, I held up my hand, almost but not quite touching his lips.

"Don't even start," I warned. "If I try to meet my mom again—and that's a big if—then it will be on my terms. Surprising her by showing up unexpectedly on her front porch just isn't going to work for me."

After a long pause, most of which Joshua spent glancing between my fingertips and my mouth, he nodded.

"If that's what you want, Amelia. I promise I won't push the issue again."

I widened my eyes in mock surprise. "Joshua Mayhew *not* insisting that I do something risky yet supposedly rewarding? What is this world coming to?"

"Hey, I'm a guy who proudly learns his lesson. You know, after about a million screw-ups." He laughed, and then leaned forward with a suddenly wicked grin. "Besides, that's my sister's job now."

I shrieked, jerking fully upright on the bed. "Oh, holy crap, I completely forgot. That thing is tonight, isn't it?"

Joshua laughed again, but this time he sounded sinister, like the villain from a black-and-white movie.

"You're not afraid, are you?" he asked in his best Bela Lugosi voice.

"Wouldn't you be?"

"Of a roomful of girls watching chick flicks while they paint each other's nails and gossip?"

I chuckled and rolled my eyes. "You have a seriously skewed view of girly sleepovers. You know that, right?"

His smile softened as he sat up beside me. "Probably. But it doesn't matter—I prefer *our* version of the sleepover anyway."

He leaned in, erasing the inches between us until we were nearly touching. Sitting this close, I could feel the warmth rising from his skin. And, of course, I felt the blush rising on my own cheeks.

"Me, too," I whispered, trying to keep my cool although I suddenly felt like I might ignite. Funny how he never stopped having this effect on me.

But even with the heat flooding me, I had a fleeting moment when I missed our *old* sleepovers. The kind where I spent every night in his bed, placing my hand on him whenever I wanted, kissing him whenever I felt the urge. But things were so different for me as a Risen ghost. So different for us.

In this new version of our relationship, I pretended to be Jillian's "old" friend and Joshua's "new" girlfriend—an ironic inversion of reality. For the benefit of his parents, I also pretended to leave his house every night. Later, I returned in my invisible state to curl up beside Joshua in bed, as close as I could without actually touching him. Because now, I could feel the wrinkles in the sheets beneath us but not the texture of Joshua's skin.

Risen ghosts regained the senses that death had taken from them. Taste, smell, even touch. But there was one tiny problem: the Risen could touch anything they wanted, except the living. It was the most ironic, double-edged gift I'd ever received.

Not that Joshua and I hadn't tried—frequently—to touch. During our first week back in Oklahoma, we took so many different approaches: slow and careful; quick and furious; even the unexpected surprise touch. But none of it worked. When I placed my hand against his, it always felt like I simply clutched the air; it was the same for Joshua. Worse, whenever we came too close, it looked as though we passed *through* each other—like *I* was made of air myself.

Nothing made me feel more like a ghost.

Still, so many things about my new existence were

amazing. The smell of Rebecca's garden after a hard rain; the taste of Jeremiah Mayhew's chocolate chess pie; the slick plastic coating on the benches outside Wilburton High. Each sensation felt fresh and new. So exhilarating, they almost made up for everything else.

Almost.

I shook my head, willing my cheeks to shift from whatever color they were now to something less neon pink. When I felt a little more in control, I met Joshua's eyes again and—a little reluctantly—returned to the subject of my upcoming torture.

"You know, I still can't figure out why Jillian insists I go to this thing tonight."

"Because you and Jill are now BFF?" he offered. When I glared at him, he grinned and went on. "Honestly, I think Jill just wants to make up for how she acted before New Orleans. And in New Orleans. And pretty much how she acts in general. Plus, I think she's trying to make you some more . . . friends."

He dragged the last word out awkwardly, grimacing. I couldn't help but copy his expression. The word "friend" made both of us uncomfortable. Not because of the ones I hadn't made yet, but because of the one I'd made and then lost.

Gabrielle Callioux.

The girl who changed me into what I was now; the girl

who, in only a few days, had become my closest friend; the girl I'd watched disappear into hell.

Thinking about Gaby would probably make tonight even harder. So I forced a bright tone as I responded to Joshua.

"Making new friends. At Kaylen Patton's house. Yay." Just for effect, I shook my fists in a fake little cheer.

"Your enthusiasm is overwhelming," he said drily. "But you promised to show up to this sleepover. And 'show up' means you actually have to *show up*. No going invisible."

I sighed heavily. Then, since my feet were already dangling over the edge, I slid myself fully off of the daybed and turned around to face him. I tucked my hands into the pockets of my jean skirt—borrowed from Jillian—and gave him a small smile.

Joshua, however, didn't return my smile. He studied me, suddenly serious, and even a little . . . sad, maybe. Then he reached out to let his palm hover by my cheek, almost as though he could cup it.

"You know," he said softly, "that I'd give just about anything to touch you again?"

I didn't trust myself to answer him aloud. Not without my voice cracking. So I just nodded. We stayed silent for another beat, until he cleared his throat.

"Have fun tonight."

All I could manage was a rough "I'll try."

Before I did something I'd regret, like lean into his hand and pretend, just for a second, that this wasn't our new normal, I spun around and raced out of the gazebo.

Chapter
THREE

Cramped into Jillian's tiny car and listening to yet another generic hip-hop song, I couldn't quite believe I'd left my gorgeous boyfriend sitting on an equally gorgeous bed . . . for *this*.

Before leaving the Mayhews' house, Jillian had forced me to try on about a hundred different outfits until I looked presentable. It was ridiculous, considering the fact that most items in my wardrobe once (and sort of still) belonged to the most famous actress in America. Next came an inch-thick layer of makeup, something

I'd stopped wearing the day Gaby disappeared. Worst of all, Jillian spent most of our drive lecturing me on how to behave once we reached Kaylen's house. Which made me wonder—yet again—why I'd been invited in the first place.

"And another thing," Jillian continued, "you need to treat Kaylen's mom with a lot of respect. Like, a *lot*."

I turned away from my open window, back toward the interior of the car so that Jillian could see my exasperation.

"What do you think I'm going to do, Jill, run naked through her living room?"

Jillian laughed, but she began to drum her fingers nervously against the steering wheel. "It's not that I think you're going to do something stupid. It's just that I'm trying to, you know, prepare you."

"For what, the Miss Wilburton pageant?"

"Something like that," Jillian muttered.

Before I could ask her what she meant, Kaylen's house came into view, and I was momentarily struck speechless.

The home was absolutely enormous—at least three stories tall, maybe four. But the building's most striking quality wasn't its size. Its façade boasted every imaginable architectural element: columns, balconies, copper awnings, weather vanes. Best of all, two life-sized statues of lions flanked the double front doors. It was a triumph of wealth and excess.

"Whoa," I eventually managed. "It kind of looks like *Better Homes and Gardens* threw up all over this place."

"Yeah," Jillian said, pulling her car onto the circular driveway. "This is what we call a McMansion."

I let out a low whistle and stared up at the house while Jillian parked alongside several other cars. We kept quiet, almost reverential as we removed our overnight bags from the trunk and made the long walk to the front porch.

Finally, standing between the stone lions and waiting for someone to answer the doorbell, Jillian broke our silence with a torrent of words.

"Okay, so Mr. Patton is an oil guy *and* a state senator," Jillian hissed in a rushed whisper. "So he's gone, like, all the time. That leaves Mrs. Patton alone a lot with Kaylen and all this money. And, well, Mrs. Patton is a former Miss Oklahoma, which *should* mean that she's super nice. But in Mrs. Patton's case—"

At that moment, the front door swung open to reveal Kaylen, unbelievably glammed up and looking regal in the marble-tiled foyer. Except the person standing in the doorway *wasn't* Kaylen. She was at least six inches taller, not counting her five-inch stilettos. That also left out the four inches of gravity-defying hair, which had been sprayed into some complicated blond sculpture. All that height made her look superhuman, like some sort of suburban goddess.

"Jillian, sweetie, don't you look pretty," she cooed, pointing to Jillian's block-print dress and wedge heels. Then Mrs. Patton raised a perfectly groomed eyebrow and assessed me coolly, before breaking into a high-wattage smile.

"You must be Jillian's little friend," she said, offering me a handshake full of bedazzled fingernails. I took an instinctive step back to avoid the nontouch, and her smile dropped.

"Sorry," I offered lamely. "I, um, have a cold."

I offered a weak cough as evidence, using my shaking hand to cover it. Then I waved that hand as if to say, *See? Germ-ridden.*

Mrs. Patton's upper lip curled in disgust and she, too, took a step backward. Then she composed that lip curl into something that was only slightly less repulsed.

"You poor thing. Why don't y'all just come on inside?"

She waved us into the entryway, gestured vaguely to a grand, curving staircase, and told us that the other girls were in the theater room on the third floor. Then she hurried away on her ridiculous heels, fleeing what she clearly assumed was the black death.

Now I realized why Jillian had demanded a fashion

show before we left. And why we were wearing designer labels to a party that should have been filled with sweat-pants and junk food.

I snorted as Jillian and I started up the stairs. "You have to admit, this explains *so* much about Kaylen."

"Doesn't it though?" Jillian murmured. "I told you, Kaylen is an okay person—she's just a little . . . skewed."

"I can see why. She's living with a grade-A pageant mom."

"Aw, who's afraid of tiaras and mascara? We've fought *demons*."

"*I've* fought demons," I corrected. "You fought a crazed psycho killer with some serious girl issues."

"To-may-to, to-mah-to." Jillian waved her hand dismissively.

After what felt like a thousand miles of stairs and hall-way, Jillian paused outside a set of red double doors. She'd just reached for one of the handles when both doors swung open and Kaylen came bounding out into the hall.

"Jill!" she squealed, enveloping her friend in a bear hug to which Jillian responded with an awkward back pat.

I'd always thought of Kaylen as something of a prin-cess. But tonight, in stark contrast to her mother, she appeared in a set of comfortable-looking pajamas.

"So, Jill, I got those hot Cheetos you like even though

they make everyone else want to puke." She abruptly shifted her attention to me. "And you're Amelia, right? Josh's secret new girlfriend?"

Now *that* took me aback. All I could do was stutter, "Uh . . . y-yeah. I guess I am."

I thought I'd have to dance around this issue for hours—maybe suffer a few sly, catty comments in the process. But Kaylen just came right out and addressed the elephant in the room.

"Not so secret anymore," she noted, before I could say anything else. "Anyway, come on in—the other girls are already here."

She started to wave us inside, grinning.

"You got all done up for Mom, right?" Kaylen asked. "Don't worry: you can go ahead and change into your comfies in the powder bath."

"Thanks," Jillian breathed, immediately slipping her feet out of her tall wedges. Then she and I hefted up our bags and followed Kaylen inside.

The theater room matched the house perfectly: overdone, with heavy red drapes and gold tassels everywhere. The only difference was that this room looked a little friendlier with the addition of a rom-com on the big screen and a few pajama-clad girls gathered beneath it.

I'd seen them before, following Kaylen and Jillian around Wilburton High. One of them—a strawberry blonde with a sharp nose and pale green eyes—hung back in the semicircle of theater chairs and arranged bowls of junk food on a low table. The other two girls approached us, both sporting messy sets of pigtails. Slumber-party couture, I guess.

"Nice dress, Jill," one teased, flipping an ashy brown pigtail. "Are you going to a fancy horse race?"

"Are you running in one?" Jillian shot back, but she grinned warmly and gave her friend a playful shove. Then she moved toward the bathroom, apparently to change. Without looking back, Jillian wiggled her fingers over her shoulder. "I'm going to go un-Derby myself. See you in a sec."

As soon as the door clicked shut, the third girl moved closer to me. Too close, actually, almost like a shark. Her smirk wasn't necessarily hostile—in fact, it looked sort of pretty against her deeply tanned skin—but it made me uncomfortable. Deeply uncomfortable.

"So," she said archly. "*You're* Amelia?"

It was as if those three words were some kind of signal. All at once, the entire room seemed to focus on me. Each girl moved in concert, angling herself toward me like a missile seeking its target.

After a long, uncertain pause, I nodded and cleared my throat. "And all of you are . . . ?"

"Chelsea Qualls," the ashy brunette offered, and

then pointed behind her to the redhead. "That's Elyse Richards."

"And I'm Mya Homma."

The girl with the deeply tanned skin and black hair waved at me, a gesture that I wasn't sure whether to read as snarky or friendly. For lack of anything better to do, I waved back.

"Hi. I'm Amelia Ashley. I'm dating Joshua Mayhew. I enjoy competitive figure skating and long walks on the beach."

The other girls laughed, relaxing by separate degrees. One by one, they each shifted away from me. Sensing that the attack was over, I smiled at them as genuinely as I could and reminded myself that I'd faced far scarier things than a roomful of teenage girls in judgment mode.

Still, when Jillian exited the powder bath, I took the opportunity to excuse myself to change—and breathe easier for the first time since we'd entered the room. Maybe even the house.

Chapter
FOUR

An hour later, the awkward, interrogation-themed tension had almost dissipated. I guess a few peanut butter M&M's and more than a few sips of stolen wine just had that effect on people. It also didn't hurt when Jillian told them that my pajamas were previously worn by the actress now prancing around in the chick flick that we were only half watching.

"I can totally see the resemblance," Mya said, using a bottle of Mrs. Patton's finest merlot to draw an invisible line between the woman on the screen and me.

"Yeah," I muttered awkwardly. "My famous aunt just *loves* to share her outdated clothes."

"Outdated?" Chelsea breathed. "They're freaking gorgeous. Is that silk?"

Chelsea sat in the chair next to mine, and she moved forward to touch my sleeve. Without thinking, I yanked my arm back before she had the chance. Jillian must have seen the small, insulted O that Chelsea's mouth made, because she darted forward.

"Amelia has touch issues," Jillian said defensively, leaning around me. "You know, like a phobia."

"Oh." Chelsea gave me a smile that was equal parts polite and weirded-out. Kaylen, however, looked intrigued.

"Really?" she asked. She sat up straighter in her chair. "How does that *work*, exactly? With Joshua, I mean."

My mouth started flapping open and closed like a fish's. How did I even *begin* to answer that? Luckily, before I had to craft some believable lie, Jillian faked a loud yawn.

"Bor-ring," she grumbled. "New subject, guys. Please."

I could have kissed her. Instead, I gave her a sly wink of gratitude.

"Okay," Kaylen said. "No more phobia talk. How about a game of truth-or-dare?"

Jillian and I shouted no at the same time, almost as

loudly as Chelsea, Mya, and Elyse cheered yes. With the rest of the party on her side, Kaylen grinned triumphantly.

"Four against two. It's totally happening."

I groaned loudly and glanced at Jillian. She shrugged, as if to say, *No use fighting this.* I sank into my plush seat, waiting until the very last minute to join the other girls in the cross-legged circle they'd formed around the coffee table. Once there, I folded my arms and prepared myself for the inevitable questions from Kaylen. But to my surprise, Mya jumped in with the first challenge.

"Truth or dare, Jilly?"

Obviously Jillian hadn't expected that, either. She blinked a few times and then said, "Uh . . . truth, I guess."

Mya exchanged meaningful looks with Chelsea and Elyse before turning back to Jillian. "Are you in love with Scott Conner?" Mya asked bluntly.

Jillian blinked even faster, as did I.

I knew that Joshua's quiet friend Scott liked Jillian; his feelings were written all over his face, every time he looked at her. But I had no idea that Jillian might feel something for Scott in return, especially not after her misguided crush on Kade LaLaurie this winter.

Now, watching the red stain of a blush creep up her neck, I knew it must be true: Jillian liked Scott back.

"No," Jillian muttered, after far too long a pause. "Of

course I don't like Scott. He's like . . . a brother to me, or something. And he's not even *that* cute. I'm mean— floppy hair is over, right?"

Instead of answering her, the other girls whooped and laughed in triumph.

"Liar!" Elyse crowed. "You *do*! You totally like him."

Chelsea pointed an accusatory finger at Jillian. "You've got a crush on your big brother's bestie. Admit it."

"No," Jillian spat. She chucked an M&M at Chelsea, who caught it deftly and popped it into her mouth. Somehow, this offended Jillian even more. She folded her arms over her chest and scowled at her friends.

"Fine. So I sort of like Scott, okay? I didn't used to. But after we got back from Christmas break, he just . . . he started to look better to me. Cuter. Funnier."

I heard what Jillian didn't say: that Scott Conner, compared to a creep like Kade LaLaurie, looked like Prince Charming. Not that Scott needed the comparison—he'd always been a nice guy. But now, Jillian actually valued that quality. I couldn't wait to tell Joshua.

Jillian's girlfriends, however, continued to tease her mercilessly. And for once, she couldn't seem to muster up any sharp comebacks. So she scowled harder and flopped angrily against the footrest of a theater chair.

"Traitors," she hissed halfheartedly, after the last bit of laughter quieted. Then she turned to Kaylen. "Don't think you're going to get out of this, just because I'm embarrassed now. Truth or dare, Kaylen?"

Kaylen flashed everyone a smug half grin. "I always take the dare. You know that."

"Oh, I know." Jillian grinned back, but her smile wasn't a happy one. "That's why I already have your dare picked out."

"Bring it, Jilly." Kaylen curled her fists and flexed her arms into a strongman position. "I'm not afraid."

When I saw Jillian's smirk, I wondered whether Kaylen should have been.

"Okay, if you're so brave, then why don't you go get us another bottle of your mom's wine?"

Kaylen had already started to beam confidently, when Jillian added, "And one of her old pageant tiaras. A *big* one. Which you will wear for the rest of the night."

The other girls started cackling, but Kaylen paled faintly. I would bet anything that those tiaras, with all their sharp edges and cold sparkle, represented the worst of Kaylen's fears. Just the thought of stealing one had her broken out in a visible sweat.

Despite the jealousy I'd felt toward Kaylen, despite the fact that she'd thrown herself at my boyfriend last fall, I suddenly wanted to protect her. To keep her from risking her mother's wrath, and from having to see another tiara again, if she didn't want to.

"Jillian, I think that's one too many dares."

I spoke as quietly as possible, but the other girls heard me. As Kaylen watched me, something in her eyes shifted from desperate to hopeful.

"Actually," I went on, keeping my eyes trained on Kaylen's, "I *know* that's one too many dares. Kaylen will probably get caught stealing the tiara. And if she has to steal something, I'd rather have the wine."

Faced with a choice between the humiliation of their queen bee and more booze, the crowd quickly chose the latter. As if to demonstrate, Elyse grabbed the bottle from Chelsea's hand and tilted it back, draining the last few ounces.

"More wine, more wine," she began to chant softly, once she'd finished off the bottle.

As Kaylen pushed herself up from the floor, her feigned look of boredom barely hid her obvious relief.

"Okay, okay," she said, moving toward the doors. "I'll get us another bottle."

"Two," Jillian called out, just before the doors clicked shut. Then she whipped around toward me.

"Thanks a lot, Amelia," she said, dragging out my name sarcastically.

I shrugged, unbothered by the fact that I'd spoiled Jillian's plans. It was just too bad if she momentarily hated me for it. I'd lost too many friendships to let Jillian ruin one of her own. Besides, Kaylen might be needy and a little self-absorbed, but that didn't mean she deserved cruelty.

There was enough of it in the afterlife, I'd learned.

Oblivious to my motives, Jillian turned back to her friends, effectively cutting me out of the conversation. I shook my head and smiled.

Oh, Jillian. You are nothing if not yourself.

I settled against the foot of my chair, satisfied to listen in silence for a while. Whether or not I would make friends with these girls tonight, perhaps I'd found an ally in Kaylen.

Or at least I thought I had. Less than sixty seconds after Kaylen returned, passed the stolen wine to her friends, and flopped back into her place in the circle, she turned on me with a wide smile.

"Truth or dare, Amelia."

My eyes narrowed as I stared back at her. If I was being really honest, I'd thought that Kaylen herself would give me the biggest break, considering what I'd just done for her. But no such luck.

Though I didn't know her exact question, I knew its inevitable subject: the boy I loved; the boy I'd been through hell for, almost literally.

It should have been an easy choice. I should have picked truth, and then lied like crazy. Fibbed my way through the dark secrets about Joshua's Seer heritage and my undead status. Provided some vague answers, like "yeah, he's a good kisser," or "no, we haven't talked about what will happen to us after graduation."

Instead, I lowered my head and flashed my darkest smile.

"Dare, Kaylen. I choose dare."

Chapter
FIVE

Obviously, Kaylen hadn't anticipated my response.
She sputtered a bit, floundering to think up an
appropriate challenge for a girl she barely knew,
and secretly envied. Finally, after exchanging a few plead-
ing looks with her friends, she settled on an old staple.

"It's almost midnight, so I guess . . . I dare you to summon Bloody Mary in the mirror." She glanced around
the theater, trying to find the right venue, and then
pointed to the powder bath. "In there. So we can hear
you chant her name."

I had to choke back a laugh.

My dare is to summon a ghost*? One that doesn't even exist?*

Instead of outright mocking the dare, I put on my most intimidated face. "I don't know, Kaylen. That's kind of a creepy game."

Beside me, I could see Jillian roll her eyes; she knew as well as I did that a little spinning and chanting in the dark didn't scare me. Kaylen, however, was fooled: she preened and smiled.

"That's the dare, Amelia. Unless you want to take it back, and answer a few questions."

This time, I didn't have to fake my reaction. "No, that's okay. Bloody Mary's just fine by me."

I paused in the doorway of the bath, locked eyes with Jillian, and tried not to grin. Then I ducked inside and pushed the door shut behind me.

I just stood there for almost a full minute, shaking my head at the idiocy of this task. Most of these girls probably hadn't played Bloody Mary in years. I couldn't remember, but I was pretty sure I hadn't played it in several *decades*.

Still, when I heard someone call out, "The lights are still on," I flipped the switch.

Even with the thin strip of light filtering in from under the door, the room was surprisingly dark. I could just barely see the outline of my face in the mirror.

I shouted to the girls outside, "How many times am I supposed to spin?"

After a pause, someone answered, "Thirteen."

"Thirteen?" My eyes shot open. "I'll get dizzy and throw up."

"That's the point," someone else said, followed by a chorus of giggles.

I groaned loudly. I suppose this was the true torture of the dare: self-induced nausea in a stranger's bathroom.

Hurray for girly bonding time.

With a heavy sigh, I brushed the lip of the sink with my fingertips and closed my eyes again. Then I began to turn slowly, using the smooth porcelain edge of the sink to guide my spins.

One, I counted in my head, while calling, "Bloody Mary," loud enough for the other girls to hear.

That first chant incited another rash of laughter outside the door, but soon I was too occupied by the task of staying upright to listen. Spinning in tight, measured circles proved much harder than I'd thought. By the fourth repetition, my feet began to tangle; by the sixth, my head starting spinning in full force; by the eighth, I wasn't even sure if I could keep myself vertical.

Nine, I counted, starting a new circle. As I spun, I fumbled for the sink's edge but lost my grip before it could steady me.

Ten.

I tried to plant my palm against a wall for a moment's support, but my hand slipped and bumped roughly against the next wall in my rotation.

Eleven.

Maybe I'd tried too hard to ignore the girls outside the door. Or maybe I'd grown too dizzy to hear them. Those were the only reasonable explanations for why they'd suddenly stopped talking. Why they'd stopped making any noise at all. But that wasn't possible . . . was it?

Twelve.

Actually, it *was* possible. The other girls had definitely stopped giggling or talking. I couldn't hear the droning background noise of the theater's surround sound, either. It was as if the world outside had gone weirdly silent while I spun.

In my final, dizzy rotation, I felt the strangest sense that—even in the unnatural quiet—something waited. Something watched.

Thirteen.

"Bloody Mary," I whispered, ending my last turn with a desperate grab at the sink.

My feet skidded to an awkward stop and I bent over the basin, sucking in deep breaths as I tried to suppress a sudden wave of nausea. Below me, the drain seemed to circle itself, spinning and spinning around the center of the bowl. The sight of it made me even dizzier, so I looked up instead.

The new view wasn't much of an improvement. My face moved in the mirror, shifting from one corner to the other. Fractured pairs of eyes danced like bits of colored glass in a kaleidoscope: green on the left side, green on the right; green above, green below.

Gray in the middle.

My vision abruptly corrected itself and I stumbled backward, away from the face in the mirror. Mostly because it wasn't mine.

The pale skin and crew-cut hair; the cold, soulless gray eyes behind wire-rimmed glasses—that was Kade LaLaurie, smiling back at me from the place in the mirror where my face should have been.

Kade, the murderer; the crazy person; the dead guy who should have currently occupied a dark corner in hell instead of this bathroom mirror.

His nasty grin widened as he held one finger to his lips, soundlessly telling me to keep quiet.

As if I could even muster the will to scream right now.

I thought briefly about calling forth my glow. Even if I didn't really understand how it worked, it hadn't failed me before—especially when I'd needed it to incinerate demons. But a specter on the other side of a bathroom mirror? I had no idea how to fight such a thing.

Still, something about Kade's continued, mocking

smile helped me find my voice.

"What do you want?"

My whisper sounded harsher and stronger than I'd expected. Hearing it, Kade dropped his smile. With a cold glare, he cocked his head to one side and scrutinized me. I don't know exactly what he saw, but his smile returned. He lifted one finger to the interior of the glass and tapped it ever so slightly.

Assuming that a fight would follow, I braced myself. But instead of attacking me, Kade suddenly vanished behind a pane of frost. The entire mirror iced over, hiding him from view until I couldn't even see the obscured outline of his figure.

For a moment, nothing else happened.

Then slowly, letters began to appear in the frost, traced there by an invisible finger. As I watched, the letters scrawled backward to form words, starting with the bottom of some message and moving toward its beginning. Nothing about it made any sense until the last word completed itself.

At that point, I'm pretty sure I stopped breathing.

In even, flawlessly aligned block letters, the message read:

YOU

OR THEM.

ONE DIES PER WEEK UNTIL YOU JOIN US.

I understood its meaning perfectly: the message came from the darkness itself.

From hell.

Before my mind could process this fully—before I even had a chance to breathe—the ice melted, crashing onto the sink and floor in one noisy wave.

My feet were soaked, my hands were shaking, but I couldn't tear my eyes away from the mirror. Kade had vanished, leaving nothing but the image of a pale, terrified girl in his place.

Chapter
SIX

I must have figured out a way to black out but stay conscious. That was my only explanation for why I suddenly found myself sitting in a theater chair, staring blankly up at Kaylen.

A very angry version of Kaylen.

"What do you mean, a pipe burst?" she demanded, crossing her arms and giving me a glare that bordered on murderous.

I shrugged. In my semidelirious state, I must have dragged myself out of the hellish bathroom *and* conjured up an excuse for the sopping mess. Excellent work on my part, all things considered.

"I don't know, Kaylen," I heard myself saying. "It's *your* plumbing."

Most of Kaylen's guests snickered. But from the corner of my eye, I saw Jillian shift forward ever so slightly. Judging by her clenched fists, she knew something had gone wrong. At the very least, she knew a pipe hadn't burst.

"I've got to go," I said abruptly, pushing myself up from the chair. Without looking at the other girls, I moved toward the pile of overnight bags at the back of the room. "Jillian, can you take me home?"

"What?" Kaylen nearly shrieked. "You destroyed the bath mat, and now you're making my best friend leave *my* party?"

I hesitated, glancing at Jillian. Thankfully, she looked more than ready to leave, too. I let my shoulders slump and put on my fakest, most embarrassed frown.

"I . . . I didn't want to admit it, but I *did* get sick playing Bloody Mary. I tried to wash up in the sink, but I kind of overfilled it. I'm so, so sorry, Kaylen. This is just so embarrassing."

The apology worked . . . a little. Kaylen still looked frustrated, but the rigid line of her mouth softened and she uncrossed her arms.

"Well, after all the wine and the spinning, I figured that could happen," she conceded.

In a last-ditch maneuver, I decided to ham it up to the fullest. For Jillian's sake, since she still had to see these people at school on Monday.

"I don't want to ruin the party. And it was so important for me to make a good impression. But I feel kind of awful now. Like, I might get sick again." I wiped the back of my hand across my forehead, as if the gesture would prove . . . something. Clamminess, maybe?

"So how about I mop up all the water," I finished. "And then just go home?"

Kaylen's eyes widened and she waved her hands frantically. "No! God no. I don't want you puking on the *floor*, too."

"Okay," I said, hanging my head in fake dejection. "I'll just go then."

Evidently my pathetic but determined charade had thoroughly spooked Jillian. "I'll get our stuff," she chimed in, a little too eagerly. She practically dove for our bags, digging them out of the pile and then using them to usher me toward the door. Like I needed any additional prodding to get out of there, and soon.

After a perfunctory good-bye to Kaylen and her guests—all of whom looked a little dazed by the scene I'd just made—Jillian and I raced out of the room, down the stairs, and through the front door.

Neither of us spared the Pattons' McMansion a backward glance as we drove away. We didn't say it aloud, but I'm pretty sure we were thinking the same thing: we couldn't move fast enough to escape the house that had gone from creepily gaudy to just plain creepy.

Jillian and I hadn't been on the road for more than ten minutes before she swerved the car onto a shoulder and stomped on the brakes. She stopped so abruptly that I had to slap my hands against the dash to keep myself from slamming into it.

Jillian shifted into park and turned sharply toward me.

"What *happened* back there?"

I shook my head, frowning as I settled back into my seat. "I'm not entirely sure. An ultimatum, I think."

Her brow knitted in confusion—an expression that reminded me so much of her brother.

"Explain, Amelia," she said. "Please."

And so I did; picking absently at my sleeve, I described my strange meeting in the mirror. When I finished the story, Jillian turned away from me. For longer than I'd expected her to, she just stared out the darkened windshield.

Finally, in a hushed voice, she asked, "Do you think they mean it?"

I raised one eyebrow. "Which part?"

"The *death* part."

I studied her face for a moment, and then nodded. "Yes, I think they do. I think they really will kill people if I don't come to them."

Jillian flinched but still didn't look at me. "When are they going to start?"

I sighed and began to rub my right temple. "I don't know. They weren't terribly specific."

"How?" she asked bluntly, and then amended, "I mean, how can they *kill* people? I thought you said that they needed someone else to do their dirty work on earth."

"If Eli and the redheaded girl from my dreams told the truth, then you're right: the demons won't do it themselves. They'll need some kind of ghostly middleman. But as my little visit proved, they already have one, don't they?"

"Kade," she whispered, facing me at last.

I nodded again. "Kade."

Jillian shuddered. Even in the dark, I could see her pale visibly. "That's not exactly someone I want to see again, you know?" she murmured.

I didn't blame her. The last time Jillian and Kade interacted, he'd drugged and pistol-whipped her, and she'd subsequently killed him with a mouthful of ground oleander seeds. Not a memory that would make for a very happy reunion.

I turned away from her to stare vacantly out the passenger window. "You won't have to see him, Jill," I said softly. "This is my problem. I'll deal with it, in whatever way I have to."

Jillian stayed silent for at least a few minutes. When she eventually cleared her throat, I thought she was ready to reply. To agree with me. But instead, she threw her car into drive and swerved back onto the empty road. We skidded, fishtailing wildly between the gravel on the shoulder and the asphalt.

Jillian grimaced as the tires squealed, but she made no move to stop again. Once the car righted itself, she began to speed like hell had already started chasing us.

"Jillian!" I shrieked. "What are you doing?"

"Making it *my* problem, too," she murmured.

Gripping the steering wheel with one hand, she used the other to pull her cell phone from its little nook in the dash and dial it with one thumb.

"The road, Jill—watch the road!"

Jillian ignored me and put the phone to her ear. I heard the echo of a few rings, and then someone answer with a rough greeting.

"Meet us," Jillian said flatly, in lieu of hello. "You know where. And who to bring."

She didn't wait for a response, didn't even say good-bye. She simply ended the call and began typing wildly, still using one thumb. I could only say a prayer of thanks that she did so without looking away from the road.

Then, after finishing the text, she popped the phone into its cubby and turned back to the task of driving like a crazy person. Even then, with both hands on the wheel and both eyes on the road, she didn't speak to me. Each time I demanded to know our destination, Jillian just shook her head and drove faster.

Despite my familiarity with the roads and forests in this area, I had no idea where we were going. I didn't recognize the side streets we passed, nor did I find any help in the endless rows of indistinguishable pine trees that flew by outside the windows. It wasn't until Jillian slowed to an almost legal speed that I noticed something familiar in the woods to our right. Something black and glittering that ran parallel to our path.

A river.

"Jill," I repeated. "Where are we going?"

This time, my question was softer, more urgent. But this time, Jillian didn't need to answer me. I saw our destination soon enough, when she turned onto another road.

Ahead of us, I saw the hulking outline of High Bridge. We were still a little far away—the route Jillian had taken from Kaylen's house to the bridge was a strange, twisted one—but I could see the yellow tape and sawhorses that decorated the entrance.

Obviously, the county was in no hurry to take down the condemned structure. It made me wonder what the county officials would do if they really knew what lay beneath that crumbling monster.

Whoever Jillian had contacted had beaten us to the bridge: a green sedan waited on a gravelly shoulder, just above the steep hill that led to the riverbank. Jillian parked behind the sedan and flashed her brights twice before killing the engine.

She put her hand on her door, about to get out, when she thought better of it and faced me in the dark. She didn't say anything—just watched me until she turned abruptly and exited the car, too fast for me to react. I sat there, blinking and confused. Then, for lack of any better ideas, I followed her.

Here, the night felt colder than it had at the Pattons' house. I didn't know whether that had something to do with the breeze now coming off the river, or whether this place just made everything seem chilly and unwelcoming.

Jillian stood a few feet ahead of me, facing the other car and rubbing her bare arms furiously against the cold. I closed the distance between us warily, still unsure of how Jillian intended to make my problems hers. The fact that High Bridge obviously played some part in her plans didn't help my mood.

Nor did the fact that Joshua stepped out of the sedan's passenger seat. He saw Jillian first and gave her the barest of acknowledgments. Then his eyes caught mine. Through the darkness, I could see the apology in them.

I tilted my head to one side and frowned. I had no idea what warranted the Mayhews' strange behavior. At least, not until the driver stepped out of the sedan.

Scott Conner—Joshua's good buddy and Jillian's newest crush—had no business here. Yet there he stood, his shaggy hair sticking up in peaks and curls, as if someone had recently woken him up from a deep sleep. Which, I realized, had actually happened.

Although we'd never technically met, Scott gave me a shy, close-lipped smile. It was a kind look, gentle, but it was far too familiar. Too knowing.

I took an involuntary step backward, away from Scott. I was afraid of him, then—afraid of the boy who shouldn't be smiling at me in a way that suggested he knew my secrets, and felt sorry that I had them.

Joshua confirmed my suspicions, speaking quietly although no one else was around to hear us.

"Scott knows, Amelia. About you, and what you are."

Joshua gave me a few seconds to process this news. Then he turned and pointed to the ugly heap of metal and concrete behind him.

"Scott knows, and he's here to help us bring High Bridge down. Tonight."

Chapter
SEVEN

N o." I tried to speak firmly, but my voice came
out edged with hysteria. "No, no, no."

My nerves vibrated as though they'd been
strummed, echoing back anger, excitement, uncertainty,
and even a touch of betrayal. I felt a sudden flush of
heat, like my glow might break free and cut a path of fire
across the road.

When Scott took a step forward, I held up both palms
as a warning.

Come any closer, pardner, and I'll blast ya.

I heard someone choke out a strangled laugh and then realized it was me. In an effort to control myself, I took a few deep breaths.

"No," I repeated, locking eyes with Joshua again. "No to all of it."

In the past when I'd been so clearly shaken, Joshua had approached me cautiously. Almost like I was a wounded animal. But tonight he rushed to my side, unafraid. He stood as close to me as he could, brushing one hand through the air above my shoulder.

"I'm so sorry," he said. "Jillian asked him to pick me up. Apparently he already knows—"

"I already know a thing or two about the afterworlds," Scott interjected.

I blinked back, stunned. Not because Scott had just interrupted his friend—something I'd *never* heard him do—but because of what he'd said. His casual use of the word "afterworlds" was particularly interesting. It wasn't a term that the average teenage boy threw around lightly.

The average *Seer* boy, however, was a different story.

I raised my eyebrows at Joshua, signaling him to let me work through this, and then turned back to Scott. Slowly, tentatively, I took a step forward.

"What do *you* know about the afterworlds?" I asked softly.

"Probably not as much as you guys." Scott gave me another sheepish smile. "But enough to help."

That answer didn't satisfy me. I narrowed my eyes and moved one step closer, all the while keeping my gaze trained on him. "How? *How* do you know enough, Scott?"

He held up one hand in a motion of caution and, with the other, pulled something from his pocket. He raised the object into the light of a nearby streetlamp so I could see it, and then took his own slow steps toward me. When we were within reaching distance, he handed it to me. It looked like a thin, cheaply made wallet, its fraying edges held together by duct tape.

"Flip it open," Scott urged. "To the pictures."

I did so gently, opening to the small plastic sleeves that held a handful of wallet-sized photos. Scott pointed to them.

"Go to the third one. It's a group shot."

I flipped to the one he indicated and examined it, frowning. The photo was tiny, almost too small for me to make out the individual features of the seven or eight people seated in it.

"It's my whole family," Scott explained. "At least, all of them that live in Oklahoma. We took it a few years ago, during my freshman year. See? That's me in the front row."

He smiled shyly and pointed again. I peered back down at the photo and saw a younger version of Scott, with shorter hair and a few less inches of height, smiling up from the first row.

Then my eyes trailed to the back row, where the elders of his family stood. On the far left, standing a few feet apart from everyone else, was a white-haired woman with thick glasses and a broad smile. She looked strangely familiar, though I didn't know why.

Noticing my stare, Scott leaned closer and pointed to the old woman.

"That's my gran. She was on the decorating committee at First Baptist. The same church Ruth Mayhew used to attend."

Suddenly, I knew where I'd seen her face before. She'd been in the church the day Ruth marched me outside and threatened me with exorcism. More importantly, this old woman had been at my cemetery, standing in a circle of Voodoo dust, the night Ruth called off my exorcism so that I could save Jillian's life.

The woman in the photograph was a Seer. And Scott's grandmother.

Which means that Scott is . . .

"How long have you known?" I whispered aloud, still staring at her picture. "What you are?"

"Not long. My gran never told me about this stuff, and

she didn't raise me with the superstitions, like Ruth did with her grandkids. But I know Gran believed in ghosts. And I know she had some pretty creepy after-church activities, judging by all the jars of weird crap she kept in her house."

"'Kept'?" I asked, catching his use of the past tense.

He shrugged, but I could see a glint of sadness in his eyes. "Yeah, she passed away this January."

"I'm sorry," I said softly. And I was, even if the woman had tried to end my afterlife. Loss hurt, no matter who it was you lost.

I closed the wallet and handed it back to Scott carefully, making sure that our hands didn't touch. He took it from me and slipped it into his pocket. Then he shrugged again, more awkwardly this time, and cast an uncomfortable glance at Joshua.

"Jillian and I have been . . . hanging out a lot lately. She needed someone to talk to after everything that happened at Christmas, and when we put together all the different pieces about my gran—"

"Jillian realized that she had a new Seer boyfriend?" Joshua concluded bitterly. "One who was willing to listen to all of *Amelia's* secrets?"

"No, no!" Scott flapped his hands desperately in the air. "Jillian never bitched about Amelia, not to me. She just warned me that something bad might happen again, and that we needed to be ready with a plan to fight it."

"Like the 'something' that happened an hour ago," Jillian added forcefully. She gestured to me emphatically. "Tell them, Amelia. Tell them about your little truth-or-dare disaster."

I startled, surprised that I hadn't done that yet. I'd been too wrapped up in the shock of another person knowing *what* I was, and why.

With a shudder that had nothing to do with the cold night air, I repeated my conversation with the dark visitor in the mirror. As I spoke, I saw Joshua's jaw tighten and his fists clench reflexively.

Scott trembled too—with fear, not anger. But somehow, he found the courage to interrupt the end of my story.

"Amelia, we have to do something," he urged. "Don't you see that? For your sake, and Jillian's."

I wouldn't have wanted to stand on the receiving end of the look Joshua now gave his friend.

"And who," Joshua seethed, "appointed you safety inspector for my girlfriend *and* my baby sister?"

While Scott floundered to explain himself, I shot Jillian a similar glare. She'd betrayed my confidence, in more ways than one. At least she had the decency to look *somewhat* contrite, but that didn't stop her.

"Okay, *enough*," she ordered. "So I told Scott. So we've

secretly been dating. So what? None of this is going to help us destroy High Bridge."

I threw my hands up in the air. "And what exactly would the destruction of High Bridge accomplish, Jillian? Except maybe a little therapy for some of us."

"Oh, I don't know, Amelia," she drawled. "Only close the gate into the netherworld forever. No big deal."

"That's . . . that's not possible."

Jillian crossed her arms and flashed me a smug smile. "Well, *we* think it's possible."

She signaled to Scott, who turned and opened the back door of the sedan. He rummaged around before pulling out a small, unmarked book.

"My gran's journal," Scott said, closing the car door. "It has all these Seer spells in it, and notes about how the afterworlds might work."

Jillian plucked the book from his hands, rewarding him with a small kiss that made him blush and Joshua wince. Unbothered by the obvious conflict she'd created between her brother and his friend, she thumbed through the notebook until she found the appropriate page. Then she pressed the book flat and carried it over for me to read.

Beneath Jillian's thumb, I saw the spidery scrawl of handwriting. But other than a few key words—"gate," "darkness," "dust"—I couldn't make out the rest of it.

I shook my head, blinking awkwardly from the concentration.

"I can't read it, Jill—either it's too dark out here, or she was too old when she wrote it. Maybe both."

Jillian uttered an exasperated curse. "Well, I can read it. And it says that demons seem to link their gateways to certain structures—particularly those associated with rivers; these structures not only function as lures, but also as sources of the demons' earthly powers. The journal says if we lace one of these haunted structures with Seer dust and then destroy it, we should be able to stop any harmful spirits from escaping."

I paused, still studying the page in front of me. Then, softly, I asked, "What about nonharmful spirits, Jill?"

Beside me, Joshua stirred. Probably because he'd already followed my question to its logical answer. *I* hadn't intended any harm to Ruth, yet her Seer dust— or Voodoo dust, according to Kade—had limited my movements. Kept me from entering or exiting wherever the dust had been poured.

The same rules applied to all ghosts, "harmful" or not. Intentions meant nothing to a line of gray powder. I couldn't use something so pitiless, so final, to bar the doorway to and from the netherworld. Especially when a certain few ghosts still resided there.

Gaby, for one, and possibly my father. Even Eli, dark

as he could sometimes be. Not to mention all the other souls that Eli and his predecessors had unfairly imprisoned there.

I couldn't trap them in the darkness, just to save myself from it.

"No dust," I said, shaking my head. "I'll agree to do the rest, but no dust. We can't risk the afterlives of all those trapped souls. Even if it means that the demons themselves might break loose."

Jillian started to protest, but Joshua waved her silent.

"Amelia's right—we can't condemn the other ghosts like that. We'll just have to do what we planned to do tonight, without the dust. And if anything bad happens later . . . then we'll deal with it *later.*"

When he finished, Joshua gave me a small, reassuring smile. I knew what he was doing: asserting a compromise between Jillian's plan and my own. Between the total destruction of the netherworld, and the total destruction of my soul.

Joshua just saw through me that well. He knew that this situation could end badly for me, if I thought I had no other choice.

Huffing angrily, Jillian stomped over to where Scott stood near the entrance to High Bridge. She started to complain to him, but he took her hand in his and leaned close to whisper in her ear. Instantly, her frown softened and the fury went out of her eyes. She hesitated, just for a moment, before whispering something back. Then she turned to me with a strangely rueful smile.

"Your dad, Amelia. I forgot."

At that moment, I wanted to hug Scott. Instead, thick tears welled in my eyes. I tried to brush them aside quickly, but a few drops still fought their way to the surface.

"Thank you," I managed to croak. "Thank you all for understanding why I can't . . . why I just won't . . ."

"Write your dad off like that," Joshua finished gently. "Or Gaby."

"Or *any* of them. Jillian, Joshua—you've seen part of the netherworld. You should understand."

Slowly, and a little begrudgingly, Jillian nodded. She may not have liked it, but she knew I was right. Very few souls deserved to spend eternity in that place.

I cleared my throat of the remaining lump that my tears had left.

"So, now that that's all settled, how do we do this? How do we destroy High Bridge?"

Scott and Jillian exchanged a look—one I couldn't quite identify—and he grimaced. Then he reached into his coat pocket, pulled out a small, rounded object, and lifted it into the glow of the streetlamp. Light glinted off the object's metal shell, like some cold, sadistic wink.

No one said anything. No one even moved.

Well, aren't you just a bag of tricks tonight, Scottie-boy?

I let out a noise that sounded like the offspring of a hiccup and a hysterical giggle. Then, in a bemused voice that I almost didn't recognize, I asked, "Would someone please tell me that that's not a grenade?"

Chapter
EIGHT

N
o one spoke again for a while. Not until Joshua broke the silence with a low growl.

"What the hell, Scott? What is that thing?"

"It's one of my dad's hand grenades," Scott replied evenly. "From his ammo closet. Which is stupidly easy to break into, by the way. This was the best thing I could come up with to collapse the bridge, since I'm pretty sure none of us carries around a spare stick of dynamite."

Joshua leaned forward to glare at Scott and his sister.

"So you two have been planning this demolition

project for a while, huh? Without consulting Amelia and me, even though we're the ones who have the most at stake. Do I have that about right?"

Clearly unruffled by her brother's harsh tone, Jillian snorted. "Well, it's not like we could have told either of you—you would've just said no."

"Damn straight," Joshua hissed. "We would have told you both to go to—"

"Actually," I interrupted softly, stepping around Joshua, "I think it's worth a shot."

From the stunned looks on all their faces, you would have thought I'd pulled out my own grenade. To be honest, I surprised myself. But the longer I watched that tiny bomb glitter in Scott's hands, the more this plan made a terrible, wonderful kind of sense.

The end of High Bridge? The end of a place that had taken my life and so many others? Wasn't that worth the risk?

Of course it was, especially if the burden of risk fell squarely on me.

Before Joshua could talk me out of it, I strode over to Scott. Then, with one hand held up in a signal of extreme caution, I used the other to take hold of the grenade. He relinquished it with surprising ease, probably because he was still a little shocked that I'd agree to this plan at all.

I took a few steps closer to the bridge, handling the

grenade delicately, turning it over in my palm so slowly that my movements probably looked comical from the outside.

Of course, no one was laughing. If anything, Joshua's frown had deepened and his eyes had grown even wider. Although he was my voice of reason—my heart—I turned away from his horrified gaze; I couldn't let him weaken my resolve.

"So, now that *that's* settled," I said with forced nonchalance, staring at the miniature bomb in my hands instead of the people around me, "how does this thing work?"

"As . . . as far as I know, you hold the lever down, pull the pin, and throw. Then, you know . . . run like hell."

Although Scott had cleared his throat before speaking, his voice still hit a few nervous high notes. Judging by his stutter and Jillian's sudden fidgeting, neither of them had thought we would *actually* detonate the grenade. Then again, neither of them had seen pure evil in the mirror tonight.

I was still examining the grenade, wondering exactly how I should go about releasing its destructive power, when I caught a glimpse of movement. When I looked up, Joshua now stood less than a foot from me.

"Amelia," he whispered, "I don't think we should do this."

I lowered the grenade so that it wouldn't hang in the

air between us like a threat, and leaned toward him.

"I know, Joshua. And on most days, I'd agree with you. But what if we can stop the demons *tonight*? What if we can end the threats to your family? To *us*?"

Joshua shook his head, but I saw his eyes dart involuntarily to the bridge. Although his gaze only lingered there for less than a second, I knew I'd struck a nerve. Joshua hated that bridge almost as much as I did. Still, he wasn't quite on board with this plan yet. Which meant I needed to give him one last push. . . .

Holding the grenade slightly behind me, I reached out my free hand to brush my fingers against his. Except our fingers didn't connect. Instead, our hands floated through each other like passing currents of air. Like nothing.

"Joshua, listen to me," I whispered. "Please. As long as the rest of you take cover, all the risk falls on me. And what's the worst that could happen? I die, lose my Risen abilities, and get to touch you again? Sometimes, that's all I really want. So if the three of you are safe, then there's no downside to this."

The reluctance in his eyes shifted into something that resembled hurt.

That look didn't mean *I'd* hurt him; it meant that he knew I would die again—and eagerly—if I had to. And in that glint of hurt, I saw everything clearly: even though Joshua understood me, even though he might agree with me just a little, he wouldn't go along with something like this. Not now, not ever.

Keeping the grenade tucked behind my back and out of his reach, I lifted onto my toes. With my eyes shut, I planted a small kiss on what I hoped were his lips. I lingered near the warmth of his skin. Even without a real kiss to precede it, that warmth felt delicious, and I wanted to remember it.

After a slight hesitation, I moved closer, until my lips were only an inch from his ear. There, I said a single, simple word:

"Run."

I didn't wait for his reaction; I followed my own orders, spinning away from Joshua and sprinting as fast as I could for the entrance of the bridge.

While I ran, I heard desperate shouting behind me as Joshua ordered Jillian and Scott to dive behind their cars. Thankfully, none of them had tried to follow me.

I skidded to a stop at the center of the bridge and stared down at the dark, incomprehensible thing in my hand. I gripped its safety lever tightly and felt it press against my palm.

What did Scott say? I thought feverishly. *After I pull the pin, do I let go of the lever?*

No matter how much I tried, I just couldn't remember

how this thing actually worked. After far too long a pause, I thought:

Only one way to find out.

With the lever still held tight, I slipped one finger of my free hand through the ring of the pin. Using more force than I'd thought I would need, I yanked the pin loose. It dangled on my finger, like some macabre ring, and I just stood there for a blind second, watching it.

Suddenly, instinct took over. I felt my grenade arm pull back behind my head and then propel forward. During the forward arc of my arm, I had the briefest flash of memory—a sunny day; my father, adjusting the throwing position of my elbow while I clutched a grass-stained softball.

The memory faded into the darkness and, without another thought, I released the grenade.

I heard a small snick as the safety lever snapped back out. Now armed, the grenade continued on its trajectory above the bridge. I watched, temporarily dumbstruck by how small it looked in comparison to the tall support girders. Then another instinct took over: one of self-preservation.

I spun around on one heel and pumped my arms and legs as hard as I could. Although I moved fast, a fuzzy, molasses feeling sank into my thighs, making me feel as if I had to run harder if I wanted to escape.

Once I finally reached the end of the bridge, I threw myself at the shoulder of the road, rolling down the steep embankment toward the river.

The ground hurt me badly each time it connected with my shoulders. But that didn't hurt half as much as the painful boom that suddenly rang in my ears, or the pieces of blasted bridge that began to rain down upon me. I dug my hands into the ground to stop my rolling and then curled into a protective ball. Just before I tucked my head under my arm, I caught a glimpse of a piece of concrete flying toward me. It was huge—the size of a small car, with bits of sharp wire poking out from its edges—and I knew I wouldn't survive when it hit. At least, I wouldn't survive like *this*.

So here was the moment. The one I'd been dreading and anticipating in equal measure since December. I steeled myself for it as best I could, summoning up my brightest memories to wrap around me when it happened.

By the time I'd relived those memories twice, I knew that something was very wrong. Like the fact that a thousand-pound chunk of concrete was taking minutes instead of seconds to fall, for starters. After waiting a few more seconds, I *had* to look up.

What I saw made me uncurl instantly and skitter backward like a crab along the embankment.

There, about ten feet above my head, the enormous block of concrete looked just as it had when I first glimpsed it, all brutal rock and shredded wires. Thick and sharp and very lethal. But clearly lighter than air, too. It floated, suspended impossibly on the breeze.

As did every other piece of High Bridge. Chunks of concrete, strips of asphalt, even slices of the metal girders—they hung in the night sky like unnatural constellations.

Apparently, the only things that actually made it to the ground were the smaller rocks that had initially rained on me. Road debris and gravel, by the looks of it; pebbles that had no structural connection to the bridge. Everything integral to the bridge itself—every bit of foundation, of support—remained in its strange stasis in the sky.

Until the rubble *did* move again. Instead of falling toward the earth as it should have, it started to drift slowly back to where the bridge originally stood. Once there, rock and metal began to link together like pieces of a puzzle, moving of their own will to re-create the structure I'd tried to destroy. Within the span of only a few minutes, the dark outline of High Bridge began to reform.

I watched, openmouthed, as a tangled set of wires straightened and then slipped into corresponding holes in an upright wall of concrete. A girder set itself upon the newly stabilized wall, as if placed there by an invisible carrier.

But not *quite* invisible, I realized.

If I looked closer, if I squinted just right, I could make out the occasional inky trace of black smoke drifting beneath the individual components of the bridge. Yet the smoke wasn't insubstantial. Though thin and nearly transparent, this black smoke could evidently carry hundred- and even thousand-pound pieces of construction.

I'd seen smoke function like this before—smoke that moved in ways it shouldn't. Which led me to the conclusion that the shadowy vapor now rebuilding High Bridge wasn't smoke at all.

"Wraiths," I gasped, crawling farther up the embankment on my hands.

As if to confirm, the individual tendrils of smoke rearranged themselves while they worked, taking on thin but near-human forms. During the transition, they never slowed or faltered in their reconstruction project—even when their environment shifted into something cold and ghastly.

All around them, all around *me*, the riverbank darkened and hardened until the icy purples of the netherworld appeared. The grass beneath my hands frosted over, and I had to jerk my fingers off the ground to keep them from freezing to it.

I only had time for one chilly breath when a slick, unfamiliar voice echoed across the river and silenced me.

"Amelia Ashley," it hissed. "This was a mistake. Your mistake."

Although the voice echoed, it didn't boom; it crept through the netherworld like a whisper, intimate but discomforting in my ear.

"This error will cost you," the voice continued. "Instead of seven days in your first week, you have one. Agree to stay here now, or someone dies. Immediately."

I'd been wrong earlier: *this* was my moment. *Now* was the time.

I parted my lips to do the only thing I could: say yes, and commit myself to the darkness forever. But nothing intelligible came out—just one strangled syllable that sounded an awful lot like "No."

Despite my unclear response, the darkness didn't hesitate. The netherworld seemed to collapse in upon itself, each garish color disintegrating until nothing remained but real trees, a real river . . . and a very real, very intact High Bridge.

And in that cruel, impossible moment, I knew that my little bomb hadn't freed anyone. It had condemned someone to death.

Chapter
NINE

N o amount of reassurance from Joshua could dispel the leaden ball of guilt in my stomach. Almost three pitchers of coffee and nine Mayhew Bakery day-old pastries didn't do the trick, either, although they had officially proved that I was a nervous eater. During our drive from High Bridge to the Mayhews' house, I'd felt strangely calm. Impassive, even. Now, I just felt overstuffed with food and foreboding.

I pushed my half-eaten, stale palmier away in disgust

and looked around the kitchen. Across from me, Jillian and Scott had fallen asleep on each other's shoulders, slumped awkwardly in their dining chairs. On this side of the room, Joshua leaned with me against the counter of the kitchen island. He still watched me warily, as though he thought I might try to blow up his parents' house, too.

I raked one hand through the ends of my hair. "I'm not going to do anything crazy again, Joshua. I promise."

"I know, Amelia," he said, keeping his voice low. "That's not what I'm worried about."

"You're *not* worried that I tried to detonate a weapon of mass destruction tonight?"

Joshua shook his head. "Even if I don't like how you did it, I don't blame you for trying. And I don't think this is your fault, either. It's not like you *invented* demons and made them evil."

In response, I held my hands up in a pose of surrender. "But does that matter? Will that matter to the person who dies tonight?" Then I peeked at the kitchen clock. "Or this early morning, I guess?"

I dropped my palms to the countertop in defeat. As he'd done since we arrived home, Joshua placed his own hand comfort-close to mine. I stretched my fingers toward his, aching to tangle both sets together.

"I don't know the answer to that, any better than you

do," he said softly, running his thumb across the granite counter, near the length of my wrist. "All we can do is wait out the night, and then spend the next six days coming up with a better plan."

I laughed mirthlessly. "You mean: a 'better than last-minute, ineffective demolition' plan."

He smiled sadly but said nothing. Frowning again, I looked away from him and motioned to the view outside the wide kitchen window, just behind Jillian's and Scott's slumped forms.

"Well, fortunately or not, we don't have much longer to wait out the night."

Through the newly leafing branches in the front yard, we could see the first traces of sunlight. Without taking his eyes off the window, Joshua walked over to another counter and removed a fresh pot of coffee from the maker. Once he'd poured it into our mugs, we waited in silence, drinking and watching dawn break over the Mayhews' front garden.

Only when the sunrise shifted fully into early morning did Joshua set down his cup and stretch his arms high above his head. Then he settled back against the countertop with a wide yawn.

"Well," he said, stifling the last bit of his yawn, "the demons haven't attacked the house, and we haven't gotten a tragic phone call from one of my friends.

So . . . no news is good news."

"Maybe," I murmured. I took another long sip of coffee and kept my eyes trained on the brightening sky. As I watched the colors shift from pink and peach to pale blue and gold, I let myself hope. Just for a few, indulgent minutes.

Maybe Joshua was right. Maybe the demons were bluffing. After all, Eli had told me that demons weren't omniscient. They didn't innately know the identity of everyone I'd ever met; the demons merely targeted those unlucky people who happened to be in my proximity. A simple glance around the kitchen showed me that all my companions from last night were very much alive, if thoroughly exhausted. And Joshua had already checked on his parents—more than a few times, actually. So it looked like I could claim the night as a victory.

With one important exception.

Although my mother hadn't been anywhere near our ill-fated grenade attack, I couldn't help but worry about her. She was the only other person I'd visited lately, which made her a possible victim. Not a likely one . . . but still. I'd feel much better after a quick, invisible peek in her living-room window.

I laced my fingers and reached my arms forward, across the island, in an attempt to stretch away some of my cramped tension. Then I turned back to Joshua.

"Feel like driving me to my mom's house again?" I asked him. "Just for a quick check?"

In response, he pulled his car keys out of his pocket and began twirling the ring around his index finger. Seeing the exhausted lines around Joshua's faint smile, I briefly considered plucking the keys from his hand and giving the whole driving thing a try. But I doubted a wrecked pickup truck would help anyone, especially Joshua. I kept my hands to myself and followed him outside, stifling my own yawns as I climbed into his truck.

On the drive to my mother's house, Joshua and I agreed that music was a necessity: the louder, the better. We rolled down the windows to let in the cool morning air. As I drummed my fingers against the outside truck door in time to my new favorite song, I felt a twinge of guilt about blasting guitar riffs at seven a.m. on a Sunday. One look at the purplish shadows under Joshua's eyes made my guilt vanish. On impulse, I started to sing as loudly as possible to keep him awake. Joshua took a surprised, sidelong glance at me, so I added an air guitar, just for effect.

I thought he would laugh, or at least beg me to stop singing. Instead, he joined me, belting out the lyrics in a painful, off-key pitch. While he wailed, he shot me another sidewise glance, smiling a little during a particularly screechy chorus of "baby, baby, bab-eeee." The performance continued long after I'd dissolved into a fit of tired, giggly snorts.

When we pulled onto my mother's street, however, my laughter died.

I could see a faint, shifting light in her front window, a sure sign that she'd woken up early to watch the Sunday-morning newscast—a ritual to which she'd strictly adhered for as long as I could remember. That glow, and her brown sedan parked out front, meant that she'd spent the night in the relative safety of her house.

But inexplicably, my stomach began to sour with fear. I pressed one hand to my abdomen, willing myself to breathe normally as Joshua parked the truck a few hundred feet back from my mother's driveway.

He turned toward me in the cab, his eyes suddenly serious. "I'm coming with you this time," he said.

Just yesterday, I'd asked him to wait in the car. Although I'd appreciated his support, I didn't think my mother could take the added stress of meeting her undead daughter's living boyfriend. But this morning, I wasn't sure I could make the trip across my mother's tiny yard all by myself.

Watching the flicker of light in her window, I nodded and, without thinking, reached out to give Joshua's hand a grateful squeeze. Immediately, my hand slapped against the steering wheel. I looked down to see my hand shimmering, transparent, above his.

"Perfect timing," I growled, and yanked my hand back.

Joshua sighed, pulled his own hand from the steering wheel, and ran his fingers through the air beside my cheek. An uncomfortable jumble of desire, anger, and fear shot its way through me and came to life as a blush on my cheeks.

"One thing at a time," Joshua reminded me gently.

"You're right," I whispered, shaking my head at myself. "It's just that I'm . . . I'm just . . ."

When I trailed off, he laughed softly but without humor. "I know. Trust me, Amelia: I know."

He dropped his fingers and let them hover, a millimeter from the delicate spot above my collarbone. Then, with another heavy sigh, he pulled away and got out of the truck. I waited, fighting the urge to shriek with frustration—about Joshua, about the demons, about what I might view through my mother's window. After a few embattled seconds, I climbed out of the truck too.

I trudged behind Joshua, dragging my feet through the thick, dewy grass of my mother's lawn. The yard really needed a good mow, but if I had to guess, my parents' mower had died sometime after me and my father. I made a mental note to drag Joshua over here, while my mother was still at work, for a day of covert yard cleanup.

If she's still alive to need it. If any of you are.

The cold, slithery voice in my head was my own, but I jerked back as though I'd been slapped. *Shut up*, I silently told the other voice. *I don't need your input.*

Unaware of my nasty inner dialogue, Joshua glanced over his shoulder to give me a small, close-lipped smile as we stepped together onto my mother's porch.

You okay? he mouthed.

I just set my lips into a grim line and moved to peer in the front window, praying that my mother had left the curtains parted at least an inch or two.

To my eternal gratitude, she had. Even better, she was sitting on the couch just to the side of them. From that position, I could easily see her profile as she faced the TV.

I gusted out an enormous breath of relief and began to count off each indication that my mother was alive and well: the flick of her ponytail as she moved her head quickly from side to side; the tight clench and unclench of her hands to her closed lips; the almost violent lift and fall of her shoulders. . . .

I stopped counting. Something was wrong. Very wrong.

My mother's entire body moved as though someone had attached puppet strings to it—she was jerking and shaking on the couch.

Is she having a seizure?

At that thought, I didn't care if I alerted her to my presence; I practically threw myself against the window to get a better look inside. From that vantage point, I could see that, aside from the heavy crisscross of tears across her cheek, she seemed perfectly healthy. Alert, upright, and in relative control of her limbs. But as she pressed her fingers to her lips and shook her head again, I frowned harder.

TV, I realized. *She's crying about something on TV.*

My gaze trailed upward to the program that had affected her so strongly. When I saw what my mother was watching, I froze.

It wasn't a sad movie, as I'd hoped. Not even a particularly moving commercial. The news played out across her small, outdated screen, just like I'd expected it would. And right now, the news featured a very familiar face.

At first, I desperately hoped that she was just a newscaster. That she only appeared on the screen because she was giving a report on a violent car crash, as the headlines indicated. After a few more seconds, however, it became clear that the blond woman on the TV wasn't smiling prettily from a newsroom. The picture was a head shot, the kind of photo that reporters place on camera when they can no longer show the real thing. When the person in the picture no longer exists to interview.

As if to confirm my fears, the headline beneath the

photo shifted. Previously, it had read:

VIOLENT MIDNIGHT CAR CRASH

Now, in two lines of garish, breaking-news red, the banner proclaimed:

FORMER WILBURTON RESIDENT SERENA TAYLOR, 32,

DEAD IN CRASH AT HIGH BRIDGE

I didn't have the chance to catch any more of the story because the sourness in my stomach finally rose to the surface. I dove to the edge of the porch, just in time to be violently ill off the side of it. Then, without a backward glance at my mother or even at Joshua, I ran away from that house as fast as I could.

Chapter
TEN

I didn't remember when Joshua stopped me, nor did I remember how he convinced me to get back into the truck without being able to touch me. All I knew was that I went from tearing a feverish path through the wilderness near my mother's home to sitting motionless in the passenger seat of Joshua's truck as it bounced us down a roughly paved road.

"What . . . what happened?" I asked hoarsely. I had a bad taste in my mouth, and I had a bad feeling about how it got there.

"You were sick," Joshua replied plainly. He kept his gaze trained firmly on the road, almost as if his life depended on how hard he could concentrate on the task of driving. I'd never seen him so intent on *not* looking at me.

"Do you hate me now, knowing that I caused someone's death?"

My question dripped with self-pity, and I hated myself a little for asking it. But that didn't mean that I didn't want to know the answer anyway.

For a long time—an eternity, to someone who's asked that kind of question—Joshua said nothing. When he eventually cleared his throat, I cringed, ready for something awful. Ready for him to tell me, finally, that I'd put him at too great a risk.

"Amelia, I love you."

He said it so earnestly, so fiercely, that I leaned back in surprise.

"I love you," he repeated. "And hell itself won't stop that. Sorry to put it so dramatically but, well, it's the truth. And I'm terrified because I can't keep you or me or anyone we know from what's coming. From what's already *here*."

I nodded bleakly.

"It must have happened right after we left. I don't know how they convinced her to drive on *that* road again."

Then I recalled one image from the night of my death: a young girl with crazed, possessed eyes, watching while I drowned in the river below her.

"Actually," I amended, "I have a pretty good idea how they did it. But I just can't believe they would choose . . ."

When I trailed off, unable to finish, Joshua spoke one, low word.

"Serena."

For some reason, I chose that moment to lose it. I dropped my face into my hands and began to sob messily, not bothering to hide my misery from Joshua. I cried like I hadn't done in months, letting the full force of what I'd seen on my mother's TV wash over me in a brutal, guilty wave. And as I sobbed, other things started to seep in along with the details of the morning news report.

Memories.

The image of an eight-year-old Serena on the day we met, beautiful and a little wild in her grass-stained soccer uniform. A whiff of the rancid volcano we'd tried to make together for a seventh-grade science credit. The slight chip on her right canine, from a rock-hard jelly bean we found in her mom's couch that I'd dared her to eat. The heart she'd drawn around Doug Davidson's name in bright-red ink, right on the front cover of her Government book, our first day of public school.

Our friendship had been the lifelong kind . . . for as long as I'd lived, anyway. Now, *neither* of us had a "life-long" existence. Not anymore.

It was the thought of her, lost and alone and probably tormented in the netherworld, that ultimately made me stop crying. I swallowed back the last of my sobs and wiped furiously at my eyes, smearing the tears away haphazardly across my cheeks. As my vision cleared, I could see that Joshua had pulled his truck to the shoulder of the road, and he now waited patiently for me to work through this outburst of misery.

Yet another reason why I loved him; yet another reason why he deserved so much more from me than self-indulgent misery. He deserved my action, as did Serena, and Gaby, and my father, and every other wrongfully imprisoned soul. I wasn't exactly sure *how*, but I knew that I wouldn't go into the darkness without freeing the people I loved from the demons.

And I wouldn't go without one hell of a fight.

I kept silent until the force of tears and sickness and loss no longer controlled me. Then, when I felt like my body would better obey my mind, I finally turned to Joshua.

"Please take me back to your house."

Joshua began moving fast, as if he was dealing with an unstable situation—or person.

"That's a good idea," he said hurriedly. "We'll get you back there so you can rest for a while, have some of my dad's cooking, and then maybe—"

"No."

My interruption wasn't cruel, but it didn't leave any room for argument, either.

"I'm done resting," I continued, a touch more gently. "I've been resting since Christmas—since Gaby—and look what that's accomplished. First, you and I love each other, more than ever, but our relationship is stalled. It will be, until something about *me* changes. Then, the demons are obviously a bigger threat than they were the day we met. And now, another one of my friends is dead."

"None of that is your fault, Amelia—"

"I know," I interrupted again. "Really, I do. Like you said: I didn't create hell. I didn't invite this evil into our lives. But I'm tired of my loved ones hurting because of the darkness. I'm tired of being its victim too. And I'm ready to do something about it. *Now.*"

Once I'd finished that pronouncement, I leaned back against my seat and did a quick self-assessment. I felt . . . *good*, actually. Surprisingly good. Galvanized, even.

But Joshua clearly didn't know how to respond. As he drove, he opened and shut his mouth several times without saying anything. Finally, after taking more than a few miles to collect his thoughts, he nodded.

"Okay, then. What do we do next?"

Joshua's question sounded just as fierce, just as deter-mined as his earlier declaration of love. Which meant that both came from the same, good place inside of him. The place I loved most.

Despite everything that we'd gone through, despite everything to come, I couldn't help but give him a wide, bright smile.

"I think it's time to gather a coven of Seers."

It was a good plan. Not to mention, it was the only plan I could come up with on short notice. But that didn't make it any easier to implement. First, sheer numbers were not on our side, as Jillian wasted no time in tell-ing me.

"It's just math, Amelia," she mumbled through an enormous bite of cold fried chicken. "One, two, three."

To illustrate, she used her cleaned drumstick to point at Scott, then Joshua, then herself. She swallowed her huge bite and added, "Three versus—what?—thousands of demons and their ghost slaves? No offense to anyone at this table, but I don't like our odds."

I groaned and let my forkful of potato salad clatter to my plate. *Math*, I laughed to myself. How quickly Jillian forgot that I'd helped Joshua to an A in Calculus last semester, while she almost failed basic algebra.

Aloud, I said, "That's why we're going to get a lot more Seers, Jillian. Because the larger our circle, the greater power we have to open the netherworld. And that's the most important part."

"Aside from the killings?" she asked drily.

"That's *not* going to happen again."

I answered so sharply that Jillian actually sank back in her chair, temporarily chastened. She should consider herself lucky that I hadn't followed my first impulse and thrown my fork at her.

For the second time today, the four of us were gathered around the Mayhews' breakfast table—this time, with a Southern-fried lunch of the weekend's leftovers. When Joshua and I had arrived back at the house, Rebecca and Jeremiah were already awake; this necessitated a flurry of explanations about why the two couples were together so early in the morning, instead of sleeping safely apart. Jillian and I crafted some impromptu slumber-party lies that, although thin (*nail painting! gossip! chocolate!*), convinced the older Mayhews to leave us alone with a few plastic containers of leftovers and an entire afternoon to plan our attack.

"Personally, I think we should talk to Ruth's and my gran's old Seer group," Scott offered.

Joshua and I replied simultaneously: "No chance," on

his part, and "That's a fantastic idea," on mine.

Joshua turned to me, blinking rapidly. "What? You can't be serious, Amelia."

"I'm very serious. We *need* them. As your little sister so sweetly pointed out, there's strength in numbers. And in the old coven's case, experience. Two newbie Seers and one who hasn't technically been triggered yet aren't going to keep the netherworld open for very long."

"Hey," Scott protested. "I could, like, hold my breath for a really long time, or something. You know: get 'triggered' or whatever."

I smiled at him gently. "Scott, in a weird way, that's very sweet. But I don't think an intentionally failed suicide attempt is what we're really going for."

When he grinned back at me sheepishly, I noted, "A-plus for enthusiasm, though."

"I think it's a mistake," Joshua insisted, running one nervous hand through his hair and then resting it on his neck. "We can't forget that the Wilburton coven wanted to exorcize Amelia. Just a few months ago, actually. I'd bet none of *them* have forgotten that fact."

To my surprise, Jillian actually took my side and began to argue with her big brother.

"So what?" she challenged him. "I doubt that would matter, if they knew we were all after the same thing. Besides, they're probably leaderless without Grandma

Ruth, anyway. If we ask them really nicely, maybe bring them a few extra cases of Ensure as a peace offering . . ."

Although Jillian kept talking, I stopped listening. Not because she offended me with her disrespect, but because of something she'd just said. Something that gave me an interesting, if dangerous, idea. I turned it over in my mind, treating the idea as carefully as I would a delicate seashell with sharp edges. Razor sharp, if past experience served.

But worth it, I ultimately decided. Maybe even necessary to our mission. I mentally rejoined the conversation as Jillian continued to poke fun at her Seer elders.

". . . you know, throw in some denture cream. Ask them if we can see pictures of their great-grandchildren—"

She stopped short when she caught my determined stare.

"What?" she demanded. "Why are you looking at me like I'm a crazy person?"

"Actually, I'm looking at you like you're a *brilliant* person."

One corner of Jillian's upper lip lifted in suspicion. "What's that supposed to mean?"

Ignoring her hostile sneer, I flashed a knowing little smile. "It means that someone should give your grandma Ruth a call."

For a moment, no one responded. Then Joshua and

Jillian burst into raucous laughter. Joshua actually started to tear up, and Jillian curled sideways across her chair as if all the cackling had given her a cramp. But their laughter died when they noticed that I hadn't joined in.

"I'm not joking," I said evenly, once they'd quieted down. "Ruth Mayhew is the most powerful Seer we know. We'd be idiots to try and do this without her."

Jillian snorted lightly, reached into the pocket of her dress, and flipped out her cell phone. She used it to gesture meaningfully at me.

"Okay, Fearless Leader. Why don't *you* call her, then?"

Again, she wore that derisive sneer. But I could tell from the glint in her eyes that she didn't actually hate the idea; she was just too afraid to make the call herself. So I glanced over at Joshua. He met my gaze squarely, but like his sister, he clearly balked at the thought of making such a call. I understood this fear far better, coming from Joshua.

To put it mildly, Joshua's relationship with his grandmother had been strained for the past few months. Because of me—but also because he'd chosen a different kind of Seer life. The kind that included coexistence with the dead, something Ruth staunchly opposed. This opposition should have struck her from our list of possible partners. And yet . . .

"I'll make the call."

Thankful that I'd practiced dialing a few times on Joshua's cell, I snatched the phone out of Jillian's hand and scrolled quickly through her list of contacts. The photo that corresponded with Ruth's phone number made me shiver a little, but I clicked Dial before I could chicken out—and before anyone around the table could stop me.

Ruth answered on the second ring.

"Jillian, honey? How nice to hear from you."

Immediately, I could tell that Ruth had recovered from her poisoning last Christmas. Lucky for her and the New Orleans Seer community, Kade LaLaurie's serpentwood cocktails apparently didn't have a permanent effect. She sounded so strong, so imperious, that it struck me mute for half a second.

"Jillian? Jillian, dear, I'm awfully busy—"

"It's not Jillian, actually."

My voice came out strained and unfamiliar. But Ruth nonetheless recognized it. After a tense pause, she growled, "What do *you* want?"

"A chance," I said weakly. Then, in a firmer tone, I repeated, "A chance, Ruth. I need one, your family needs one—the entire town of Wilburton needs one."

I heard a faint, rhythmic clicking on the other line, as though she was tapping her fingernails against a marble surface. She stayed silent for so long, I thought she might have hung up on me. But finally, she commanded, "Explain yourself."

I took a deep breath for courage, and then did just that. It took me a while to go through the whole story—I actually started from the beginning, with Eli, and made my way to the present threat. I only left out a few details, mainly steamy ones concerning me and Joshua; in my opinion, those memories belonged solely to us.

I felt a little breathless as I finished. Checking the clock over the Mayhews' stove, I could see why: I'd talked for almost thirty minutes straight. I took a quick, peripheral peek at my tablemates. Joshua and Jillian looked far more somber than they had earlier, and Scott looked downright queasy. I guess Jillian didn't give him the *entire* story, after all.

Ruth's voice drew my attention back to the phone call, which, up till now, had been more of a monologue than a conversation. As Ruth continued to speak, it seemed that the call would remain a monologue—she talked ceaselessly for another thirty minutes, telling me *exactly* what she thought about me and my plan. She even told me when the conversation was officially over, hanging up on me without so much as one word of good-bye.

I stared at the phone in my hand long after the call ended, not really noticing when the screen went blank from inactivity. My tablemates stared at me, too, waiting silently for the bad news. While they waited, I played Ruth's most important words over and over in my mind. Then I shook my head and raised my eyes to Joshua's.

"She's in," I said. "Ruth's on our side."

Chapter
ELEVEN

Four tense but uneventful days later, neither Joshua nor I had quite recovered from Ruth's shocking change of heart. Or change of methods, at least.

On the phone with me, she made it perfectly clear that she still thought I shouldn't exist in this realm. But as long as I intended to fight the powers of darkness, she'd stand with me. Until High Bridge fell, of course. After that, we would return to our respective sides of the dead/living divide.

For the last few days, Joshua and had I spent every

spare minute planning the big picture. Before we knew it, it was already Thursday night—only forty-eight or so hours away from our epic showdown. So we lay on the gazebo's daybed, avoiding his Physics homework and plotting the smaller details. Unfortunately, most of our plotting involved *waiting*, since everyone agreed that we should let Ruth convince the Wilburton Seers to join us. God only knew what would happen if four teenagers, one of whom was a Risen ghost, asked them.

Without looking at Joshua, I tugged nervously on my bottom lip with my teeth.

"Ruth said she could get a flight out of New Orleans Friday," I told him. "And she promised that she'd spend this week working on spells. But since she won't get here until tomorrow night, we only have one full day to rally the Wilburton coven *and* prep for Saturday's midnight attack, before the demons strike again. Assuming they even keep their word on the one-death-a-week thing."

Joshua shifted uneasily beside me. "We can't afford to think like that, Amelia."

"You're right," I said softly. "I'm not sure I can wrap my brain around the idea that someone else might die before then."

To distract myself from that very real possibility, I reached up and drew invisible patterns in the air with one finger. Joshua watched me for a minute and then reached up as well, to try to clasp my hand. Even though our hands passed through each other midair, it was the thought that counted; with Joshua, it *always* counted.

I angled my head toward his on our shared pillow. "You know the only thing that makes all this bearable?"

"That you love me?" he guessed.

"Bingo." I smiled faintly and dropped my hand to trace the outline of his jaw.

"Do you need me to tell you that the feeling is mutual?" he asked. When I shook my head, he beamed at me. Then his smile faded into a grimace.

"Damn," he murmured, raking his fingers through his messy, post-baseball-practice hair. "I forgot to tell you—I've got a game tomorrow night. I won't be there to help you with my grandma."

The thought of speaking to Ruth in person, without Joshua as a buffer, made me go cold. Still, I shrugged and gave him a blasé wave. "It'll be okay—Ruth and I can handle the planning that night by ourselves. And on Saturday . . . well, you'd better not miss Saturday."

"I wouldn't, not ever. But you know what's weird? I'm actually a little sad that *you* have to miss Friday."

"Me, too," I said, and I meant it. I'd attended each of his spring ball games, albeit invisibly: I'd never felt ready to introduce myself to Joshua's friends. Kind of ironic, considering the fact that just a few days ago, I'd introduced myself to one of them with a literal bang.

"Maybe if I'm not there," I joked, "you'll play even better. You know, since my freaked-outedness won't be subliminally freaking *you* out."

Recently, college scouts had started attending the Wilburton High baseball games to watch Joshua and his friend David O'Reilly play. Since the scouts arrived, I'd spent every game in near agony, both hopeful and fearful that Joshua would finally earn his scholarship to some faraway college. Each pitch, each hit, had me clawing at my wooden seat. Now, I didn't know if either of us would survive this weekend to see another game.

Unaware of my real fears, Joshua laughed. "Maybe you *do* affect how I play. But it's not like I can see you up there in the bleachers."

His reference to my invisibility problem brought up another, far less pleasant thought. I curled up into a seated position next to him, tucking my legs beneath me on the bed.

"Speaking of Friday," I said, abruptly changing the subject, "I think I've decided that I *am* going to go, tomorrow morning."

Joshua's eyebrows drew together with worry. "You shouldn't have to go by yourself, Amelia. I can skip school tomorrow. Go with you."

I shook my head firmly. "No, you can't. Besides, you'd

get some pretty weird looks, standing all by yourself at the funeral of a woman you didn't even know."

Joshua's expression darkened further as he shifted to sit up beside me. "So, you're really going to stay invisible for the whole thing?"

"It's Serena's funeral, Joshua. You read the newspaper: my mother will definitely be there. I can't let her see me, especially not on a day like that."

Two days ago, Jillian had found Serena's obituary in the *Latimer County News-Tribune*. Other than the few details I'd learned from the TV news report, I discovered some unexpected items in the obituary as well.

The first thing out of place was Serena's burial site: it would be the same cemetery where I'd been buried, instead of her family plot in the neighboring town of Hartshorne. Next, the obituary listed only one person as Serena Taylor's next of kin. Not her mother, father, or little brother Aaron, but one Elizabeth Louise Ashley. My mother.

"If you want to go by yourself," Joshua said, drawing me out of my confused thoughts, "then I won't stop you."

Although he spoke the words, I could tell that Joshua didn't like the idea of me being alone at the funeral of my ex–best friend/murderer. Truth be told, I didn't much like it either. But I *couldn't* miss the funeral—just as I suspected that Serena hadn't missed mine.

Suddenly, Joshua's face brightened with a new idea. "You could wear a disguise," he suggested. "So that your mom won't recognize you."

I released a small snort of disbelief. "What, like wear oversized glasses with a fake mustache attached?"

Joshua grinned a little. "Could I get a picture of that, please? But seriously: Jillian obviously loves to dress you up like a paper doll, so we could at least see what she comes up with."

I was about to reject the idea completely, when I hesitated. At worst, I could turn invisible at the cemetery gates if I didn't feel sufficiently disguised.

"All right," I said, looking up at Joshua. "I'll give it a shot."

He blinked back, clearly surprised that I'd actually agreed. Then he pulled out his cell phone. After a quick text and its reply, he slipped the phone back into his pocket.

"Jillian's in her room—she says you should just go on up so that you two can look through some clothes."

I swept away a few leaves that had fallen onto my jeans from the plants above us and then peeled myself off of the daybed. "Don't you think it's a little ridiculous," I asked him as I rose, "that the two of you *text* each other, when you're less than a hundred feet apart?"

Joshua grinned good-naturedly and settled back on

the daybed with his previously discarded Physics book.

"How would we have known how far apart we were, unless we texted first?"

I shook my head, moving toward the entrance of the gazebo. "I'm not sure I'll ever understand this century."

I heard Joshua chuckle as I let the heavy outer drapes of the gazebo fall shut behind me. I trudged through the dark backyard into the house, dragging my feet a little. Once I entered the house I turned myself invisible, just in case Jeremiah or Rebecca had decided to stay up later than their children, and made my way to Jillian's bedroom. I knocked on her door, feeling a strange sense of déjà vu—I'd gone to her room to get dressed up only a few days ago. But considering what had happened since then, it felt like something I'd done in another lifetime.

The door opened and, instead of Jillian, a dress greeted me. It swung slightly on its hanger, which Jillian held in front of her like an offering. The dress was surprisingly understated: cleanly cut black silk, almost retro with a wide neckline and three-quarter-length sleeves.

"Perfect," I said quietly, running my fingers across its fabric. "Very . . . funereal."

Still hiding behind the dress, Jillian produced a black, floppy-brimmed hat in her other hand. "This, and some oversized sunglasses, ought to hide your face."

Finally, the dress swished aside and Jillian came into

view. Without letting me cross her threshold yet, she scrutinized my face as if I had a smudge of dirt on it.

"What?" I asked, wiping self-consciously at my cheeks. "What is it?"

Jillian tilted her head to one side, still giving me that thoughtful look. "Have you always worn your hair down? I mean—did you wear it like that, when you were alive?"

I tugged at the ends of my long brown hair and frowned. "Yeah, I did."

Jillian nodded decisively. "Then tomorrow, you're a ponytail girl. Sleek and sophisticated—none of your usual bohemian crap."

"Thanks, Jill," I drawled. "You're a big help."

"Don't mention it," she muttered, entirely missing my sarcasm as she continued to study me. "A little makeup wouldn't hurt you, either. Mascara, blush, maybe some red lipstick—you'll look like a totally different person. I'll leave everything out on my bed for you tomorrow morning. I'd help you get ready before I go to school, but . . ."

"The no-touching thing sort of preempts that," I finished awkwardly.

She was obviously not as concerned by the problem as I was. Without bothering to end the discussion properly, she shut the door in my face.

"Night," she called belatedly, her voice muffled by the wood.

Although Jillian couldn't see me, I rolled my eyes at her door. Even with all we'd been through together, I guessed some things never changed. I took a quick peek at Jeremiah and Rebecca's door, to make sure they hadn't heard me talking in their house so late at night. Then I crept back downstairs, through the back kitchen door to where the gazebo—and Joshua—waited for me.

When I woke the next morning, I found myself curled as close to Joshua as I could get on the daybed in the gazebo, where we'd stayed up talking. I pushed myself into a stretch, yawning.

I cast a glance back at Joshua, and my yawn transformed into a soft smile. I loved the way he looked as he slept: frowny and disheveled like a little kid. Not as heart-wrenchingly handsome as I found him while he was awake, but somehow just as appealing. Sitting this close to him, I experienced that familiar, curling ache within my core, the one that awakened each time I *really* let myself look at him. Physically, it felt as though I'd slept alone in an otherwise empty bed. Emotionally . . . well, that part never changed.

My gaze drifted upward, to the mesh skylights that Rebecca had sewn into the cloth ceiling of the gazebo. I wasn't surprised to see that it was still dark outside. On a day like this, there was no way I would sleep past dawn. I was too edgy. Too anxious.

I slithered off the bed—no need to rouse Joshua, since no one in the Mayhew household could possibly be awake yet. I stepped carefully across the creaky gazebo floorboards and parted the drapes, slipping quietly through the backyard. I almost laughed at myself as I crept into the Mayhews' house like a cat burglar: for a girl who could go invisible, I was acting a bit ridiculous.

Yet something about my goal this morning felt a little clandestine. Maybe because I hadn't told anyone, including Joshua, my full plan.

With my lips pressed tightly shut, I climbed the stairs and then paused outside Jillian's room. Did I really want to do this? Like a crazy person, I answered myself by nodding. Then, as slowly and delicately as possible, I turned Jillian's doorknob.

Inside, Jillian was sprawled diagonally across her bed, taking up every available inch of space with weirdly angled arms and legs. And she was snoring. Loudly. I stifled a snicker: the wry, jaded Jillian Mayhew *snored*. That was something I could file away for later use, I told myself as I passed the foot of her bed.

A slight hitch in one of her snores made me pause, midstride. But when the jackhammer-like chorus started back up, I continued to tiptoe across the room. There, draped over an armchair, I found what I needed.

I wasted no time changing into the black dress, struggling only momentarily with the back zipper. After placing the floppy hat on Jillian's vanity, I took my discarded clothes to the closet, where the rest of my wardrobe was secretly stored. I shoved my jeans and top into a bag of dirty clothes—which Jillian begrudgingly washed with hers each week—and dug around for the pair of black heels that Gaby's brother Felix had given me as I was leaving New Orleans. I stood and slipped into them unceremoniously, trying not to think about the fact that the shoes probably cost more than my mother's mortgage payment.

Next, I sat on the bench in front of the vanity and squinted at my dim reflection. As much as I hated to admit it, Jillian was right: I needed to do something about my face, which didn't look a day over eighteen. Probably because it wasn't, and hadn't been for over a decade.

Breathing a quick prayer for good luck, I tried to re-create the makeover that Gaby had given me in New Orleans. After an additional swipe of blood-red lipstick, I smoothed my hair into a low ponytail and put on the floppy hat. With just the slightest catch in my throat, I slipped on Gaby's huge pair of Fendi sunglasses—the ones I'd handed to Jillian the minute we left Louisiana. Then I leaned back to assess my handiwork.

I couldn't believe how transformed I actually looked. The dress, the ponytail, the lipstick—combined, they made me look at least five years older. Best of all, the hat and sunglasses obscured my face so well that I could pass as any random woman in her midtwenties. One of Serena's friends from work, maybe.

Satisfied, I snuck out of Jillian's room as quietly as I'd snuck in and made my slow, stealthy way back outside. As I crossed the back porch and prepared to descend to the driveway, I caught a glimpse of the gazebo and faltered. I hated to leave Joshua there alone, to wake up in a few hours and find me gone. But if I woke him up now, he might insist that he come with me after all. So, with a guilty heart, I took the last few steps to the driveway and began my long, lonely walk.

I'd seen this place at dawn, many times. Yet today, it seemed different. More watchful, more *alive*, if that was possible.

Just outside the cemetery gates, I paused to inspect the changes. Every other time I'd seen my graveyard, it looked a little dilapidated and ignored—a burial place for people who couldn't afford better. Now, the rusted gates had been polished up and adorned with a new sign that announced the name of the cemetery in wrought iron curlicues. All along the front fence line, someone had planted a thick row of irises, which bloomed in bright purples and pinks and yellows. Even the gnarled trees seemed more welcoming with rustic wooden bird-houses nailed to their trunks.

My cemetery actually looked *cheerful*. More like a pretty little park than a place where the poor buried their dead. But somehow, the differences made me more ill at ease than ever. Maybe because I just couldn't imagine a living person—or even a team of living people—spending any significant time in this place. Especially when you considered all the secrets and souls that lay deep beneath its soil.

Still, the irises presented me with a solution. I made my way over to a particularly thick clump, knelt as best I could in the black dress, and plucked a few of the more vibrantly flowered stems. I laid them across the crook of one arm, careful to keep the petals off the fabric of my sleeve, and stood. Then, with just a slight falter in my steps, I entered the graveyard.

I walked slowly down the main cemetery corridor, pull-ing my heels up whenever they sank a little too deeply into the unpaved path. When I'd covered the overpriced shoes with a sufficient amount of grime, I yanked them off and continued barefoot. Old habits died hard, I supposed.

As I passed a freshly dug grave, in front of which someone had placed a few rows of white plastic chairs, I tried not to look at it. I would deal with *that* problem later.

Finally, I'd gone far enough into the cemetery that I could stop at my first destination. Funny that I remembered the location of *this* headstone, even though I'd only visited it once. I dropped a single yellow iris on the grave and said a quick prayer before turning away. That small tribute was the most Eli Rowland deserved, and probably the most he'd received since being buried here almost forty years ago.

Now that my respects to Eli's grave were paid, I made my way over to the headstones I really wanted to visit. Or head*stone*, as the quick glance at my own was mostly obligatory. I dropped a purple flower on the small mound of my grave and then turned to the most important slab in this entire cemetery.

I was happy to see that my father's grave still looked well tended. If the mowed plot and cleanly swept marker were any indication, then my mother visited pretty regularly. A pot of slightly wilted flowers sat on top of the headstone, so I added two irises to the bunch. For lack of anything else to do, I rearranged them, moving the freshest flowers to the front and plucking out any stems that were brittle or brown.

Pleased with the new bouquet, I let my fingers trace down the headstone until they found the carved indentation of three words. TODD ALLEN ASHLEY—I outlined each letter with my index finger, trying not to think about the fact that this memorial was the only physical reminder of him I had left. Done outlining, I placed my hand flat against the stone to block out the date of his death.

"Hi, Daddy," I said aloud, and I could hear the longing in my own voice.

"Hi, Amelia."

The unexpected response made me jerk my head back so fast I felt a muscle in my neck wrench. I hardly noticed the pain, though; I couldn't seem to focus on anything but the person standing behind my father's headstone.

I'd half expected this meeting; half hoped for it, too, although I didn't think the odds of it happening were very likely, given the tragic events of Saturday night. Still, I couldn't help but ask the million-dollar question:

"Serena—is that you?"

Chapter
TWELVE

Serena had only been dead five days—not long enough to look so alert. More importantly, the *demons* themselves had killed her. She should be a mindless, shadowy slave in their wraith army right now.

Yet there she stood, not four feet away, smiling down at me with perfect awareness, as though she were still alive. She wore the same suit that I'd seen her in on Saturday morning—a shame that she hadn't had the chance to change into something more comfortable and eternity appropriate. But she must have loosened her ponytail sometime before she died, because her corn-silk hair now floated in pretty waves around her shoulders. When the early sunlight hit it at the right angle, it glowed.

Almost like a halo.

"Hi, Amelia," she repeated, in a voice that was simultaneously familiar and otherworldly. It had a sweet, lilting quality that spread through me like warm honey. The sound of her voice made me feel happy. Giddy, even. I couldn't understand the feeling, couldn't understand how she looked exactly the same and yet totally different, until something clicked in my mind.

"The light took you," I breathed, "instead of the darkness."

In lieu of an answer, Serena flashed me a mysterious, close-lipped smile and took a step closer to my father's grave.

"How, Serena?" I blurted out, too impatient to wait for her to speak. "How could you be with the light now, if the darkness killed you? I don't understand how."

Again, she didn't answer my question. Instead, Serena folded her hands and leaned casually on top of the headstone. With a thoughtful frown, she cocked her head to one side and stared at me for a moment. Then the enigmatic smile returned, and she shook her head.

"You know what your problem always was, Amelia?" she mused. "You never knew how to relax. Even as a kid, you were so freaking straitlaced."

"W-what?" I stuttered.

Now *this*, I didn't expect. Maybe an explanation for how she stood here, in the living world; maybe an apology for *killing* me. But not this.

Serena went on with a widening grin, untroubled by my distress.

"God, do you remember when we were eleven and you let me cheat off your math exam? Our parents didn't even have a clue, but you basically went nuts with guilt and told them in less than a *day*. Little Miss Good Girl, to the rescue."

I remembered now. She'd begged me for days to let her cheat, and I'd caved. Even though I eventually tattled, the guilt burned acidic in me long afterward. Because ultimately, I'd betrayed my mother *and* my best friend. It was one of the few dark memories in our bright history, yet Serena was laughing like it was our best.

"Or how about the time we smoked that entire pack of clove cigarettes with my cousins behind my dad's pool shed when we were fifteen? You were the only one who threw up, and then you insisted on taking about nine showers and staying over so your parents wouldn't smell the smoke on you."

Again, she spoke of one of our darkest moments. Another situation in which she'd pressured me to do something I hadn't wanted to do . . . another situation in which I showed weakness, in one form or another.

"Why are you bringing these things up?" I asked softly.

Hearing her snicker cruelly about these memories—which were few and far between, when compared to all the good things we'd shared—I had the urge to show her how strong I'd become. But God help me, my eyes started to sting. This woman had been my *best* friend. Now, during our first meeting since my death, she seemed intent on rehashing the worst of what was once *us*.

If that was how she wanted things to be, then I certainly wouldn't give her the satisfaction of seeing me cry. I narrowed my eyes and kept them from watering by sheer force of will.

Serena still wore that cold smile. She unfolded her hands and let them rest over my father's headstone, her long, slender fingers almost brushing the carved scroll-work near the top of his stone. Then, without warning, her face fell and she sighed heavily.

"I'm saying these things, Amelia, because you're my bestie."

Serena's tone was sincere, but it made me scowl at her. The last time she'd called me "bestie," she'd shoved me over the guardrail of a suspension bridge. That kind of thing could really take the shine out of a word.

"What are you talking about?"

This time, my question sounded colder, angrier. Not like the timid little girl in Serena's memories. She must have noticed the shift in me, because her expression hardened, too. When she spoke again, her tone was clipped. No-nonsense, like we were discussing a business proposal.

"I'm talking about the choice you've been asked to make, Amelia—I'm here to help you make it."

I had to give credit to the newly dead version of my old friend: she was just full of surprises. Not only had she shown up here, away from the dark place where I assumed she'd be trapped, but she also knew about the demons' ultimatum. Those two facts—her freedom and her knowledge—seemed like they should be mutually exclusive.

"Okay, I'll bite," I said icily, folding my arms across my chest. "How would *you* choose, if it were your decision?"

Serena lurched forward so quickly, her grip on my father's tombstone was the only thing that kept her from pitching over the stone and onto the grave.

"If I were you," she whispered harshly, "I'd march my skinny ass back to that bridge and *beg* them to take you in."

I automatically recoiled and spat out a curse word,

low and soft. Then I forced myself to stop shaking and looked her right in her suddenly demented blue eyes.

"And why would *your* crazy ass do that, if you were me?"

Still leaning precariously over the stone, she shook her head sadly. "You just don't get it, do you, bestie? If you don't turn yourself over, then you'll have to fight them. And we both know that you're not strong enough."

"I am strong enough," I growled, suddenly angrier than I'd been in my entire life.

"You're weak, Amelia Ashley," Serena insisted in a singsong voice. "Weak, weak, weak."

I rose then, pushing myself up from the grave until I stood slightly above her. And for the first time that morning, something other than confidence flickered in Serena's eyes. I couldn't be sure, but I thought I saw a glimmer of fear as she finally leaned back across the headstone.

"That's where you're wrong, Serena." I kept my voice even and low, but in my core, my emotions boiled. "You always underestimated me—always mistook morality and kindness for weakness. That was *your* fatal flaw, not mine."

She raised one pretty blond eyebrow. "Oh, really? Are we forgetting the night of your eighteenth birthday?"

I bristled. "You mean the night you murdered me, Serena? Because I'm pretty sure I'll never forget that."

"You mean the night you screwed things up for *yourself.*

You should have gotten the hell off that bridge. You knew something was wrong: you saw it, before anyone else did. But you stayed to look for me." She shrugged, flashing me a condescending smirk. "Weak."

I felt that strange, floating sensation people get right before the bottom drops out from beneath them. "How . . . how do you know that? You were possessed that night."

Serena lifted one shoulder in another, half shrug. "I know it now. And it's enough reason for you to do the right thing and turn yourself in."

Despite how much her words angered me, despite the hot swell of indignation in my stomach, my eyes began to sting again. Especially when the image of an eight-year-old Serena, flashing me a gap-toothed smile, rose unbidden in my mind.

"Don't you understand, Serena?" I pleaded, sounding so fervent that I surprised myself. "Turning myself over to the dark could *never* be the right choice, because it wouldn't really save anyone. The demons never stop killing people, never stop acquiring souls. There would be more murders after I gave in—maybe even ones that *I'd* commit. I can't do that to myself. And I can't let your death be so . . . so pointless."

Serena's smile made my skin crawl. There was something terribly wrong about that smile: it pulled hard at her cheeks, stretching her lips so far that too many of her teeth showed. Instead of looking like some angelic vision, lit up by the morning sun, she looked malevolent.

Demonic.

"Oh, bestie," she hissed, still wearing that ghastly smile, "my death wasn't pointless. My death was miraculous."

Before I could ask what she meant by that, a thread of black smoke began to weave its way around her shoulders and through her beautiful hair. It moved across her like a caress, so intimate and foul I nearly gagged.

"You're not light," I choked. "You're dark. They *did* get you."

I didn't think it was possible, but her nasty grin actually widened. Serena gave me one shiver-inducing wink. Then, in a voice that sounded like it rose from a rotted corpse, she rasped, "The choice, Amelia: make it soon. Or someone else joins me in paradise."

As she hissed out the last "ssss," the smoke enveloped Serena and she vanished, leaving nothing but a trace of handprint-shaped black ice where she'd gripped my father's gravestone.

Chapter
THIRTEEN

I have no idea how long I stood there, dazed and staring blankly at the empty space behind my father's grave. I only stirred when I heard a chorus of voices near the front of the cemetery. My head turned toward the noise slowly, almost reflexively, like I didn't have the capacity to move it consciously.

A small crowd had gathered about a hundred feet behind me, milling around the freshly dug grave and the plastic chairs. Watching the black-clad figures mingle, I shuddered. At this point, I was in no mood to attend a funeral. Especially Serena's.

I had to take a deep, shaky breath and remind myself that the *thing* I'd just talked to wasn't Serena. Not really. That thing was a puppet—a newly created wraith that the demons used to terrify me. I couldn't let their tactics work, not today.

Still, I made a mental note to discuss a few details of this new threat with the Seers. Like the fact that the wraith-Serena could still access memories from her life—the darkest ones, at least. I was bothered by the fact that she had appeared here in the living world, instead of the netherworld where I usually saw the wraiths. This appearance could mean only one thing: that the demons had a new soul reaper working for them. One that might still be somewhere close, watching me.

In case that was true, I stood a little taller and wiped the frightened wince from my lips. The phrase "game face" came to mind, and I actually smiled. My grim, close-lipped expression might not have been any prettier than Serena's corpse grin. But if anyone—like Kade LaLaurie, for instance—watched me right now, I knew they wouldn't see me rattled. If anything, my resolve to fight back had just strengthened exponentially.

With my shoulders pressed firmly down and my head erect, I turned from my father's headstone and went to join the other mourners. Once I entered the crowd, I tried to keep as anonymous as possible—I moved with the flow, exchanging sorrowful looks with people just long enough that they wouldn't bother to notice me further. I didn't see my mother in the crowd, which was both a relief and a disappointment.

As I circled the area in which the funeral would take place, I realized that I didn't recognize *any* of the other mourners. That was a little odd: I'd known Serena over half of her short life, so I should have known almost everyone there. The fact that I didn't . . . well, it bothered me. More than it should.

I glanced over at a man in a navy pinstripe suit who was sweeping away a few stray leaves from Serena's otherwise pristine new headstone. While I watched him work for a moment, I imagined this same man performing this same ritual on my own stone so many years ago. I shook my head, trying to rid myself of the morbid thought. As a distraction, I let my gaze trail down to Serena's epitaph. Seeing it, I frowned harder.

I'd expected something along the same lines as mine: loving daughter, too soon lost, etc. Instead, beneath the usual information one finds on a headstone, Serena's slab read:

THE NIGHT WILL SHINE LIKE THE DAY,
FOR DARKNESS IS AS LIGHT TO YOU.
PSALM 139:12

An ironically appropriate memorial, but not something Serena's parents would have chosen for her. At least, not the parents I knew.

Like an answer to my unasked question, a hearse and two black Town Cars finally pulled up outside the cemetery gates. A group of old men who looked like funeral-home attendants got out of the first Town Car and moved in unison, opening the back of the hearse and removing the casket. The sight of it made me flinch, and I almost turned away. Until I caught a glimpse of the sole person exiting the second Town Car.

I guessed that was the family car—the car that should have carried Serena's parents and her younger brother to this service. But none of them stepped out of the vehicle. Only my mother did, wearing a worn gray dress and carrying the same purse she had used when I was in high school.

Seeing her smooth the wrinkles from her dress—something I did almost incessantly when I was nervous—I frowned. Why was she the only person in the family car? Why was she in the family car at all?

My curiosity notwithstanding, I hung back, hiding in the thickest part of the crowd while my mother followed the casket's procession. After the pallbearers had placed the casket on a steel mechanism hovering over the open grave, the man in the pinstripe suit motioned for us to take our seats. I chose one in the last row, where I could slip away easily if I needed to. Then I watched apprehensively as my mother moved to stand near Serena's headstone.

I thought one of the funeral-home employees—most likely, the pin-striped man—would start the service. But instead, my mother stepped forward and cleared her throat.

"Serena Taylor," she began, "was an exceptional woman. Most of you know that because you worked with her. You knew her as a good accountant: someone whose work could be trusted; someone who your clients could rely on; someone who you were friends with, outside of work. But I knew her . . . as my daughter."

When my mother spoke that last word—"daughter"— I gripped my plastic chair and dug my fingers into its rim until they ached.

That's not true. That's not possibly true.

I hissed the thoughts so loudly in my mind, I almost missed the next part of the eulogy. I had to pry my fingers off the chair and fold them, one by one, into little fists in my lap. Unaware of the storm of jealousy and hurt that she'd just brewed inside her *real* daughter, my mother continued.

"Although you knew Serena, most of you probably don't know me. My name is Elizabeth Ashley, and I met

Serena when she and my daughter Amelia were both eight years old. They became close friends, so Serena became like a member of my family; that's just how the Ashleys—and Serena—operated. We all stayed friends, throughout the girls' childhoods and teen years. Then, after what happened on my daughter's eighteenth birthday, Serena's parents decided to . . ."

My mother paused, obviously searching for the right words. She shook her head decisively, and changed directions.

"When Serena could no longer count on the love and support of her own family, I made her a permanent part of mine. If her mother couldn't see what the blessing of having a daughter meant, I certainly could—especially a daughter like Serena. I stood beside her through her hardest times, and she stood beside me through mine. Even after she graduated from college and found a job, she drove all the way from Tulsa at least once a month to visit me. That's just the kind of girl she was: loving. I will miss her, as much as I miss my own daughter and husband."

As she spoke, I began to understand what my mother didn't actually say aloud: after my death, which had undoubtedly seemed suspicious, Serena's parents assumed that their daughter had something to do with it and threw her out of their home. And as was often her habit, my mother ignored her own financial troubles, her own loss, to save the day.

When my mother began to weep openly, the man in the pin-striped suit reached across the headstone with a handkerchief, which she waved away. She used the heel of her palm to wipe at her at eyes and then struggled through her tears to finish the eulogy.

"So I guess what I'm trying to say," she concluded halt-ingly, "is that I hope we can all forget the tragic way that Serena died, and remember the most important things. Like how warm she was—how smart and beautiful and funny. Because that's the best memorial Serena Taylor could ask for. And it's the one we owe her."

Finally, the weight of this situation crushed my mother, and she dissolved into messy sobs. Like me, she wasn't a pretty crier. But something about her grief made her even more beautiful to me. I had to fight the nearly irre-sistible impulse to surge forward and throw my arms around her shoulders.

As I replayed her final words in my mind, I wanted to cry, too. Whatever had passed between Serena and me—whatever might still pass in the netherworld—Serena Taylor had been my best friend. I had to keep thinking of her as the smiling, laughing girl I used to know—not the rotting puppet I met that morning.

I kept my burning eyes trained on my mother as she

moved aside so that the other funeral goers could stand and pay their final respects. After what felt like ages, an attendant told the people in my row that we could file past the coffin. I stood in the center aisle behind a line of strangers, waiting dutifully for my turn, and then finally stepped forward.

No expense had been spared on this casket: its ornate metal fixtures glinted in the morning light, and an enormous arrangement of white lilies covered the top of the coffin and drooped over its edges. I faltered, just for a second, before leaning forward to add my last iris—hot pink, Serena's favorite color—to the pile.

I was just about to withdraw my arm, but a soft gasp made me look up from the casket. I nearly tripped backward over my own feet when I saw that my mother had made the sound . . . and that she was staring right at me with a mixture of fear and uncertainty. Her hand, which had been clutched firmly to the lapel of her coat, wavered midair, and for one horrified second I thought she would point at me and scream. The urge to run and the urge to reach out to her warred within me, but I couldn't seem to move. My paralysis didn't pass until my mother's hand dropped back to her lapel and she looked away, her face suddenly impassive.

I forced my own head downward and tugged at the brim of my hat so that I wouldn't be tempted to look at her again. Then I hurried away from the casket, skirting the crowd as I made a beeline for the cemetery gates. As far as I was concerned, this funeral was officially over. I needed to get away from this place immediately.

But I'd only made it within a few feet of the entrance when someone called out, "Miss? Miss!"

It was my mother's voice . . . and she was nearby. Although I didn't turn around, I knew she called out for me—who else would she be following this close to the exit? I ignored her and picked up speed, walking so fast that I almost ran out the gates. But that didn't deter her.

"Miss!"

This time she shouted it, and I knew she wouldn't give up until she'd caught me. So I had to make a choice: bolt, or finally turn around and face the person I'd basically stalked for the last few months.

I skidded to a stop, cursing myself for not going invisible when I had the chance, right after my mother looked away at the casket. Then, with a shiver of apprehension, I spun around slowly on one heel.

My mother had stopped too, and now she stood a few feet away, panting from the effort of the chase. To my surprise, she didn't say anything at first. Other than the heave of her shoulders, she didn't even move. I followed her lead, keeping stock-still and silent in the gravel parking lot of the cemetery. Inside, however, I was a riot—all spastic heartbeats and rapidly firing nerves. I was pretty sure that if someone didn't speak soon, I would start to implode.

Finally, my mother sucked in one steadying breath and stepped cautiously forward.

"Miss?" she repeated. "You forgot this."

I didn't realize that she'd been holding something until she lifted one arm and opened her hand in offering. A single, perfectly round daisy sat in the center of her palm. I frowned at it, momentarily confused. Then I shook my head.

"No, that's not mine."

I kept my voice high and breathy in an attempt to disguise it. My mother didn't react in one way or another to the sound of it, so the effort must have worked. But she still shook her head.

"It is," she said simply, stretching her arm out so that her palm was a fraction closer to me. I paused, looking between the daisy and her face. I could tell from the determined set of her mouth that she wouldn't leave me alone until I took the flower. The real issue, then, was how exactly I would take it from her.

Not sure what else to do, I reached out and, with the tips of my fingers, plucked the uppermost petals of the flower. It lifted from her hand without our skin ever touching, and I tried not to sigh in relief. When I cupped the flower to my side, I felt the petals scratch at my palm—the daisy was fake, a pretend blossom of fabric and plastic.

My mother still didn't react as I took it, nor did she say anything when, after one last glance at her, I spun back around and began to hurry down the road that led away from the cemetery. It wasn't until I'd reached the main road—the one I would take back to the Mayhews' house—that I realized what my mother had done.

She'd offered me a fabric daisy: the very kind of flower she always placed on my grave.

Chapter
FOURTEEN

"S he knows. I know she knows."

"Maybe not. Your mother could have meant anything when she handed you that flower. Maybe she really *did* think it was yours. Like she thought that you dropped it, or something."

Hearing this highly unlikely explanation, I didn't say anything. Instead, the corners of my mouth tugged into a tight, disbelieving smile, and I arched one eyebrow at Jillian. Seeing my skeptical eyebrow raise, she shrugged and leaned against one column of her parents' front porch.

"But . . . probably not."

"Probably not," I echoed.

Then I wrapped my cardigan more tightly around me and craned to peer around another porch column. It was already dark outside, but I didn't need a spotlight to see that the driveway was completely empty. It had been, since Jeremiah and Rebecca left to watch Joshua's baseball game.

"Where *is* she?" I asked. "She should have been here hours ago."

Jillian and I had been waiting far too long for Ruth's taxi. Her flight should have landed at Wilburton's tiny municipal airport late that afternoon. But five p.m. had come and gone with no sign of a car—and no contact from Ruth whatsoever.

Again Jillian responded to me with a shrug, but this time she actually looked nervous. Like she knew that each second that ticked by meant another life was put more at risk.

I leaned against the railing of the porch and sighed raggedly. I wanted a lot of things right then, but more than anything, I wanted Joshua.

Part of me hoped that he had a fantastic game—one where he didn't have to worry about death or demons or his crazy girlfriend who liked to throw hand grenades. Another part of me missed him horribly, especially after

I read the note he left for me on the gazebo's daybed:

I understand. Good luck tonight. I love you.

Such a simple note, and yet every word made me ache inside.

I should've told Joshua why I wanted to leave early for the funeral. In fact, I should've just said yes when he suggested that he go with me. It didn't help that almost everyone else in his life—his parents; Scott; his other good friend, David O'Reilly; *Kaylen*—got to watch him play that night. And I supposed that I wouldn't even get to tell him about what happened that morning until very late that night—if I ever got the chance.

If we ever get started at all.

Ruth's conspicuous absence didn't bode well for us and our little endeavor. The longer Jillian and I waited for her, the more I suspected that either something had gone wrong, or Ruth had lied to me. Taking another long look at the empty driveway, I was about to admit defeat and choose the latter.

But just before I turned away, something at the far end of the drive caught my eye. I squinted at it, and then smiled.

A light flickered through the thick line of trees that bordered the Mayhews' property. As it moved, the light doubled and grew stronger, until I could see that it came from two car headlights.

Those two headlights weren't the only ones bouncing down the Mayhews' driveway. While the car I first noticed drove toward the house, another followed behind it and another behind that one, and so on until the entire driveway had filled. Even then, I could see other headlights moving on the other side of the front tree line, as more cars found parking spots outside the Mayhews' property.

"Holy Moses," Jillian whispered, staring with wide eyes at all the people exiting their cars and making their way across her front lawn.

"Holy Seers," I amended, but I sounded just as awed. An awkward crowd of at least fifty Seers gathered at the base of the porch. But that didn't make sense: less than twenty had attended my failed exorcism last fall. I couldn't explain how the Wilburton Seer community had doubled in just a few months. Not until I saw Ruth Mayhew finally exiting the first car.

Once her driver closed the car door behind her, she brushed imperiously past the big group and marched up the porch steps as though she owned them. Then she stopped in front of me abruptly and placed one hand on her hip as if to say, *You're in my way—move.*

Standing there, looking so much healthier than the last time I saw her, she resembled a general ready to command her troops. On some level, I was relieved: I needed her angry and authoritative, so that we might actually have a fighting chance against the darkness. But I also bristled under her resentful scowl. After everything that had passed between us, it frustrated me that her hatred hadn't lessened one bit.

"You're late," I said flatly, in lieu of a greeting. The corner of Ruth's mouth lifted into a half smile, one that I suspected was involuntary since she erased it so quickly.

"As you can see," she answered, tossing her glossy white hair, "I was just a *little* busy."

"Where did all these people come from, Grandma?"

Ruth and I both startled at the question—we hadn't even noticed Jillian approach us. It seemed as though we'd immediately fallen into our old routine, letting ourselves get wrapped up in mutual dislike. Still, the cold went out of Ruth's eyes when she looked at her granddaughter.

"They're from other towns nearby," she explained. "Some of them are even from other states. I've been working all week: reinstating myself with my old coven in Wilburton, recruiting Seers from others." She cast a rare doubtful peek over her shoulder at the crowd on the lawn. "I honestly thought I'd get more people than this, but . . ."

"But nothing," I interrupted, unable to hide my admiration. "This is amazing. There are way more Seers here than I expected."

Again, Ruth looked begrudgingly amused. "Well, thank you for that high praise."

"Anytime," I offered, smirking back at her.

We appraised each other for another beat and then, without so much as a signal, we turned simultaneously to face the crowd. From the corner of my eye, I saw her toss an irritated look in my direction. There were too many generals on this porch after all, it seemed. So I swallowed my pride and took one step backward, effectively giving Ruth the floor.

As I'd suspected, Ruth needed no other concession. She threw back her head, folded her hands in front of her, and began to address her audience.

"I won't waste your time with introductions," she called out, projecting her voice at a surprising volume for someone her age. "If you're here, you know who I am. And if you are what you claim to be, then you'll be able to tell which of these girls up here is my living granddaughter, and which . . . isn't."

I heard uneasy murmurs race through the crowd: *ghost, ghost ghost*. Those whispers crawled over my skin like probing, intrusive fingers. For the first time, it struck me that every person gathered on the lawn was staring up at me with barely concealed hostility. Suddenly, my commanding posture felt a bit foolish: these weren't the kind of people who took orders from me; these were the kind who would try to blink me out of existence, if they could. I didn't shrink into myself, but at that moment I certainly wanted to.

"Let's get right to it, then," Ruth continued, without sparing me as much as a sideways glance. "You all know why we're here: to end the threat that has plagued this area for decades. Possibly for centuries. We've long known that the evil ones choose rivers as their gateways, and we know that this river is a prime example. So, what do we do about it? When I contacted you this week, some of you suggested that instead of focusing on the river, we take out the earthly tool that the evil ones have been using: the bridge. But as this girl"—here, Ruth gestured to me—"has discovered, ruining the bridge is pointless on several levels. First, the darkness won't let the bridge be easily destroyed—they have an army of souls protecting it. And second, the destruction of an evil instrument on earth won't do much to its users in hell."

At this point, I felt a little frisson of excitement. Ruth *had* paid attention to me on the phone, and she clearly understood the problem: no human effort would take down that bridge, and even if it fell, nothing mattered unless the hell gate itself closed. I leaned forward, listening more closely to Ruth's plan.

"The real solution," she said, "is to open their gateway under its earthly façade, and then make it inoperable. Will this close hell itself? No. But it will end their reign here, in this one region; it will force them to hunt elsewhere—it will keep *our* children, *our* grandchildren, safe."

"How?" someone called out from the crowd. "How do we make it inoperable?"

For half a heartbeat, Ruth's gaze seemed to flit toward me. I thought maybe I'd just imagined it, until she announced the most crucial part of her plan.

"Dust," she announced proudly. "We'll salt the very earth of the netherworld with our Seer dust, so that nothing dark can ever tread it again."

The crowd began to chatter so excitedly, so loudly, that no one could hear me shriek, "No! Absolutely not!"

Almost no one. For a second time, Ruth's gaze flickered in my direction. I tried to catch her eye—tried to plead wordlessly with her to find some other way to win this battle. But she looked away quickly, turning back to her enormous new coven with a broad grin.

"We will season the waters of their river with our potions," she proclaimed over the enthusiastic babble, "so that nothing dark will ever flow in our own river again."

Now the crowd broke into actual cheers. I could only cover my mouth with one hand to hold back a sob. There were so many Seers on board with this plan—so many Seers in general—that I would never convince them to keep the netherworld open long enough to free my friends. I wasn't even sure that once they'd completed the task of jamming the portal, they'd let *me* escape it.

I couldn't believe I'd actually *wanted* to call in Seer reinforcements. I felt cheated, tricked, furious . . . until I caught sight of someone approaching the porch from behind the crowd. At first, the figure was blurred by the darkness. But as he drew closer, I could see his face.

Joshua still wore his baseball uniform and, even from this distance, I could tell that he'd played an intense game: dirt streaked everything, from his knees to his shoulders. He must not have joined the crowd early enough to hear his grandmother's plan, because after a moment's search, he found my face and then flashed me a warm, radiant smile.

That one smile changed everything. After a smile like that, I had to go along with Ruth's plan. Mostly because I couldn't imagine a world—living or beyond that didn't include Joshua's smile. And I knew, deep down, that the demons would eventually come for him. How could they not, if they really wanted me to say yes?

So it didn't matter that I might lose my own afterlife. It didn't matter that I would have to think, *hard*, of a way to save the people I cared about before Ruth trapped them in the netherworld forever. All that mattered at that moment was that I loved Joshua, and I wanted him safe.

Without another thought, I leaped off the porch, ran down the path that the recoiling Seers made for me, and threw myself into Joshua's open arms. I didn't even have time to register his arms around me before I planted a kiss on his waiting mouth.

It wasn't until he kissed me back that my brain finally processed the miracle: I could *feel* him again.

Joshua pulled away from the kiss only long enough to gasp, "What the hell—"

"I don't know," I interrupted breathlessly, shaking my head. "But I don't even care right now."

Neither did Joshua. His lips met mine again, just as forcefully and joyously as before.

I didn't feel the fiery tingle that had accompanied each of our touches before I Rose. Instead, I just felt him—warm and insistent and real. I couldn't think, couldn't breathe from the ecstasy of kissing him again. I wanted to draw him into me, to join my heart to his. Because I couldn't do that, I let my fingers run everywhere: his jawline, his neck, his chest. Joshua dropped his hands to my waist and tugged me more firmly to his hips. In turn, I tangled my fingers in his hair and moaned against his mouth.

Shock, fear, wonder, joy all flowed through me so quickly that I grew light-headed. When my knees began to buckle, Joshua held me tighter but he didn't stop kissing me. I could read his thoughts in that kiss: just like me, he didn't know how long we had together before this miracle vanished, and he didn't want to waste a split second of it.

Which was apparently all we had left.

The instant Ruth boomed, "Enough!" the sensation of Joshua's lips and arms disappeared. I actually lost my balance and fell forward with my own arms open, so that they nearly passed through his body like an insubstantial breeze. Once steady, however, I shared a brief, fraught look with Joshua and then spun around to face our interrupter.

Ruth remained on the porch, but she now stood with her feet apart, pointing at me like I was some kind of criminal. Her expression mirrored that worn by most of the Seers in the crowd: disgust.

"Abomination."

She whispered the word, but the crowd had grown so silent that I heard her clearly. Her eyes burned with confidence, self-righteous indignation. I knew what the Amelia from last fall would have done, if she'd seen that kind of glare: she would have run away, scared and alone in the black night. But I wasn't the Amelia from last fall. I was something stronger and fiercer.

Something that had suddenly gotten out of control.

Before I'd even had the conscious thought to summon

it, my glow appeared, curling around me in licks of bright flame. The fire burned me, inside and out, and I began to storm toward the porch with wide, brutal strides.

As I walked, the Seers once again parted for me like the proverbial sea. But this time, they didn't sneer at me . . . they *cowered*. With each step, I let my head swivel from one Seer to another, grinning broadly. Several of them actually responded with gasps, which only made my smile grow. Such small game couldn't distract me. Right now, all I knew was that the vicious old woman on the porch needed to *burn*.

"Amelia!"

Joshua's voice shocked me out of my fierce trance, and the glow extinguished itself immediately. My fury disappeared with it.

I blinked rapidly, before making eye contact with Ruth. She looked *horrified*, even more than when I'd seen her poisoned. And suddenly, I'd never felt more ashamed of myself. Fighting the sting of mortified tears, I let my head hang low.

It's already happening, I thought bleakly. *I'm letting myself go dark.*

My head shot back up, however, when Ruth finally spoke. Probably because she didn't sound scared, or even angry. Instead, she sounded elated.

"Ladies and gentlemen," she announced, once again pointing at me. "Meet our new secret weapon."

"So . . . I'm basically going to be a scarecrow?"

When no one answered me right away, I snorted in disbelief.

I didn't even try to mask my bitter tone. I'd spent several hours listening to Ruth's grand plan for me while sitting on an uncomfortable wooden pew in her old church—the place she'd taken me, Joshua, and a few Seer leaders after the rest of the crowd dispersed and hugs were exchanged with Rebecca and Jeremiah (who had no idea what had occupied their front yard, only minutes before they arrived home). Now, after hearing Ruth out for what felt like the thousandth time, I added *disgruntled* to *tired* and *achy* on my growing list of complaints.

On a big-picture level, I understood that this was everyone's problem. But right now the demons weren't targeting Ruth's coven or their loved ones: they were targeting *mine*. Unfortunately, this little conclave seemed intent on pushing me to the edge of their plan. And once I'd told them about my previous interactions with the demons as well as my meeting with Serena that morning, the Seers settled on the most *dangerous* edge. The one where I stood on the bridge like some sacrificial lamb—practically offering myself up to the demons on a platter. All so the Seers could trap my family and friends in the netherworld forever.

"You won't be a scarecrow, Amelia," Ruth chided. She tilted her head to one side and offered what she probably thought was a reassuring smile. "You'll be a Trojan horse. A distraction for the demons, in case they try to stop us from distributing the dust inside the netherworld."

Despite her flattering words—and her rare use of my first name—my angry smirk deepened. "In other words," I said, "I'll be bait."

"Exactly," Joshua chimed in. In fact, he growled the words, though from anger or a lack of sleep, I couldn't tell. He leaned forward in our front pew and glared meaningfully at the Seer elders, all of whom had taken more comfortable seats in the choir loft behind the altar.

"You're treating this like some sort of holy Seer mission," he accused, "where Amelia and all the other people that the demons killed are just collateral damage."

One of the elders, a middle-aged man whose sweater vest barely covered his paunch, raised his eyebrows as if to say, *Aren't they?*

Seeing this response, Joshua made a disgusted noise and flung himself back against the pew.

"Screw that, dude," Joshua spat. "You can do this without us, then."

Unlike her companions, Ruth knew how to play the diplomat when she wanted to. She waved her hands in a sort of settle-down motion and then looked from the Seers to us with a forced composure.

"No one is saying that, Joshua." She kept her voice low and soothing, but her grandson still laughed darkly.

"Not out loud," he replied. "Not yet, anyway. Just give them until tomorrow night when it's time to destroy the netherworld, and let's see how many of them wait for Amelia to get out."

Suddenly, at the weirdest possible moment, I wanted to throw myself at him again. To wrap myself around him like silk.

I mustered up a little more self-control and then placed my hand upon Joshua's, which he'd clenched to the edge of the pew. He didn't feel my touch, but he saw it. He released the pew and flipped his hand over so that our palms would have touched, if they could.

"What do *you* want?" he asked me. I met his probing gaze for a moment, before I looked down at our not-quite-entwined hands.

"To win," I answered quietly, even though everyone in the room could still hear us. "To stop the demons from killing anyone else . . . in any way we can."

Joshua immediately blanched. But before he got the chance to argue with me, the eavesdropping Seers sent up another one of their annoying, riotous cheers. Almost in unison, they started to climb out of the choir loft to congratulate me on my decision, and themselves on their plan. They began talking all at once, and soon it seemed as though everyone in the church was excitedly repeating the words "dust, demons, and defeat."

Everyone except Joshua. He watched me silently, still wearing that stricken look. Probably because he alone knew what my concession meant. By agreeing to play the sacrifice game, I'd basically agreed to the demons' original terms. Whether the Seers won or lost, I would likely be dragged into hell. Not that the Seers cared—they continued to chatter and clap each other on the back, walking out of the church without even one backward glance at the distraught teenagers who'd just solidified their crusade.

"You can't," Joshua whispered harshly, after the last of the Seers had gone. Suddenly, he looked so much older. So much more fearful, like all his optimism had left him in one fell swoop. I lifted my hand to his cheek, once again wishing for the ability to touch him so that I could smooth away the troubled lines around his mouth.

"I can, and I will."

I spoke gently, and I smiled to soften the blow. But the

effort didn't work. Joshua shook his head, hard, as if the strength of the shake might take back what I'd just said.

"This is crazy," he hissed.

"Yeah, it is." I felt my lips tug into a bitter half grin. "But it's also the best plan we've got."

"It's the *only* plan we've got."

"Then I guess that settles it."

When Joshua tried to argue, I raised my palm to silence him. "Do you know why I'm not as worried as I should be, Joshua? Because you'll be there too. And I know you won't let them shut the netherworld without me escaping it first."

He hesitated, obviously unsure of what to say or do next. Then he groaned, raked his fingers roughly through his hair, and dropped his hand to the top of the pew beside me.

"Okay," he sighed. "Okay. We'll do it: you'll be the demon trap, and I'll be your lookout."

He seemed so worried that I felt the ache in my chest awaken and writhe. So I offered him what little I could, in the form of a small smile.

"It'll work," I assured him softly. "This plan *will* work. Because I love you, and you love me, and we'll be together tomorrow night. The plan won't fail, because it can't."

Hearing this kernel of positivity—from me, of all people—Joshua responded with a small smile of his own. "Well, if you think we've got a chance, then we actually might. So that's it, then: the plan won't fail, because it can't."

"It can't," I repeated, ignoring the cruel voice inside of me that whispered the exact opposite.

Chapter
FIFTEEN

T his place is just so damn creepy," Jillian whispered.

She cast a wary look around the moonlit riverbank where we stood and then wrapped her arms more tightly around Scott's waist.

"Yeah," he said, pulling her to him. "After you find out that a place is impervious to hand grenades, you kind of lose your desire to party there."

"Or die there again," I muttered low enough that no one could hear me as I drew closer to Joshua. From the corner of his eye, Joshua caught my movement and mimicked it so that we stood as close as possible.

"It could be worse," he replied to everyone in a jokey tone. "We could be hanging out with a bunch of old witches on one of our last Saturday nights of the school year. Oh, wait. . . ."

Scott and I chuckled, but Jillian just rolled her eyes. I guess I couldn't really fault her bad mood. None of us had slept well last night, after our little Friday-night hoedown with the southeastern Oklahoma Seers.

Today hadn't been much better either, at least not for me. I'd had to go invisible while I watched Joshua and Jillian spend their Saturday afternoon playing family with Ruth, who pretended that she'd just flown up for an impromptu visit—no demon-fighting ulterior motive whatsoever. Poor Scott had to stay at home all day, completely alone, waiting for tonight's battle. Frankly, I think we were *all* a little tired from the effort.

Now Joshua and I stood on the muddy riverbank with Jillian and Scott, each of us trying not to look up at the hulking form of High Bridge. Just as it had on the night of Serena's death, this area felt colder than the rest of Wilburton. Almost as if this place was so dark, so unrelenting, that it had the ability to swallow the warmth of spring and turn it into something bleak and frozen.

I wasn't the only one who felt that way. Just a few

minutes after we arrived, Jillian insisted that she and Scott make an emergency run back to the Mayhews' house for hoodies and coats. If we *had* to be here on a Saturday night, she argued, we shouldn't have to freeze for it. Of course, the four of us were only here—a full hour before showtime—because of our "orders."

Our current job was relatively simple: stand guard near the bridge until the "moon was right" for the other Seers to arrive and perform their spells. If something eerie happened, we were supposed to call Ruth so that she could get a team of Seers here earlier than planned.

Personally, I thought the "moon" part of the Seers' mandate was absurd. I'd seen the young, barely triggered Seers of New Orleans perform similar spells under extreme duress, and none of them had used the moon, as far as I could tell. But when I tried to explain that to Ruth that afternoon, during one of the few moments we were alone in a room together, she'd simply appointed me and my friends watchdogs and then given me a series of dismissive waves.

I guess that was the modus operandi of the southeastern Oklahoma Seer community: no one's vote counted unless it had a few years—and a genuine pulse—behind it.

I pursed my lips and puffed out a slow, frustrated breath. Then I glanced over at Jillian, who was still

staring around the bank uneasily. She caught me looking and grimaced.

"It's really quiet out here."

"Too quiet," I agreed.

Despite the tense mood, Joshua and Scott began snickering. When Jillian and I balked, Joshua explained, "You
two sound like you're in a bad cop show. As in, *Ashley
and Mayhew, Paranormal Investigators.*"

I groaned and slapped at the air where my hand
should have made contact with his shoulder. "You're
ridiculous."

But as Joshua and his friend continued to chuckle, I
let myself join in—the last few hours had been such a
jittery span of boredom and tension that I couldn't resist
the break. Jillian must have felt the same, because the
four of us soon made a game of renaming TV crime
dramas.

"*Law and Order: Supernatural Intent*?" Jillian suggested.

I snorted and then countered, "*Disem-Body of Proof*?"

"No, wait! Wait!" Joshua held up his hands and composed his expression into something overly stern. "*CSI:
Wilburton.* 'Where the drama never stops.'"

While Jillian and I dissolved into a fit of giggles,
Scott imitated the deep, dramatic voice of a movie
announcer. "Millions of viewers want to know: will
the town's one stoplight *ever* start working again? Find

out next week, on *CSI: Wilburton*."

He had just started to add a "dun-dun-dunnnn" for effect, when a haughty voice interrupted us.

"I assume by the singing and laughter that you're all done shirking your duties now?"

All four of us spun around to find Ruth standing just a few feet away on the riverbank and watching us with barely concealed disdain. Behind her, the horde of Seers waited upon the embankment and along the road, appearing very much like an army in their uniformly black clothing.

To my surprise, Jillian was the first to step forward and speak for our little group. "Nothing happened while we were waiting, Grandma. And we're ready."

Ruth eyed the rest of us—Joshua, Scott, and me—in a way that suggested she didn't think *we* were ready at all. Instead of saying so, she turned slightly around and addressed her troops. "Form your circles along the bank," she commanded loudly. "We'll begin as soon as everyone has taken their place."

The Seers followed their orders quickly, moving in waves down the embankment to group together in circles of ten along the riverside. After most of them were situated, Ruth faced the four of us again, focusing specifically on me.

"Why aren't you on the bridge yet?" she demanded.

No *say your good-byes*, no *good luck, young lady*—just that imperious *get your ass up there* command.

I shook my head grimly. "You're a real piece of work, Ruth, you know that?"

She smiled back just as coldly as before. But in the dark, I thought I saw the tiniest flicker of sympathy in her eyes. As if she actually felt somewhat sorry about what might happen to me that night—not enough to come up with another plan, but enough to give me that look.

Or maybe I just imagined that flicker; it *was* dark out there.

Since Ruth and her Seers obviously weren't going to provide me with another alternative in the next ten seconds, I resigned myself to this one. Trying not to tremble, I glanced first at Jillian. At that moment, she wasn't looking at me. She was staring up at Scott with the warmest smile I'd ever seen her give someone. She seemed happy, and that fact made me happy too. Not that a girl like Jillian needed me to worry about her; regardless of her previous taste in boys, I didn't doubt that she could take good care of herself from now on.

Next my eyes met Joshua's, and instantly, something clenched painfully inside my heart. He stared at me the same way that Jillian had stared at Scott—but the look in Joshua's eyes was far stronger. The look he gave me said everything that he didn't: that he loved me, that he would watch over me tonight, and that he would fight his way to me, before the darkness closed.

Without speaking it aloud, Joshua told me that we were in this together. Always.

He and I held each other's gaze for longer than was appropriate—given that we were standing near his grandmother, who happened to hate me—but I couldn't bring myself to care. Finally, when I reached a point when I would either have to look away or run away, I let my eyes drop to the ground.

Keeping my gaze trained firmly on the tips of my boots, which had already sunk half an inch into the muddy riverbank, I cleared my throat. "So," I asked roughly, "what are my specific orders now?"

"Get up there and do whatever it is that you do when the demons attack."

Ruth said it matter-of-factly, like creating my glow was the easiest task in the world. But by now, I'd realized that there was no point in arguing with her. I tilted my head back and looked squarely into her eyes—like Joshua's, they were a beautiful midnight blue, but hers were once again cold and shuttered. She and I would not share some tender good-bye.

"Okay. See you on the other side."

Then I turned away from her—from all of them— and began to trudge up the embankment to the bridge.

Although it hadn't rained, the ground felt slipperier than it had on the way down, like the very earth didn't want me to make this climb. Still, I kept going, finally cresting the hill with a deep, shaky breath.

I allowed myself one second of terrified indecision before taking that first step onto High Bridge Road. Once there, however, I forced my legs to move at a steady, assured pace until I stood near the center of the bridge on one of the few stretches of concrete that looked like it *wouldn't* collapse at any moment. I shifted my weight from leg to leg until I felt as comfortable as I could, given the circumstances, and settled into my wait. Lord only knew how long the Seers' spells would take— how long I would have to wait until this bridge shifted from mere rock to demonic metal and ice.

From this vantage point, I could still hear Ruth's voice below me, echoing across the bank as she traveled from circle to circle to make sure that everyone was ready. Between gaps in the bridge's railing, I could also see Joshua, Jillian, and Scott move to join one of the smaller circles. As they joined hands with the older Seers, a ragged breath tore its way out of my lips. Now I really *was* alone.

"Quit feeling so sorry for yourself," someone behind me demanded.

I whirled around and saw Ruth, standing between

two unstable-looking fissures in the asphalt. She had one hand placed on her hip, while she gripped an over-stuffed red bag with the other.

"What are you doing here?" I asked, in a smaller voice than I would've liked.

"Bringing you a gift."

Ruth shifted her bag forward, in front of her, and then began to step carefully over the cracks in the pavement. When she came within arm's distance of me, she reached into her bag, pulled out an object, and handed it to me.

For a few seconds, I didn't register the fact that I was holding the hilt of a medium-length, serrated knife. But once I finally processed that information, my eyes shot up sharply to Ruth's.

"What . . . ? Why . . . ?"

She lifted one shoulder in a nonchalant shrug. "Because you need a backup plan."

I made a small noise of disgust. "So, what, you think I should fall on my sword if things get bad? Is that it?"

"No, you stupid girl," she hissed, abruptly angry. "I want you to protect yourself, if you have to."

"What are you talking about? I'll *supposedly* have my glow, and anyway, I'm pretty sure kitchen knives don't work on demons."

"Of course they don't. But knives can work on other ghosts."

My frown deepened. "No, they don't."

"Maybe not if I wielded them, or Joshua." She paused, giving me a smile that was both dark and conspiratorial. "But if *you* take a knife to another supernatural being, that's a different story."

At first I didn't understand what she meant. Then I remembered: I'd hurt Eli—drawn blood, even—when he tried to kiss me. According to Eli, that was something that shouldn't have happened. Ghosts couldn't hurt each other physically, any more than they could strike out and hurt the living without demonic assistance. And yet, *I'd* done it. Twice.

I'd told Ruth about it on the phone the other day, just as an afterthought in my long story; I had no idea if what she said might actually work.

"But . . . it's an object," I continued to protest. "One from the living world. I'm pretty sure it will just go right through any ghost that isn't Risen."

"Maybe. But nonetheless, you *do* have the power to blood-let. So if the need arises . . . well, I've done what I can."

As if to emphasize what a huge indulgence she'd made on my behalf, she wiped her hands together, symbolically cleaning them of any blood I might "let."

All I could offer in return was a quiet, pensive, "Thanks." Then I moved the knife to my hip and slipped the blade through the space between my jeans and belt, so that the hilt caught and held the knife at my side. Like some modern-day gunslinger in skinny jeans and thousand-dollar boots.

Ruth nodded—in approval or farewell, I couldn't tell. She turned away and navigated back to the entrance of High Bridge. When she reached the top edge of the embankment, she paused, and I thought for one strange second that she might look back at me. Give me a salute for luck, maybe.

Instead, she began to move deftly down the side of the steep hill. As her head ducked below road level and out of my sight, I heard her call out to her Seer circles.

"It's time."

Chapter
SIXTEEN

The Seers hadn't been chanting for very long, but the sound had already started to freak me out. There's nothing like fifty or so voices speaking Latin in unison to make one's skin crawl. I almost would have welcomed the netherworld, if only to get them to stop.

Almost.

Trying not to listen to the chants, I started to play with the hilt of my new knife, using it to slap the flat side of the blade against my jeans in a kind of rhythmic beat.

Since that little sound didn't really do much to help me drown out the noises below, I began to hum and then outright sing, as I tried unsuccessfully to summon my glow.

"Glow," I sang, intentionally too loud and off-key. "Glow, glow, glow. Gloooooowwwww. . . ."

Catchy.

My blood seemed to freeze the instant I heard that word echo off the girders around me. I froze too, holding very still with my hand on the hilt of the knife. I listened intently, but after a few minutes of nothing but that damn chanting below me, I felt foolish.

It's nothing, I told myself. *Just the Seers' voices, carried by the wind.*

Still, it took me more than a few seconds to ease out of my rigid stance and shake my head. "Idiot," I chided myself, laughing quietly.

"Only because you're still here."

That time, I knew I didn't imagine the voice. It echoed so loudly, I had no choice but to admit that something had finally joined me on this bridge. Again, my hand flew to the hilt of the knife and I spun around, searching for the speaker. I wasn't surprised that I didn't find anything: it wasn't that kind of night, and it was *never* that kind of place.

"What do you want?" I addressed the air itself, since I

technically had no one to confront.

"To save you, Amelia."

By now I could tell that the speaker was male, although his voice sounded distorted, like it came through some busted-up old microphone.

"Save me?" I asked, pacing nervously around my spot on the bridge, still looking this way and that for some sign of presence. "Save me, how?"

"By telling you . . . to run. Now."

It was the pause—the slight, struggling gasp for breath—that made me realize who spoke to me.

"Eli? Eli, where are you?"

Now my pacing became urgent. If Eli was here, maybe I could find him, maybe I could get him to take me to my father and Gaby when the netherworld opened, before it was too late.

But my heart sank before he could even reply. Just as that little hitch in breath told me that the voice belonged to Eli, it also told me that Eli wasn't here in the living world. Worse, he wasn't any place where he could help himself, much less me.

"You're projecting, aren't you?" I said, answering my own question on his behalf.

"Yes."

He hissed the word, but I could tell that he made the sound more from exertion than ferocity. Afterward he panted, as though that one word, projected from his dimension to this one, might break him.

"Eli, I can't leave." I grimaced and glanced around the empty bridge. "I have to stay here and do this, or they're going to start—"

Eli's interrupting scream was so piercing that I reflexively hunched my shoulders and clenched my hands into fists. The shriek ended almost as quickly as it began, fading with a strangled gargle. Like he'd *actually* been strangled.

"Eli?" I yelled, spinning around frantically. "Eli?"

"Eli is now otherwise engaged," another voice responded. I searched for this new speaker, but of course, the bridge remained empty.

For a petrified minute, nothing else happened. Then tendrils of black smoke appeared a few feet from me. They began swirling around one another, writhing like a den of snakes until they coalesced and started to form a human figure. Initially, the person's features were indistinct, as shifting and difficult to determine as shapes in dark water. When they finally solidified, a young man in a well-cut gray suit and wire-rimmed glasses faced me. His smile seemed benign, even gracious. But I clutched the hilt of my knife more tightly.

Alexander Etienne, or Kade LaLaurie, depending on the situation. As if anyone in their right mind would want to meet this *thing*, in any situation.

"Hello, Amelia sweetheart," he purred, like we were old friends.

"Go to hell, Kade."

I spat the words without forethought, and instantly regretted them when Kade started laughing as if I'd just told the most hilarious joke. Which, considering his new home, I probably had.

Kade raised both eyebrows, just above the rims of his wire-frame glasses.

"So, Amelia, how's life?" he asked. Then he affected a bashful frown. "Oops, I forgot: how's half-life?"

"Where is she, you insane piece of trash?" I demanded, completely ignoring his taunts.

Kade's frown grew even more exaggerated, until he resembled an innocent little boy who didn't understand the question. "Where's *who*, Amelia? To whom could you possibly be referring?"

"You know *exactly* who I'm talking about."

"Your good friend?"

"Yes," I growled. "My good friend."

Kade chuckled. "Well, why didn't you say so right away? That's an easy question to answer."

He slipped his hands into his pockets, rocked onto the balls of his feet, and let loose one low whistle. A second writhing set of smoke-snakes appeared, roiling together beside Kade. Slowly, another person materialized . . . just not the one I expected.

Now Serena Taylor stood next to Kade, wearing the same wrinkled suit and corpse grin that she had in our cemetery. She didn't say anything but instead released a small, delicate sigh. Instantly, the rotten-egg smell of sulfur washed over me. It curdled my stomach, as did the sight of her grin.

Yet the longer I stared at her, the more I realized that she really was an empty shell. A puppet, just like I'd thought.

"Is this who you were talking about?" Kade asked, wrapping his arm around Serena's shoulder.

Although it pained me to do so—made me feel like I was writing Serena off—I gulped thickly and replied, "No, not that friend. You *know* the one I'm talking about."

"My mistake." Kade dropped his arm from Serena's shoulder and grinned again, looking as though he'd been caught playing a practical joke. As soon as Kade stopped touching her, Serena vanished. It made me suspect that she'd never really been there at all.

"You mean Gabrielle Callioux," Kade said. *"Gaby."*

He said her nickname with such obvious contempt that I couldn't help but make a guttural sound—one that bordered on a snarl.

"Bring her here, Kade. Now."

To my surprise, he answered, "Gladly, Amelia! Gladly."

Still flashing that bright smile, he snapped his fingers twice, the way a jerk might order a waitress over to his table. Immediately something began to shimmer above the concrete near his feet. Just a faint, swirling mist at first. Then it took a human, if transparent, shape. But it didn't take the same upright stance that Kade and Serena had. Instead, this form stayed crouched, huddled close to the ground like a dog afraid of a sharp kick.

Which was exactly what Kade delivered into the translucent figure's side. It whimpered softly, and Kade turned a satisfied smile back on me.

"Amelia, meet the new Gaby," he said pleasantly. "Gaby, show some respect to your old friend."

The form on the ground glanced up at me with wide, unnaturally blue eyes—the same kind of burning, neon eyes that Eli had, the night he projected his body here to warn me about the demons. But even though this creature's eyes were blue, I saw nothing of Gaby in them—no spark to let me know that the creature knew me, or that it even *was* Gaby.

"I don't believe you," I said, my voice shaking. "That's not her. It can't be."

Kade cocked his head to one side and delivered another brutal kick to the creature's side. This time it screamed, and I almost crumpled to my knees. There was no question that the voice behind the scream belonged to Gaby.

I cried out her name, just once, and she looked away. In terror, or in shame, I don't know. Tears welled up in my eyes, and I shook my head wildly, as if that could stop them.

"Let her go," I shrieked at Kade. "Let her go now."

Kade pretended to consider it, but after a moment, he scrunched up his face and shook his head.

"Nah. Don't think I will."

Once more, he snapped his fingers. Like Serena had done only minutes ago, Gaby vanished like a puff of smoke, leaving nothing behind but the cracked road. I stared at the empty spot she'd just occupied, temporarily stunned. Then something hot and acidic began to burn inside me.

It built so quickly and fiercely, I almost didn't realize that my glow had finally erupted—not until I caught its bright orange reflection in Kade's eyes, which had suddenly lost an ounce of their maniacal gleam. Faced with my glow again, he didn't look quite so confident; in fact, he now looked a little scared.

At that moment, I didn't think. I just flashed him a smile—one that bared as many of my teeth as possible—and lunged for his throat.

I'd almost reached him when the bridge began to

sway violently. My foot caught on a ridge of churned-up asphalt, and I dropped to the road with a hard smack. The second I hit the pavement, my glow extinguished and my shoulder made a sickening pop. The sound was so loud, I almost mistook it for the powerful crack that rang throughout the river valley.

But the echo from my fall couldn't possibly reverberate like that off the metal girders of the bridge.

"What the—," I began, but a chorus of frenzied screeches interrupted me.

At first I thought that the cries came from the riverbank, where the Seers were still gathered. But when I looked up, I saw the swooping black shapes, diving like enormous birds toward the shoreline.

Wraiths or demons, I couldn't yet tell.

I didn't spare a single glance for Kade, to see whether he was cowering or rejoicing—I pushed myself up off the road and ran for the railing. The second I reached it, I gripped the metal edge and leaned over so that I could get a better view of what was happening on the bank.

Below me, the Seers had broken their circles and were running in all directions. Probably because the diving shapes had landed and were now worming their way throughout the crowd, inciting them to frenzy. They were wraiths, then—a fact that was simultaneously relieving and disturbing. Especially since I couldn't find Joshua in the stampede.

I was still gripping the guardrail, debating whether or not to abandon my post and try to find Joshua, when my fingers suddenly began to ache. I looked down and saw that a thick layer of ice had formed upon the rail, which had shifted in color from muted gray to a mottled mess of red, purple, and black.

Those changes could only mean one thing: the netherworld was descending.

Biting my lip so that I wouldn't scream, I yanked my hands off the frozen guardrail and tried not to think about how much skin I'd left stuck to the ice. I rubbed my palms against my jeans to warm them and then started to run toward the entrance of the bridge. But before I could reach the edge, another black shape swooped down and landed in front of me.

I shut my eyes, praying that my glow would return and blast the wraith off the bridge. When I opened them, however, I found a nasty surprise waiting for me. The black shape hadn't formed a wraith at all. Instead, a female demon stared back at me.

"Little lamb," she whispered. "Are you here for your slaughter?"

My mind went blank with terror. I spun away from the demon, running blindly in the other direction. Which was unfortunate, really, since I barreled right into Kade.

The instant I collided with him, he wrapped his arms around me like a straitjacket, loosening them only to twist me around so that I faced the bridge again. From that vantage point, I could see a small group of demons, moving toward us at a maddeningly unhurried pace. They stopped at the same time, making a sort of flock formation a few feet from us.

The female demon stood at the center of one flank, while a male demon stood at the head of the V. Although I hadn't seen him in a long time, I recognized him immediately. He was one of the first demons I'd met, the night his companion dragged Eli into the hellpit below the bridge. This male was also the first demon to suggest that I join them—the first demon to *covet* me.

"It's lovely to see you again, Amelia," he said, proving that he remembered me, too. But of course he did—none of us would be here, otherwise.

I didn't respond, partly because Kade gripped me so tightly and partly because I didn't want to give any of them the satisfaction of hearing my voice waver.

"Master Belial," Kade greeted this lead demon slavishly, "this is the girl you've sought. I've captured her for you."

The lead demon—Belial, apparently—ignored Kade's toadying. Instead, a light smile creased the demon's bloodless skin.

"You're looking well," Belial continued, addressing

me. "Much prettier than when my colleagues met you in New Orleans."

At the mention of New Orleans, I began to struggle—however ineffectively—to free myself from Kade's grasp. I'd wounded a huge number of demons in New Orleans . . . maybe even destroyed them, judging by the fact that a legion had come to attack me and only a few were left to retreat. Suddenly, I could see the demons' true intentions: they'd created this little game to lure me into turning myself over to them, so that they could punish me for what I'd done. They didn't want a new servant—they wanted revenge.

Even as I struggled, Belial continued talking. "However pretty you look tonight," he said, sighing grimly, "the fact remains that we require blood. From either you, or one of your compatriots. Someone goes with us tonight. I'm afraid those are the rules we've set out . . . and God forbid we break them."

His reference to God elicited a chilling round of laughter from the other demons. Belial bowed his head to each side of their formation, acknowledging that they'd picked up on his joke. Then he turned back to me.

"So, Amelia, what's it to be?"

"I can't . . . with his arms . . . so tight."

I cringed and stretched, as if to emphasize the fact that

I couldn't fully answer them under such constraints. Seeing this, Belial jerked his head at Kade, and immediately, my bonds loosened. Even without seeing his face, I could tell Kade didn't want to release me. But like the well-trained dog he was, he obeyed his master and let me go.

I made a show of rubbing my arms, as if their comfort was the thing that would help me make my decision.

"Okay," I said, more to myself than the demons. "You need a life, right? That's what you're taking tonight, no matter what?"

Belial didn't speak, but he bowed his head in mock civility.

"Any life?" I pressed.

The demon smiled, flashing his sharp, glistening teeth—far more than any human mouth contained. "Well, I'm sure that will suffice. Of course, we'd prefer *your* life. But if you feel like turning over one of your friends as this week's offering . . . maybe you *are* the girl we'd like you to be."

I smiled back demurely, batting my eyes at him. "I guess I am that girl, since I think you should take someone else in my place."

"Consider it done," Belial crowed, clapping his hands together. "We'll even let you *pick*!"

My smile widened into something dark and twisted.

"I was hoping you'd say that," I hissed. Then, before the demons could react, I yanked the serrated knife from my belt, spun around, and plunged the blade deep into Kade LaLaurie's heart.

Chapter
SEVENTEEN

I'd stabbed Kade without thinking about the conse-
quences. To be honest, I didn't even think it would
work. Like Ruth had said, I could blood-let, but I
didn't think I would actually be able to use a solid, liv-
ing-world weapon against Kade.

Apparently, I was wrong.

After I sank the knife into him, Kade sputtered for a
few, stunned seconds. Then a trail of bright, arterial-red
blood trickled from the corner of his mouth. Nowhere
else, though—the knife wound in his chest never bled.

He reached up, digging his fingers painfully into my upper arm. They loosened when his entire body began to stiffen. His back went rigid, his fingers drew up into claws, and his face froze into a permanent, ghastly scream; it was exactly what I imagined rigor mortis would look like. When his cold gray eyes whitened over, he let out a final, gargled sound and then fell backward.

By the time he hit the surface of the bridge, Kade LaLaurie was nothing but a months-old corpse with my knife in its chest; a ghost ended once and for all. And I didn't feel the least bit sorry about it.

With grim resolve, I turned to face the demon horde. But to my surprise, they weren't preparing to attack me. They didn't even look angry . . . not exactly, anyway. Their solidly black eyes had widened to even more inhuman proportions, and their smiles had grown ravenous. Lustful, in fact.

Finally, after a few more seconds of slavering, the demon named Belial made a small noise that sounded an awful lot like laughter.

"That was unexpected, Amelia. And—I have to say—absolutely delightful." The demons behind him murmured in agreement, each of them moving a fraction closer to me.

"You'll have to forgive us," Belial went on. "Violent deaths always make us a little . . . tipsy, let's call it." He chuckled lightly, as if their sudden bloodlust was charming. Then his smile turned pensive. "You know, Amelia, with instincts like yours, it's no wonder that the light has given you such unique . . . *gifts*."

"What are you talking about?" I spat. "The light hasn't done *anything* for me."

Once more the demon assessed me, but this time I saw a glint of doubt in his black eyes.

"Oh, it's clear that the light chose you as a vessel for the task," he mused, not really answering me. "But poor Kade aside, I'm still not entirely certain *why*. Eli and Kade were strong, wild, and hungry; both were willing to kill, and to die. You, however . . ." He paused and then passed another questioning glance over me. "I just don't think your heart is in this fight."

Serena's taunts in the graveyard rose, unbidden, in my mind. So it was true, then: the demons had never wanted to acquire me. At best, they wanted to end me; at worst, imprison me for an eternity of torment in the darkness.

"I'm not weak," I said firmly, taking a small step toward Belial. "You may think that, but you're wrong. The reluctance to kill people isn't weakness. Neither is love."

"In our world," Belial whispered, "love is most certainly a weakness."

As if on a cue, a chorus of whooping howls filled the air. Belial smiled again, but he could no longer mask what he truly was: pure darkness; pure evil. When I heard a familiar voice, calling to me from the entrance of the bridge, I knew why Belial had smiled, and a cold ball of dread settled into my stomach.

"Amelia?" Joshua shouted from the entrance of High Bridge. "Amelia, Ruth and I can't cross onto the bridge to get you—you have to run!"

I wanted to run to him, wanted us both to escape. But I couldn't seem to take my eyes off the demon's taunting smile.

"I told you," Belial continued to whisper to me, "we *will* have a life tonight. One of our own certainly doesn't count. So I'm afraid the person you love most will just have to take your place."

All of a sudden, a mass of wraiths swarmed up over the edge of the bridge and began to fly toward the entrance. Whatever power Belial had over my gaze, it broke at that moment. I whirled away from him and screamed.

"Joshua, run!"

I only had time to catch his horrified gaze when the wraiths converged upon him like a wave. They would kill him in seconds, I knew it. I whipped back around to the demons, my heart hammering so hard that I could hardly gasp, "Me. Take me inst—"

"No," Ruth's commanding shout interrupted my surrender. "You'll take neither of them."

Belial, who had been watching me intently this entire time, allowed his head to swivel leisurely toward Ruth. I could see something register in his eyes, and a slow, disquieting smile spread across his face. He raised one hand and, with a simple flick of his wrist, the swarm of wraiths fell away from Joshua, who fell gasping to his knees. Then Belial gestured grandly to Ruth.

"By all means," he called out loudly, "join us."

Whatever had prevented Ruth and Joshua from entering the bridge earlier must have fallen away, because she now moved decisively across its length, to where the demons and I stood. As she came toward us, I could see something shimmer back into place at the entrance of the bridge, like a transparent mirage.

By then, Joshua had regained his strength and stood. But no matter how much he screamed, I couldn't actually hear him—I could just see his mouth opening and closing as he shouted soundlessly. No matter how hard he threw himself at the entrance, he couldn't cross onto the bridge.

If Ruth noticed this new development, she didn't show it as she stopped several feet away from the demons' formation. Once he was sure she wouldn't come any closer, Belial flashed his most congenial smile.

"It's a pleasure to meet you, madam. What can we do for you on this fine evening?"

The other demons snickered at his fake, ingratiating tone. But Ruth kept her face impassive. She tossed back her gleaming white hair and met his gaze squarely.

"You can make a trade with me. For me, actually. I offer myself, so that you will end the war that you're waging on this girl."

My mouth dropped open in shock, but the demons seemed vaguely amused by Ruth's proposal. For the first time since they'd arrived, the female demon stepped out of rank and approached Ruth, smirking.

"What makes you think *you're* a sufficient replacement for the girl?"

Ruth returned the smirk and then caught my gaze. I saw something flicker in Ruth's eyes—apology, I think—before I suddenly couldn't see *anything* anymore. A blazing pain tore its way through my head, and I felt my knees buckle. Images blurred through my mind, like a reel of old-fashioned film spinning too fast for me to discern any individual panel. I clutched at my pounding temples and gasped, "Stop. Please!"

And just like that, the images vanished and the pain dissipated.

"A Seer witch," the female demon whispered, giving Ruth a wary, almost respectful look. The other demons hissed in agreement, clustering closer together in their pack. Obviously, they recognized an act of near exorcism when they saw one.

Ruth didn't confirm or deny the label. She simply folded her hands in front of her and released an impatient sigh.

"Well?"

Belial studied Ruth harder now, taking in her regal stance, her annoyed frown. "I assume that you're someone of importance in your coven?" he asked.

She gave him a withering glare. "I'm the *leader* of two major covens, including the one in New Orleans—the young members of which defeated your kind this winter, I believe."

I could see Belial bristling, but he didn't immediately retaliate. Instead, he continued to evaluate Ruth—probably weighing their intended revenge upon me against her worth as a possible addition to his army. If he accepted Ruth's trade, I didn't doubt that he would give her a position of some power; a woman with Ruth's abilities didn't end up as a mere wraith.

"You do understand," he said, "that once you join us, you will be unable to work against us; your mind will not be your own."

Ruth's answering smile was close-lipped and caustic. "I assumed as much."

Neither side said anything further until, after some considerable time, Belial nodded decisively. He didn't consult his fellow demons, which made me wonder whether he had the final say, or they just shared a hive mind. Judging by the similarly determined looks on their faces, I guessed the latter.

"It's settled then: you die tonight, and the girl goes free."

Ruth shook her head vehemently. "Not just her. All the people around her, too. Anyone that you might hunt, in order to get to her."

He considered this additional demand for a moment, and then nodded a second time. "It is agreed upon. The death shall be administered by the wraiths, and then your new form will join us in the netherworld, forever."

His voice deepened with this pronouncement, booming off the icy girders of the bridge. In response, the temperature seemed to drop, as if the air itself understood that a dark bargain had just been made. The wraiths understood, too: they began to swarm again, writhing and churning about twenty feet above our heads. They were gathering for an attack. A final one.

A shiver crawled its way across my skin, and I turned to Ruth. "You can't do this," I pleaded desperately with her. "There's got to be another way."

For the first time Ruth offered me a sad, genuine smile. "I don't think there is."

She turned slightly and eyed the entrance of the bridge,

where Joshua was still clawing at the invisible barrier and screaming his silent screams. When Ruth looked back at me, her eyes shimmered with the only tears I'd ever seen her shed.

"Please," she begged quietly. "Please watch over them. And when the time is right . . . please *leave* them and don't come back."

"I . . . I'll try," I stuttered, unsure of how else to answer her.

Above us, the wraiths began writhing faster and screeching. Any minute now, they would dive. For a wild second, I thought about shielding her with my own body.

But Ruth was no longer looking at me. Staring up at the black swarm, she fumbled frantically with something in her pocket. Finally, as the wraiths began their dive, she yanked her hand out of her pocket. Through the cracks in her bulging fist, I could just make out a few tiny, white discs—*pills*.

I screamed, "No!" But the shrieking wraiths drowned out the sound of my voice.

It took Ruth several quick swallows, but she'd gulped down all the pills by the time the black mass crashed into her. Just before the wraiths fully engulfed her, she clutched one hand to her chest and fell to her knees with an unexpectedly peaceful smile.

When the wraiths disbanded several minutes later, Ruth lay prone and motionless on the road. Her arms had fallen into a T shape, and her head had lolled to one side so that she faced me. She still wore that enigmatic smile, and her eyes were wide open. But I knew she couldn't see me. Not anymore.

Suddenly I couldn't breathe. I began gasping for air as the demons laughed and cheered. I hardly even noticed when the colors of the netherworld began to seep away, returning the bridge to a plain, ordinary gray.

Before the darkness disappeared entirely, Belial pointed one finger at me.

"The witch died before we could take her soul. Whether or not she intended this outcome, her soul is already gone, and we cannot claim her," he hissed as he began to fade from sight. "Therefore her bargain is void, and our mandate still stands: give yourself to us, or in one week, another person dies. And this time, we'll take *him*."

Belial's arm swung toward Joshua, who'd finally pushed through the vanishing barrier and was now running toward me. Then, with a last malevolent smile, the demon vanished too.

Ruth Mayhew was dead. By her own hand, no less.

No one could seem to accept that fact. Not Joshua,

even though he'd witnessed the event, nor Jillian, who'd heard about it immediately after. Not Jeremiah and Rebecca, who arrived at the bridge an hour later. And especially not the officers from the Wilburton police department.

As a few of them mentioned just after the ambulance arrived, most of the officers had known Ruth Mayhew their entire lives. They'd eaten her apple cobbler at Easter picnics; they'd tried not to squirm through a church service, lest she catch them from the choir loft and tell their parents; and they'd suffered through the Sunday-school classes that she'd ruled with an iron fist. The Ruth Mayhew *they* knew was not the type of woman who would take her own life with an overdose of heart medication; the Ruth Mayhew they knew would never have been that careless.

And yet no one really doubted Joshua or Jillian when they told the story of how their grandmother demanded that they go for a late-night hike to the town's biggest river—a hike that brought on a sudden heart attack, which she was overzealous in fighting. Too many nitrate pills had caused almost every organ in her body to fail all at once.

And that, as they say, was that.

The story was so plausible, so tearfully told, that the police never thought to explore the rest of the riverbank, where they would have found the shuffled footprints of fifty Seers, fleeing the scene less than an hour earlier. Only Scott had remained, constraining Jillian on the part of the road that hadn't plunged into the netherworld. But once the netherworld vanished—and once we determined that Ruth really was dead—then Scott and I both had to disappear too. After all, the story of Ruth's death grew less believable the more random teenagers you added to the equation.

So for the last hour, I had watched invisible as Joshua and his family slowly broke into pieces. It was the hardest scene I'd ever witnessed—and I'd just watched two beings *die* tonight. Almost as bad as watching the Mayhews' suffering was the fact that I couldn't do anything for them.

Finally, after all the stories had been told and the reports filled out, the Mayhew family was free to leave. Too tired or disoriented to pretend that he wasn't looking for me, Joshua began wandering the edges of the bridge, hissing my name. Seeing one of the remaining officers give him a funny look, I stayed invisible but rushed over to Joshua and whispered that I would meet him at his house. His eyes still searched for me in the shadows, but then he nodded bleakly and rejoined his family on their way to their SUV.

Although I desperately wanted to join them as well,

I hung back, waiting around the bridge so that I could make sure the police didn't start expressing suspicions, now that the family had left. To my relief, none of the officers said anything out of the ordinary as they wrapped things up and left too.

After the last cop car pulled away, I shifted back into visibility with a heavy, painful sigh. With one hand, I probed the shoulder that had popped, making sure that it hadn't dislocated. Then, feeling like I'd just been punched repeatedly, I began to trudge down the road toward the entrance of the bridge. I'd almost reached it when, inexplicably, I stopped, threw my head back, and screamed out the foulest curse word I knew.

I clenched my hands, digging my nails into my palms, and began to scream the word over and over. It echoed back at me from the girders and the tree line. At some point, my screams incensed a nighthawk, who began to shriek with me. Other than those noises, however, nothing else answered me. Nothing called out, from this world or another, to tell me what to do next.

Chapter
EIGHTEEN

B y the time I finally returned to the Mayhews' house, dawn had started to break. Still, I could see a yellow light from the front window—a sure sign that at least some of the Mayhews were awake. Making arrangements, I supposed, or mourning together. So I moved past the house without hesitation. Joshua needed me, but not quite yet; right now he needed his family more.

I was so exhausted that I could hardly muster the energy to soften my steps up into the gazebo. Once inside, I pulled the curtains shut and fumbled my way over to the daybed. Then I collapsed onto its surface, fully clothed and still wearing my muddy boots.

I craved peace so badly, I could almost taste it. Every part of my body ached for some rest from these nightmarish attacks. Still, I thought I knew myself too well to believe a moment's peace was possible—I thought I would stay awake for hours, crying perhaps, or just turning in restless circles on top of the covers.

But to my surprise, I must have immediately fallen asleep instead. What else could explain why a gorgeous, endless prairie had suddenly replaced the gazebo? I'd also gone from lying on a bed to standing in the grass— a change that, for some reason, didn't bother me. At that moment, *nothing* seemed to bother me. For the first time in months, I felt at rest.

A light breeze swept over me, pleasant and warming. It brought with it the aroma of earth, wildflowers, and that strange, indefinable scent that lets you know the day was sunny, even with your eyes closed.

The air smelled like spring. Like new life.

In an unhurried manner, I stretched my arms above my head and sighed contentedly. Maybe it was because of how starkly this place contrasted with the netherworld, or maybe it was just my exhaustion, but the prairie looked more beautiful then than the first time

I saw it. And I *had* seen it before, during my car ride to New Orleans with the Mayhews.

But now, the grass in which I stood seemed taller, reaching well past my knees. All around me bright colors burst through the grass: yellow sweet clover, white larkspur, and purple wild indigo. Flowers my father had taught me to recognize, when they appeared each spring. I reached for a nearby blossom—a round cluster of pale yellow petals that looked like some iridescent bubble floating above the field—when I thought I heard him speak.

"That's prairie parsley, darlin'," he whispered, from somewhere behind me. I turned toward the sound of his voice, but the field was just as vacant as before.

"Where are you?" I whispered to the empty breeze.

"He's not here," a feminine voice answered.

I turned back around and saw the redheaded girl from my dreams, standing where only prairie grass waved moments before.

"Hello again," she said, almost apologetically.

"Where are we?" I demanded. "I thought you promised that you'd stop making me hallucinate."

"It's not a hallucination. This realm is as real as it was the first time you came here. But since you're not *part of* this realm, you're only allowed to access it in your dreams."

"You didn't answer my entire question," I pointed out.

The girl smiled slightly, and explained. "It's an entrance of sorts, just like the netherworld. The netherworld leads to the darkest place in existence; this prairie leads to the lightest."

I glanced around me at the blue sky, the soft sunshine, the lush prairie. The lightest place—heaven—waited, not far from here. I could feel it now, just like I could feel the nearby presence of hell whenever I stood in the netherworld. That explained my tranquility when I'd arrived in this prairie.

"Do you like it here?" the redhead asked quietly. "Would you . . . like to see what lies *beyond* this prairie?"

I didn't respond, choosing instead to fold my legs beneath me and sit cross-legged on the grass. The girl mimicked me, tamping down the blades between us with her hands so that we could see each other. Once she'd finished, she stared at me again, obviously waiting for my reply.

But I simply placed my chin on my hands, rested my elbows on my knees, and considered her: auburn curls, bright green eyes, old-fashioned white tunic over bell-bottomed jeans. Finally, after a long silence, I leaned back.

"I think I know who you are."

She raised her eyebrows but didn't speak.

"You're Melissa, Eli's dead girlfriend. The one who

dumped him before he started stalking me."

She barked out a surprised laugh. "Yeah, I am."

"I'm guessing you have a new job. One that doesn't involve helping a demon's slave." When I quirked my head to one side, she confirmed my guess.

"I'm a guardian of this world," she said. "Just like Eli Rowland and Kade LaLaurie were for the netherworld. Ultimately, we're all competing to claim souls. My side just does it a little differently than theirs. Meaning that the other side . . ."

"Cheats," I finished, thinking back to what Eli had once said about stealing souls for the darkness.

Melissa nodded. "They pick out some of the living as targets—victims. And when someone dies at the hands of one of the dark guardians, it's far more likely that the dark will be able to claim that soul first. That's what we thought had happened to you. We didn't even realize that Eli hadn't actually claimed you, until . . ."

When she trailed off, I waited for a beat and then prompted, "Until?"

"Until someone here alerted us to your presence in the living world. Problem is, we don't interfere with ghosts who still wander, unsettled. Especially ones like you, who've gone unclaimed for so long. There's a really tacky name my fellow guardians have for your kind—damaged goods."

By now, my pleasant mood was starting to crumble. I crossed my arms over my chest and scowled at her. "I'm not some forgotten piece of luggage at the airport, Melissa. I'm a person. With a soul."

"Trust me, I know," she said hurriedly. "When my friend told me about you, I bent the rules a little and made sure you'd be at the scene of one of Eli's conquests last fall. So that Eli would *have* to notice you again."

I blinked back in surprise. "Wait—what? Are you saying *you* made me find Joshua on the night of his car accident?"

"I didn't mean to place you in Joshua's path, specifically. I just wanted to make sure your nightmare occurred at the right time, in the right place. I thought that would draw Eli's attention back to you—make him finally do what he was supposed to do after you died."

I sucked in a sharp breath. "You were *trying* to send me to hell?"

Melissa waved her hands anxiously. "No! No, not . . . technically. I was just trying to get things resolved, as far as your afterlife was concerned. No matter what my friend wanted me to do for you, I couldn't just bring you to the light immediately. And anyway, you didn't end up in the darkness, did you?"

"No," I growled. "And just so you know, Eli hadn't forgotten about me—he'd been toying with me for over a decade."

"I know," she said, shaking her head sadly—for me or Eli, I didn't know. Then she brightened, suddenly smiling widely. "But instead of Eli winning, the most *amazing* thing happened. On the night of Joshua's accident, you did something that none of us anticipated. Something that robbed Eli of *two* souls."

I stared at her blankly for a moment. Then realization hit me.

"I saved Joshua's life," I whispered.

Her smile grew even brighter. "You saved his life. And that act of kindness showed the light who you really, truly are. So, even though they determined that you still weren't quite ready, the Highest Powers decided to give you extra abilities that could save you from the darkness. That's why you have that protective glow and the ability to harm those who might try to hurt you. The Highest Powers also gave you a connection to everyone whose life you've saved since: Joshua *and* Jillian. That's why you can touch both of them."

I snorted. "Well, that's not true at all. I haven't been able to touch anyone since the Lazarus spell."

She raised one eyebrow and gave me a suggestive smile. "Oh really? Because that's not what it looked like in the Mayhews' front yard the other night."

The kiss. She was referring to that inexplicable kiss.

"But . . . but how?" I sputtered. "How did I touch him,

just that once, when I haven't been able to for months?"

Melissa shook her head. "Not everything that Gabrielle told you about your current state was true. She thought that you couldn't touch anyone just because you couldn't touch Felix. But you can still touch those people you saved. Only the Highest Powers can take that ability away. It's just that you now need—what should I call it?—extreme concentration."

I leaned back, stunned. Then, after I'd thought through a few things, I began to speak haltingly.

"If I'm hearing you right," I said, "then I have all these—I don't know—extra-ghostly abilities, because I did something out of the ordinary. But . . . it had nothing to do with some unknown quality of mine. It was a reward for my willingness to protect the living. Right?"

Melissa nodded emphatically, her red curls bouncing. "Right. Which is why you're so lucky."

I closed my eyes, tuning her out as she droned on about why I was "so lucky." Right now, I had more important things to think about. Like what it meant if the things Melissa said were true. Was she right when she said that these extra abilities—the capacity to touch those I'd saved, the protective glow—could have been granted to any ghost, if they'd done what I had?

If that was truly the case, then I was . . . *thrilled*.

In fact, the longer I thought about it, the more it felt

as though an enormous weight had been lifted off of me. Because I'd concluded something that Melissa *hadn't* said.

My afterlife wasn't predestined.

Even if the "Highest Powers" or the universe or whatever had granted me extra abilities, that hadn't happened by some random twist of fate. It had happened because of my choices. I was this ghost, this person, because I chose to help people. I chose to fight.

The demons, the light, even Ruth, who used her final words to beg me to disappear—none of them knew what would happen to me until it actually did. They could plot and plan and scheme all they wanted, but I still had power over my own future. I still had the power to decide.

This realization brought with it an almost overwhelming sense of relief.

And somehow, the realization made things with Joshua seem better, too. He and I had been thrown together by chance, not fate. We weren't star-crossed lovers, moving on some doomed, predetermined path. We were just two souls who saw each other, and in seeing, loved.

That simple bond was stronger than any supernatural connection. Stronger than any threat posed to us by the afterworlds. For the first time since the demons had threatened me, I allowed myself to hope.

I opened my eyes to find Melissa staring quizzically at me.

"Didn't you listen to anything I just said?" she asked, clearly exasperated. "I'm asking you again to come into the light now. To join us. Tonight."

I arched one eyebrow. "What do you mean? You're ready to—what?—finally let me go to heaven now, after what happened on the bridge?"

Melissa smiled in confirmation, but I couldn't help my dry laugh.

"You know, a friend of mine taught me that you don't get one blessing without giving up another. So . . . what's the catch?"

Melissa shook her head, frowning as if I'd disappointed her with the question. "Like I said earlier, Gabrielle Callioux wasn't all-knowing."

I flinched. "'Wasn't all-knowing'? Are you telling me that Gaby doesn't exist anymore?"

"My best guess is that she's with Eli and a lot of other lost souls," Melissa said, "somewhere in the darkness beyond the gateway at High Bridge. In a place you can't reach her."

"I won't accept that," I said automatically. "I could *try* to reach her. I saw her tonight—I know she's not beyond help. With light on my side, I could try."

Melissa winced. "No, technically you couldn't. If you

accept my offer, then you'll be bound by the same rules that I am. I guess that's part of the 'catch.' You'll have to give up your desire to save people once they've entered the netherworld. And you'll have to remove yourself from the living world. That means no more visits to your mother. No more nights with Joshua. In fact, you don't get to 'protect' any of your living friends . . . unless, of course, we end up claiming them after they die. You'll be a guardian of our gateway . . . *not* a guardian angel."

My stomach pitched, even though I wasn't exactly surprised by this ultimatum. After all, *everyone*—from Seers to demons to pieces of filth like the former Kade LaLaurie—wanted to keep Joshua and me apart. Why should a guardian of goodness and light be any different?

As it stood, Melissa's offer didn't sound very appealing. Not if it meant abandoning my father and Gaby and forsaking my mother and Joshua and all my other friends in the living world. I'd all but made up my mind, when Melissa shifted closer and shook her head at me.

"You're going to say no—I can see it in your eyes. But before you do, Amelia, there's something else you should know about the person who told me to find you in the living world, while you were still wandering unclaimed."

"I don't care," I muttered, fighting a losing battle with my anger. "I don't care about any more of your explanations or stories. You're delusional if you think I'll give up on everyone I love just to save myself. I won't stop protecting my mom and Joshua; I won't stop trying to find a way to save Gaby and my father."

"Ah, but that's the thing," Melissa said, her eyes suddenly sparkling. "You don't have to save your father."

I gave her a withering look. "You think that I would just leave him there? In the netherworld?"

Melissa shocked me by laughing. "Amelia, your father has never set one *toe* in the netherworld. It may surprise you to find this out, but he's my friend."

I felt my heart drop. My hands splayed upon the grass, clutching at it in an effort to anchor myself to something stable.

"What . . . what are you saying?" I breathed. "That he's here? That he's safe?"

When Melissa nodded, I dove forward, plucking her hands from her lap and grasping them tightly in mine. "Let me see him," I begged. "Please, let me see him."

"I can't," she said, looking genuinely sorry. She gave my hands a light squeeze. "I wish I could, but he and I have already broken so many rules with you: waking you up; giving you the visions in New Orleans; letting him speak to you—"

"That was really him?" I interrupted. "The first time you brought me to this field? And earlier today?"

"Yeah, it was really him. He misses you, Amelia. He wants you here."

I shook free of her hands and fell back onto the seat of my jeans. This new piece of information changed things. I couldn't pretend otherwise.

Almost reflexively, I pictured my father's face: his sunny blond hair; his easy smile; the crinkles around his vibrant green eyes. The man who'd tied my first shoe and taught me to ride a bike. The man I'd sought for the last few months, under the misguided assumption that he'd been trapped in the netherworld.

If my father really did serve the light, then that meant Eli *hadn't* claimed my father's soul when he died. I guess that explained why Eli seemed so confused when I accused him of my father's death. Maybe I shouldn't have let it happen, but at that moment, a tiny part of my heart forgave Eli. And another part forgave Melissa for treating me this way, when I realized that she'd probably been the one to usher my father into this beautiful afterworld.

Thinking of those people I needed to forgive, another question struck me. "Is . . . Ruth up there?" I asked quietly. "In the light?"

Melissa rolled her eyes. "Are you kidding? That woman would bring down the whole system if we let her go anywhere else. Besides, she gave her life in an attempt to save all of you—a fact that she's not going to let us forget anytime soon. She's been here less than an hour and she's already trying to run the place."

I couldn't help but laugh softly. Then I looked back down, studying the tiny threads in the knees of my jeans. I didn't really see them—instead, I saw my father's face again. Heard his voice, telling me to be brave, to do what I knew was right.

"What if I wanted to do something else first?" I whispered. "Before I enter heaven so that I can escape hell?"

I couldn't see Melissa's reaction to my question, but I sensed curiosity in her silence. Finally, she asked, "What is it that you want to do, Amelia?"

"Destroy the netherworld," I said in a rush, looking back up at her. "I want to destroy the netherworld."

Melissa shook her head. "Haven't the last few days been any indication that you *can't*? Besides, the netherworld is eternal, just like this prairie—just like heaven and hell themselves."

My heart sank, but only until my next thought struck me. "What about the gateways into the netherworld? Are they eternal too?"

"Well . . . no," Melissa replied, blinking in surprise. "They can be taken down, actually. I know that it's been done before, millennia ago—pretty spectacularly in Gomorrah, so I've heard." When Melissa saw my hopeful expression, however, she shook her head. "But a human can't do that, Amelia. Not even a ghost can. Only the Highest Powers themselves can do that."

Frowning, I asked, "By Highest Powers, do you just mean the rulers of light?"

"No, I mean all of them—the rulers of darkness and light. Only they have the power to destroy the gateways. . . ." Melissa trailed off when she saw my grim, triumphant smile. She didn't really know me as well as she thought she did, but even she could see that I was beginning to form a new plan.

"Amelia," she asked, "what are you thinking?"

"I'm thinking that I want you to make me a deal. A deal that involves more souls than just mine."

"Go on," Melissa said, with a note of caution in her voice.

"If I do something to the High Bridge gateway, if I find a way to close it from the inside, then I want the light to take not only my soul, but the souls of those people who helped me."

Immediately, Melissa began to shake her head. "You know I can't make that kind of—"

"Think about it," I interrupted. "Just think about it."

She opened her mouth to say something else, and then thought better of it. After another moment's hesitation, she said, "All right. I'll present your idea to the Highest

Powers. I don't know if they'll go for it, but . . . I'll try."

I gave a sigh of relief, and then asked, "When will I know whether or not they've said yes?"

She smiled sadly and stood, brushing grass off her tunic. "You won't. You'll just have to make the leap of faith that they'll answer your prayers."

Then Melissa held my gaze, obviously trying to figure me out. I thought that she might say something more— give me another unsolicited piece of advice about my future. But as we stared silently at each other, the air began to shimmer and blur around us. Suddenly, the field seemed hazy and insubstantial. Looking at it made my eyes hurt so I blinked, just once. When I opened my eyes, I could once again see the interior of the gazebo, yet the scent of summer still lingered in the air like perfume. Like a hint of happiness. Of a place I'd only dreamed of, and might finally, *finally* see . . . but only if I didn't fail. And only if they said yes.

Chapter NINETEEN

F or a long time I sat in the gazebo by myself, puzzling over the things Melissa had explained, and struggling with the choice she'd given me. With the plan that I'd barely begun to form.

My father. My *father*. If I believed everything that Melissa told me, then he was waiting for me in the light. So it should have been an easy choice. But obviously, it wasn't.

If it was just a simple matter of choosing between heaven and hell, between the total absence of my father and an eternity in his presence, I would have already made my decision. Especially since neither light nor dark seemed content to let me stay here, in the living world. But the decision became far more complicated when I thought about Gaby, Serena, Eli, and all those trapped in the netherworld. Not to mention those I loved here, on earth, like Joshua, my mother, and the Mayhew family. My head literally ached from the sheer impossibility of it all.

But I wasn't the only person with too much to handle. Many of those living people I loved were mourning right now. So I peeled my body off the daybed, cleaned myself up as best I could without a mirror or a change of clothes, and then slipped out of the gazebo surreptitiously since I wasn't technically supposed to be in there in the first place.

Luckily, none of the Mayhews seemed to have left the house yet—all their cars were still in the driveway, parked in the same haphazard formation that they'd taken late last night. I climbed the patio steps and knocked softly on the back door. I didn't even realize I'd been holding my breath until Jillian opened it—now I wouldn't have to awkwardly dodge Rebecca's hug like I usually did. But still, the sight of Jillian disturbed me. Her eyes were ringed red, and her beautiful hair was ratted up on one side as though she'd thoughtlessly twisted it in her fingers all night.

"Come on in," she rasped, stepping out of the way so that I could enter the back hallway. After we both walked into the kitchen, Jillian announced, "Amelia's here." Rebecca caught my eye and, when her face crumpled into tears, I hurried around the far side of the breakfast table to take a seat beside Joshua.

"Oh, Amelia, honey, thank you for coming over," Rebecca said, trying very hard to talk around a sob.

"Of course, Mrs. Mayhew. I wouldn't be anywhere else."

I meant it, too. Once I saw Joshua's face, everything about last night's battle—and everything about my offer from the light and the plan I'd started to consider—just faded away. He looked so worn, so defeated, that I nearly sobbed, too.

I could tell that it wasn't just the loss of his grand-mother that had almost broken him, although that loss would've been bad enough by itself; but Joshua was also crushed by our loss of the battle. He'd genuinely thought we had a chance, especially with Ruth on our side. Now, my sunny-eyed optimist had started to accept the fact that this story might not have a happy ending. Although he'd never really suffered a crisis of faith before, he certainly did so now.

Thinking back on what Melissa had said about my

abilities, I concentrated hard on Joshua: on the way I felt about him, on the way I'd always felt about him. I ignored the frustration and grief and uncertainty, and just focused on *him*. Then I reached over, very slowly, and wrapped my hand around his upon the tabletop.

He jerked at the touch, almost as though he'd received an electric jolt like the ones we used to give each other. This touch, however, was just like what we'd experienced the other night: solid, and real. Joshua's eyes widened and darted to mine questioningly. I gave him one small nod and, keeping my hand tight on his, turned back to his parents.

Jeremiah had been on the phone when I'd entered the kitchen, and he was still talking to what sounded like a relative. Every few words, he would stop to rub his bloodshot eyes.

"Yeah, it's going to be this Friday morning. We'll take the kids out of school for the whole day." He paused, and then added, "No, we'll just hold the service grave-side, like we did for Dad."

Dread started to prickle along my neck: another funeral, only a week after the last one that I'd attended; another event during which the darkness might attack.

I'd just started to imagine all the horrible things that could happen during the funeral, when Jeremiah mentioned the name of the cemetery where the service would take place. It was a traditional, well-kept cemetery on the edge of town—a site where the relatively affluent were buried. Most important, it wasn't my graveyard, which seemed to be a hotbed of supernatural activity. The different location didn't guarantee anything, nor did the fact that the demons didn't actually claim Ruth. Still, I felt a touch calmer as I tuned back in to the last portion of Jeremiah's phone conversation.

"No," he said, shaking his head, "don't worry about it, Trish: I'll get you guys some cabins at Robber's Cave. You tell everyone else to make reservations at the Express hotel. Then we'll just see you Thursday night, okay? Okay . . . okay, bye."

With a weary sigh, he returned the phone to its cradle and turned toward his family. "Well, the whole Louisiana clan will be here Thursday night. I'm going to get a cabin for Trish, Ben, and the girls, and another one for Penny and Drew. The rest of the family can get rooms at the hotel."

While Rebecca, Joshua, and Jillian processed this information numbly, I got lost in my thoughts. One detail from these travel arrangements stood out in particular: Annabel, Drew, and maybe even Hayley would be in town, in just a few days. This meant that I would have access to the young Seers of New Orleans, all of whom had inadvertently betrayed me but all of whom had also helped me defeat a huge gathering of demons.

Suddenly, my plan began to take further shape in my mind.

I got so wrapped up in it that I hardly noticed when Joshua tried to get my attention. Only after he placed his other hand on the tabletop did I glance over at him. He frowned, shifting his gaze between his hands and mine, which was still lying on the table. I hadn't even felt him let go of it.

Taking advantage of the fact that Rebecca and Jeremiah were now talking, I leaned in closer to Joshua. "Sorry. I guess I lose the ability if I don't concentrate hard enough."

He moved his lips to my ear and whispered, "We can touch again?"

I nodded, focusing on his face as I let my cheek brush his. "Yes, we can. And I have a lot of other things to tell you, too."

Looking a little stunned, Joshua sank back into his chair and arched an eyebrow. *Later*, I mouthed, once more taking his hand and folding it into mine on the tabletop. By now, Jillian had joined us at the breakfast table, so she easily noticed our touch. She raised her eyebrows as well, but thankfully, she chose not to comment yet. Instead, she let the surprise go out of her eyes before she looked back up at her parents.

"Mom, Dad, do you guys mind if the three of us just get out of here for a while? You know, for a break."

Rebecca turned away from Jeremiah, who she was comforting, and gave her daughter a distracted wave.

"Go ahead. Your dad and I need to meet with the funeral director this afternoon, anyway. I think some folks from Ruth's church are bringing food by later, so you two will be on your own for dinner. And unfortunately, I've got to go into the shop tonight to start sorting orders from the florist. Prom season really was the worst possible time for this to happen."

The three of us at the table froze. Then, after a long pause, we exchanged worried glances. *Prom*. With all the death and demons and decisions, we'd completely forgotten about it. Not that any of us had planned on going. Well, maybe Jillian and Scott wanted to go together, but Joshua and I hadn't even discussed it.

Without thinking, I glanced at the calendar on a nearby wall and then suppressed a gasp. Saturday of this week had a big star drawn on it, just below the word "prom" and a few inches below the date. Which just happened to be April 29.

The day before my birthday. I hadn't even noticed that, before now.

But apparently Joshua had. He caught me looking and gave my hand a firm squeeze. I shook my head, trying to rid it of that terrible coincidence. Trying not to think about what I would have to do, the day before my birthday; trying not to think about the fact that this birthday would be the first I'd spent conscious since my death . . . and I probably wouldn't even be on earth to experience it.

I smiled weakly at Joshua as we slid from our chairs to follow Jillian out of the kitchen. Once outside, I had to resist the impulse to spill everything right there on the back porch. I kept quiet, even after we piled into Jillian's car and she drove us someplace relatively safe to talk. I could have kissed her when she took the turn-off to Robber's Cave Park. I'd had some of my happiest memories there, and it seemed like the perfect place to regroup.

Jillian parked a little ways away from Joshua's and my picnic table, where we'd shared our first real conversation. The three of us got out of the car, but instead of moving to the table, Jillian guided us to a nearby swing set. We each took a seat and, for several minutes, just swept our feet in the dirt below, moving our swings a few inches back and forth. Eventually, I broke the silence.

"So . . . we're all going to prom this Saturday. Sort of."

Joshua shot me a surprised look, but Jillian cackled. "Are you freaking kidding me? After everything we've just been through, you expect us to tolerate frilly dresses and bad DJs?"

"We won't actually be attending the prom," I replied evenly. "We'll just be stopping by the school, before our next showdown with the demons, to get our newest recruits."

"Our newest recruits." Joshua repeated my phrase flatly, like a statement instead of a question. "You and I are going on our first—and possibly last—real date . . . for recruits."

I smiled. "And for the bad DJ. Obviously."

In spite of himself, Joshua grinned back faintly. Jillian, however, still hadn't bought it. "Wait, wait, wait," she interjected. "Let me get this straight: you want to recruit non-Seers to try and do something that several experienced covens just failed at?"

"Not just any non-Seers." I held up one finger in a sort of aha motion. "Your closest friends."

"What?" she nearly shrieked. "You want my friends to know what you are? What *I am*? Are you crazy? After that, I'd be a pariah!"

Joshua shot a glare at his little sister. "Aside from that self-serving comment, Jillian makes a good point . . . sort of. We let non-Seers in on this secret, and we're going to put them at risk."

I shook my head sadly. "Don't you see? They're already

at risk. No matter what I do, no matter where I go, the darkness will keep claiming the people of Wilburton. And I think we all know that the attacks are going to stop being so random. The demons know about the people I love, and they'll have fun destroying them, even after I'm gone. Worse, they targeted *you* last night, Joshua."

"Okay, maybe that's true," Jillian said. "Maybe Joshua is about to become Public Enemy Number Two. But how would playing demon slayer help my friends?"

"Because if your friends join us on Saturday night, then at least they'll be more aware."

"Of what?" she snapped.

I let out a short, frustrated puff of air. "Of the fact that I'm probably screwed anyway, therefore you and yours are next on the kill list. That's just the damn cycle, Jillian. And I'm not going to let what happened to Serena and Gaby happen to Scott and O'Reilly and . . . hell, even Kaylen. Not without preparing them for what's coming their way. So I think it's unbelievably selfish of *you* to do otherwise, just to protect your stupid reputation."

I answered more harshly than I'd intended, as evidenced by the fact that tears started to well up in Jillian's eyes. Immediately, I regretted my tone, but I didn't regret the words—Jillian needed to hear the truth.

She sniffed once and then quickly looked away,

probably so that we wouldn't see her cry. Joshua's and my eyes caught, and held. I thought that he might be angry with me for chastising his sister about a plan in which he didn't even believe. But I could see that that wasn't the case. Joshua obviously agreed with me on one thing: whatever happened this Saturday, Jillian needed to start thinking about other people. Unless, of course, she *wanted* them killed and turned into mindless shadow puppets.

Joshua watched me for a while, studying me. And slowly, I saw him figure out what was really going on in my head. I wanted to cover every possible scenario, because—one way or another—I wouldn't be here next Sunday. Realizing this, Joshua leaned forward and wrapped his hand around mine on the swing's chain.

"Amelia, what *happened* last night, after we left you?"

Still holding on to the chain, I let my fingers slip through Joshua's until our hands were entwined. Then, as I had promised I would always do, I told him all about my discussion with Melissa. I didn't mince words. As plainly as possible, I explained to him that, whether the darkness captured me or the light finally allowed me to join it, I couldn't stay here in the living world with him. That was the awful punch line of our love story: until he died and joined me on one side or the other, we wouldn't be together after Saturday.

By now, Jillian had rejoined the conversation, albeit silently. Like Joshua, she stared at me with a dawning kind of horror. But unlike her brother, she wasn't too stricken to interrupt me, just as I finished.

"That's not fair," she insisted, wiping angrily at the fresh set of tears that had sprung up in her eyes. "They can't do this to you."

Seeing those tears, I came to my own realization: against all odds, Jillian Mayhew cared about me; she might even have considered me her friend. I glanced between her and her brother, and then smiled softly.

"If it makes you guys feel better, I haven't completely decided what I want to do yet. But I do know one thing: no matter where I go, I want your friends safe, and I want *you* safer."

Neither of them replied, at least not verbally. Instead, Joshua untangled our fingers and stood up from his swing. Then he moved in front of me and held out one hand for me to take. I did so, allowing him to pull me up from my swing as well. When he turned and began tugging me gently toward Jillian's car, I gave him some resistance so that he would pause.

"Where are we going?" I asked, sharing a frown with Jillian as she joined us.

With a quiet sigh, Joshua turned back around to face me. "I guess we're going home to plan our next attack."

Chapter
TWENTY

I t had been almost four days since Joshua and Jillian had agreed to enlist their friends in our fight, but Joshua still hadn't touched me. Not once. He had plenty of incentive: we were finally able to touch again, we had less than one week together, and he obviously needed something to distract him from the grief of losing Ruth. Yet Joshua wouldn't so much as let his arm brush mine when we sat next to each other, eating leftover sympathy casseroles at his dining table.

Granted, he and I hadn't been able to spend much

time alone together since Sunday. Between school, the Wednesday-night baseball game he couldn't get out of, and the family's frantic preparations for what promised to be a hugely attended funeral, we hardly had time to share three words, much less a kiss. Still, I knew Joshua well enough to recognize when I was on the receiving end of a cold shoulder.

I'd been patient—quiet even, considering the fact that I might only have a few more days to speak freely. But by Thursday afternoon, I'd finally had enough. Joshua had just arrived home from baseball practice—something he couldn't avoid, even for family reasons, if he wanted to earn a college scholarship this spring. Jillian and I were sitting at the breakfast table, discussing how best to break the news to her friends that they were possible demon bait.

When Joshua breezed past us with a brief, noncommittal hello, I pushed away from the table and stormed up the stairs after him. Once I caught up to him at the top of the landing, I tapped firmly on his shoulder and mentally prepared my tirade. Joshua paused, one hand on the doorknob to his bedroom, and then turned slowly around to show me his irritated scowl.

"May I help you?" he asked flatly.

I sputtered for a second, confused. Then, without warning, I reached around him, opened his door, and yanked him into the bedroom with me. Using the back of my foot, I slammed the door shut behind us.

"What are you *doing*?" I demanded.

Still wearing that annoyed scowl, Joshua folded his arms across his chest. "I don't know what you mean, Amelia."

"Of course you do!" I threw my hands in the air in exasperation. "You've been avoiding me ever since we all came back from Robber's Cave."

"I've been busy."

He shrugged, as if that was explanation enough for ignoring the girl you supposedly loved, during what might be your last week on earth together. For a second I blanched, fighting the wave of nausea that threatened to overwhelm me. So many feelings rushed through me: sadness, fury, loss, disbelief. Finally, all I could do was shrug, too.

"I understand."

I let my head fall so that I couldn't see his eyes anymore. Then I turned away from him and reopened his bedroom door. Before I could cross the threshold, however, Joshua's hand shot past my shoulder and landed flat against the door. He didn't slam it like I had, but instead waited until I'd let go of the knob to push it softly shut.

For an endless, fraught moment, we both held our positions: him, propped against the door by his palm; me, facing it because I couldn't bring myself to look at him again. Eventually, I mustered enough courage to turn back around. My knees nearly buckled at what I saw in his face.

Joshua wasn't crying, but his tired eyes were redder than I'd ever seen them. His mouth had twisted in its attempt to hold back his emotions—a battle that I could tell it would soon lose. Apparently, his crisis of faith had finally resolved itself, in the worst possible way. My beautiful, sunny Joshua had been breaking for weeks, and now the break was complete.

"I'm sorry," he whispered shakily. "I'm . . . I'm not as good at dealing with loss as you are. And I . . ." Here he paused to draw an unsteady breath. "I'm not ready to lose you. I'm just not. I just . . . can't."

At the last word, his shoulders slumped forward and he seemed to fold in on himself. I should have said something comforting, or tried to convince him that he wouldn't lose me. In other words, I should have lied.

Instead, I focused every part of myself upon Joshua and then threw myself against him. Within the span of a few seconds we went from standing apart to falling together onto his bed. I kissed him until I couldn't breathe—until he kissed me back just as fiercely. I wrapped one of my legs around his hip and spun with him across the bed, tangling myself in his sheets and in his arms.

In between our kisses, I whispered feverishly, "I love you, I love you." He panted the words back to me, running his hands through my long hair and using it to tug me gently to him again. Other than those whispers, we didn't speak, and we didn't have to. Both of us felt the same need to consume each other, to breathe each other's breath until one of us stopped breathing altogether.

Joshua paused, midkiss, and then pulled away slightly. By this point he'd positioned himself over me and now he looked down on me with so much tenderness that I felt the fissure in my heart crackle and expand. With one hand on my hip and the other cupped softly around the back of my neck, Joshua leaned in close to my ear.

"Please," he whispered. "Please."

I knew what he was asking, and it wasn't for me to make love to him; it was for me to stay—to find some way to stay here, in this world, with him. Unfortunately, that was the one request I had no power to fulfill.

In lieu of an answer, I slipped my hands beneath his shirt and, in one swift motion, tugged it over his head. He didn't try to stop me but instead moved his hands beneath my shirt as well. After he'd positioned his fingers along my hemline, he hesitated, clearly asking me for permission. I gave him a quick but fierce peck on the lips, and he nodded in acknowledgment. Then he slid my shirt off slowly, so that the silk brushed deliciously along my stomach and arms.

Once he'd done that, however, he surprised me by catching my gaze fully and holding it.

"I love you," he said simply.

I smiled and traced his lower lip with my forefinger. "I love you, Joshua. And I always will."

He returned my smile, and then returned his mouth to mine. *This is it*, I thought. *This is finally it.*

My heart began to knock loudly against my ribs. So loudly that I thought my heart sounded like someone knocking on a wooden door. *Exactly* like it, in fact.

"Joshua?" Rebecca's voice called from the other side of the closed door. "Joshua, are you doing homework?"

Damn, I thought. *Damn, damn, damn.*

With no small amount of reluctance either, Joshua pulled his lips from mine to answer, "Uh . . . yeah, Mom. Just . . . finishing up some Anatomy."

I had to clap my hand over my mouth to keep from giggling. Even though we'd been interrupted, I some-how felt lighter, happier. Strange, how his touch could do that to me: reconnect me to him in away that I doubted would ever break again. No matter what happened this weekend.

"Well, when you get to a stopping place," Rebecca con-tinued, "can you come downstairs? A few of our guests arrived early, and I'd like you to say hello."

My stomach did a little flip. I knew that I would see the young Seers in just a few minutes, and that I would need to be ready to brief them on our plans. But even though I knew what I needed to say, I hadn't entirely prepared myself to actually *see* them. Particularly after how our first meeting had ended.

"I'll be down in a minute," Joshua called out to his mom, rolling away from me with a final brush of fingertips across my bare stomach. Despite my worries, I smiled, luxuriating in the touch for another few seconds before joining him off the bed.

While he dug around on the floor for our clothes, I couldn't help but stare at him hungrily. Joshua bent back up, caught me looking, and grinned. He held my shirt out for me and, when I reached for it, he pulled it back slightly so that I had to stretch to grab it. I laughed and took it easily from his hands.

We began to slip our shirts back on, but neither of us could stop peeking at each other. Still laughing, Joshua yanked his shirt into place and then wrapped me in a playful hug as I finished with my clothing.

"Hey," I teased, "if you keep doing this, I won't be able to fix my haystack hair."

"You're beautiful, even with bed head," he whispered into the nape of my neck, and I shivered happily. Then I pulled away so that I really could put myself back together. Once we both looked somewhat presentable, I placed my hand in his and let him lead me out of the bedroom and down the hallway.

I had a fleeting moment of worry that his mother would notice we'd come downstairs together, and rightly suspect what we'd been up to. But when we crossed through the archway leading into the kitchen, an entirely new set of worries replaced that one.

The three young Seers I'd met this Christmas in New Orleans were sprawled across the Mayhews' kitchen like they owned the place, all but ignoring their older relatives. Drew and Hayley were practically slobbering over each other at the breakfast table, near a disgusted Jillian and Scott; and Annabel looked cool and collected as she leaned against the kitchen island.

None of their behavior was particularly unnerving. But my mouth dropped open when I saw the person leaning against the island with Annabel. Actually, I saw his eyes first—a clear, gorgeous blue, offset by his smooth coffee-and-cream skin. He caught my shocked stare and flashed me a wide grin.

"Hey, Amelia," he drawled.

"Felix!" I cried out joyfully.

"It's good to see you, too. And it's good to see you looking so . . . happy."

He was referring to my flushed, post-make-out-session

appearance, obviously. My blush deepened as Rebecca turned away from the dishes that she'd been washing in the kitchen sink.

"Oh. Do you two know each other, Amelia?" she asked, clearly surprised.

"Uh . . . yeah," I replied awkwardly. "He was . . . at that party that Jillian picked me up from in New Orleans. Felix was one of the nice guys."

"Yeah, that's how we met, too," Annabel offered, slipping her arm around Felix's waist. I watched her do so, confused until it hit me: Felix had arrived *with* Annabel. And they were . . . dating? Felix noticed my confusion, and his grin widened.

"Annabel brought me for moral support," he explained. While Rebecca wasn't looking, Felix used his free, non-Annabel-occupied hand to make air quotes around the phrase "moral support." The two of them winked meaningfully at me, and I finally understood: Annabel must have contacted Felix for help this weekend, and he had tagged along under the pretense of being her new boyfriend. Funny, they seemed awfully cozy for a fake couple.

"That's sweet of you," Rebecca said, her voice once again muffled by the sounds of clanking dishes. "Just so you kids know: there's going to be a big family dinner tonight, up at the community center. Y'all are welcome to eat with us, but we figured that you teenagers would want to spend some time away from all the adults. Considering . . . what we have to do tomorrow."

The mood among the young Seers grew solemn for a moment. No matter what we had planned for Saturday, tomorrow's first order of business would be Ruth's funeral—an event that no one had expected to attend. Not yet, anyway.

Annabel broke the melancholy silence first, shifting forward from the island and gesturing to the rest of us. "That's a good idea, Aunt Rebecca. I think we'll all go outside to talk about what we want to do tonight."

Annabel made a sort of round-'em-up circle with one hand. In various states of enthusiasm and reluctance, the rest of us followed her down the back hallway and out onto the patio. Annabel waited until the back door had shut solidly behind Drew and Hayley before she turned toward us with an intent expression. But before she spoke, she caught my eye.

"Okay if I talk about *my* ideas for Saturday?" she asked me. "Jillian's already briefed us on what happened the last two times you guys tried to fight the demons."

I blinked back, startled. Then, for lack of anything better to do, I nodded at her and resisted the urge to say "proceed."

Now that she apparently had permission, Annabel

settled against a deck chair and shifted her messenger bag forward. I'd assumed it was a purse, but as she began to remove strange, witchy-looking items from it, I realized that the bag served as some sort of supply kit. None of the items themselves—candles, spell books, etc.—really surprised me. Not until she pulled out a wide-mouthed jar full of what looked like gray powder.

"Seer dust?" I hissed. "Seriously? After everything that you guys did at Christmas, and after last week's disaster in the netherworld, you still think Seer dust is a good idea?"

Annabel shook her head. "Not Seer dust, Amelia. Transfer Powder."

Sensing my confusion, Joshua tugged me closer to him and then leaned forward, toward his cousins. "What exactly is Transfer Powder?"

"Well, it's kind of a new invention," Felix interjected. "We used Voodoo and some Seer spells to create this powder. In fact, Marie even helped." He flashed a brief smile that was both mischievous *and* a little sad. "After I convinced her that she needed me to rid the Conjure Café of its 'wandering spirit.' Apparently, Gaby broke a *lot* of expensive bottles while she was invisible."

I almost grinned in spite of myself. "What does the powder do?" I asked, moving cautiously toward Annabel and her mysterious offering.

Still keeping eye contact with me, Annabel lowered her head and smiled darkly. "It transfers supernatural power, from the dead to the living. If you and I both ingest this in a Seer circle and say the right spells, then I *should* be able to absorb whatever power you're exhibiting at the time. So for instance, if you go invisible when we both take the powder, we should both be able to turn invisible."

"Neat trick," I murmured, reaching out gingerly to touch the surface of the glass jar.

"Yeah, but not all that helpful. You see, what we *really* need is the one thing that Ruth got right about her attack: the one thing that can turn you into a weapon."

With a wave of her hand, Annabel gestured at all of me, from my head to the toes of my boots. The gesture meant something, but for the life of me, I couldn't figure out what. Until suddenly, I *could*. Then I smiled, too.

"Glow," I whispered. "If you all take the powder, then you'll all be able to glow."

Chapter
TWENTY-ONE

After some debate, Annabel and I agreed that we couldn't practice with everyone—there just wasn't enough Transfer Powder to go around. So that evening, after the older Mayhews gathered at the community center for the dinner, the young Seers and I drove to Robber's Cave Park, where we could test the powder without too many witnesses.

We found a relatively secluded fire pit, a good distance into the woods—far enough away from the nearest campgrounds that no one could see our fire burning under the moonless sky, or even hear us scream. Still, I feared that someone might wander past. I paced nervously around the edge of the clearing until Annabel finally shut the spell book she'd been consulting and set it beside her on the rock bench where she'd been sitting.

"Okay," she said in a commanding tone. "Now that it's full dark, shall we get started?"

"Yes, let's shall," Hayley mimicked, and then composed her smile into something more serious when Annabel shot her a disapproving glare. Taking that as their cue, everyone formed a circle around me as I took my place in front of the fire.

The young Seers linked hands, drawing together until they all stood only a foot from me. Quietly, they began to chant—strange words that would bind and give strength to the spell. I thought that Annabel would be the test subject. But to my surprise, Joshua broke free of the circle and joined me at its center, holding a small handful of Transfer Powder.

"I don't think—," I started, but Joshua cut me off with a shake of his head.

"Who could make a better guinea pig than me?" he joked, offering me his powder-free hand. Not knowing what else to do, I took it and pulled him closer to me.

"I don't like this, Joshua."

"What's the worst that could happen?" When I quirked

the corner of my mouth, he laughed softly. "I know, I know: everything. But I'm willing to try, if you are."

I hesitated, tugging nervously on my bottom lip with my teeth. Then I lifted my other hand and allowed Joshua to pour half of the powder into it. Once we both held a palmful, I glanced over my shoulder at Annabel, who stood to my right and slightly behind me. She didn't stop chanting but she jerked her head at us—apparently, as a signal to move forward with the ritual.

Holding tight to both Joshua and the powder, I closed my eyes and began to whisper my own sort of chant. I ran the word "glow" through my mind like a song. Like a prayer. But the longer I prayed, the more I felt like I was wasting my time. I released a deep sigh and opened my eyes.

"It's not working, is it?"

I didn't answer Joshua, but instead turned my powder-filled fist over for him to examine its total lack of shimmer. I sighed again and let that hand fall to my side.

"It's no use. Like Melissa said, I've got to be in some kind of mortal peril for this to happen. Well . . . me or someone I care about."

By now, the Seers' chanting had stopped and they'd dropped hands. They all listened intently to Joshua's and my conversation. Except . . . two of them weren't waiting. At the periphery of my vision, I saw Felix take something from Annabel. Then he began walking toward us with the object raised to chest height. In the shifting firelight, I couldn't tell what he was carrying until he'd already pointed the small gun directly at Joshua.

My breath caught in my throat.

"Put the gun away, Felix," I finally said, trying very hard to keep my voice even. "Everyone knows that you're not going to shoot Joshua, just to get me to glow."

Felix tilted his head to one side quizzically. "I'm not?" he asked, just before lowering the gun and planting one bullet in the ground near Joshua's left foot.

"Whoa!" Joshua shouted, jerking wildly to the side without letting go of my hand. I moved with him, scurrying as far away from Felix as the Seer circle would let me.

The sound of the gunshot still rang in my ears, so loudly that I almost couldn't hear myself shriek, "What the hell are you doing? Are you *crazy*?"

Felix didn't respond but instead raised the gun so that it pointed at Joshua's shoulder. Suddenly, the ringing in my ears silenced, and everything around me seemed to sharpen into focus. Because the cold set of Felix's mouth told me that he *would* shoot again . . . if he felt like he had to.

From somewhere on my right, Annabel spoke in an apologetic tone. "I'm sorry, Amelia, but this is the only way. So you'd better hurry. I don't know if anyone at the campgrounds heard that shot, but they're certainly going to hear the next one."

My eyes darted to Joshua's; even in the firelight I could tell that he shared my feelings of panic. We kept staring at each other, silently communicating about what to do next, when Felix began counting down to his next shot.

"Ten, nine, eight—"

"Felix, this is ridiculous. I can't just do this on command like some trained—"

"Seven, six—"

"This isn't fair." Hysteria edged its way into my voice. "This isn't how it's going to happen on Saturday."

"Five, four—"

"Stop," I pleaded as my eyes started to well up with tears. "Please just stop this."

"Three, two," Felix said flatly, moving his gun so that it now pointed directly at Joshua's heart.

"Stop!" I screamed, louder than I'd ever screamed before. And with that scream, the glow ripped across my exposed skin like a wildfire.

"One," Felix breathed, dropping the gun to his side. Then, without an apology or explanation, he rushed to rejoin the Seer circle, which had begun to frantically chant again.

For several incomprehensible seconds, I didn't really even register that my glow really had reappeared. But when I saw it, dancing brighter than the reflection of firelight in Joshua's eyes, I realized that our window might close at any second.

I signaled to Joshua with a flick of my chin. At first, he seemed too dazed to react. But after a violent shake of his head—probably to clear it of sheer terror—he followed me. With our other hands clenched tightly together, we simultaneously raised our powder-filled fists. Then, like some bride and groom at a twisted version of a wedding toast, we tilted our heads back, opened our hands, and dumped as much of the Transfer Powder as we could into our mouths.

It tasted . . . not great, but not as bad as I'd thought it would, either. Dry and powdery, obviously, but also a little sweet and herby. As I continued to swallow it, I had a sudden flash of memory: my father and I, sitting in the Indian restaurant that he'd insisted we drive all the way to Tulsa to try; in front of us was a near-empty plate of rich, creamy korma, which I'd complained about but had secretly loved. The image vanished with the last traces of powder.

I raised my head, swallowing around the knot of powder that seemed stuck in my throat, and then peeked at Joshua. He, too, made strange motions with his mouth, as though he had tried to chew a bit of it; not a terribly pleasant effort, judging by the look on his face.

"Done?" I asked, my voice rough.

"Done." Joshua nodded, obviously trying not to gag as he spoke. "So . . . what now?"

I looked back over my shoulder at Annabel, who was still chanting solemnly with her eyes closed, and then turned back to Joshua.

"To be honest," I told him, "I have no freaking clue. I don't know if we're *supposed* to hold hands, or turn in circles, or tap dance, or—"

Joshua surprised me by darting in for a kiss. His fingers rested softly on my neck, and as we kissed, his thumb stroked my cheek. He tasted gritty from the Transfer Powder, but also impossibly sweet. And his kiss told me that he'd been afraid, too; that I wasn't the only one scared by Felix's gun.

Our kiss lasted a few more seconds. I kept my eyes closed after it ended, leaning back and sighing happily. When I opened my eyes, however, I gasped.

Before the kiss, Joshua's skin had looked like that of any normal, living boy. Now it shined with a spectral fire, curling over his arms and face without burning them.

"Joshua," I whispered reverently, "you *glow*."

With a disbelieving frown, he lifted his hand. The moment he saw its new light, he jerked backward as though he really had been lit on fire. He waved his hand violently, like that might put out the glow. But soon, his expression shifted from one of horror to wonder.

"It doesn't hurt," he marveled, turning his hand over more slowly. "I always thought it would hurt."

"No, it never hurts. In fact, it's kind of—"

"Exhilarating," Joshua finished. He grinned widely and flexed his fingers outward, so that his hand resembled a torch. But then his smile disappeared.

"How do we even know if it works?" he asked, loud enough that the entire group of Seers could hear. No one replied, but they didn't need to: the answer struck me, almost as soon as he asked the question.

"Burn me," I said softly.

"What?"

"Burn me," I repeated, stepping closer to him. "The glow only works on supernatural beings, and I'm the only supernatural being here. You *have* to try to burn me."

Joshua shook his head, grimacing. "I won't."

"Just try," I urged. Then, as a weak joke, I warned, "Or Felix might shoot at you again."

"No, Amelia . . . just no. And besides, you're still glowing, too."

He had a point. I had no idea what the two different fires might do to each other, and I didn't necessarily want to find out. So I closed my eyes and focused on something less . . . glow inspiring, I supposed. I pictured the Mayhew family, sitting around their living room, laughing and safe and demon-free; just for laughs, I threw my mom into the image too. However silly, the exercise obviously worked; when I reopened my eyes, the glow had left my skin.

I glanced up and saw Joshua staring at me in disbelief. "How did you *do* that?" he asked.

"I focused on something that didn't . . . get me too worked up, I guess. Anything calm or safe seems to make it go away."

Then I held out my unlit arm to Joshua as an offering. He shook his head again, harder this time.

"Try," I said, gesturing emphatically at him with my outstretched arm. "Just one burn. To see if you'll be able to use the glow against the wraiths on Saturday. One burn, Joshua. For Ruth. For me."

I thought he would refuse me again, but instead he shot his hand forward like a snake and wrapped his fingers, hard, around my wrist. Although we'd previously touched without hurting each other, Joshua must have decided to take the exercise seriously because it felt as though his hand was a hot iron on my wrist. My brain had barely registered the searing pain before I was yanking my arm back with a cry.

"Holy hell," I gasped, and immediately, Joshua's glow extinguished. He rushed forward to comfort me, and it took everything I had not to shy away from him. With a slight, reflexive twinge of fear, I allowed him to take my arm carefully into his hand again.

"I'm sorry, I'm so sorry," he said, talking fast, as though the speed at which he spoke might heal the pink, hand-shaped welt that had started to form around my wrist. As my burned skin darkened and wrinkled, I shook my head in awe.

It had worked: I'd transferred one of my greatest weapons into another being. And with that, another piece of my plan to destroy the netherworld gateway snapped into place.

Chapter TWENTY-TWO

J oshua couldn't stop apologizing. Lying tangled
with him in his bed that night, I constantly had
to reassure him that I wasn't angry. But even as
I helped him with his tie and suit coat the next morning, he kept running his hands lightly over my burn and
wincing.

"I hate this." He motioned once again to the nasty
pink welt on my wrist.

"I know you do. But you might stop regretting it, come
Saturday night."

"I don't think I will," he said, moving away from me so that he could slip on a pair of shiny, rarely worn dress shoes. "I hurt you. And I . . . I *meant* to."

I gave him a small, close-lipped smile and checked my reflection in his dresser mirror; I'd done my own makeup this morning, in an attempt to look more put together for his family. Then I pulled on the elbow-length black gloves that Jillian had lent me—now, a necessary addition to my funeral outfit.

"Good," I told him. "I'm glad you meant to use your new powers. So now you'll know exactly what to do if one of those wraith minions attacks you."

"What if an actual demon attacks me?"

Trying not to cringe, I swept some imaginary lint from the hem of my black dress. "As far as I know, the same rules apply to them. But please: stay out of their range, okay?"

"Not happening," he said, coming over to wrap his arms around my waist. "I'm staying close to you all night."

When I made a little *humph* sound, he grabbed my unburned hand and placed it on his chest.

"Just like I'm staying close to you for the next two days," he said quietly.

Two days, I thought. *Only two days.* All I could do was lay my head on his chest, next to my hand. After a while, I sighed, pressing myself backward to look up at him.

"Time to go downstairs for the family breakfast."

"I know," he said, sighing too.

He took my hand from his chest, gave the back of it a tender kiss, and then led me out of his room. Halfway down the staircase, he released my hand so that I could go invisible. I let the current run over my skin just as we hit the bottom of the stairs, wishing for a moment that I didn't have to keep up the pretense that I hadn't slept there the night before.

When we entered the kitchen, I was surprised to find that most of Joshua's extended family—aunts, uncles, and cousins—had already packed into the space and were milling around with mugs of coffee and handfuls of Jeremiah's breakfast pastries. I scanned the crowd and was relieved to see that Felix hadn't joined them. I still hadn't forgiven him for the previous night; I wasn't even sure if I could.

Although the Mayhews' kitchen was huge, I couldn't find a spare corner where I could hide without touching anybody. Finally, I had to separate from Joshua and move toward the back hallway. I settled against the wall, waiting until someone gave the signal that it was time for everyone to leave for the funeral.

Luckily, my wait wasn't entirely wasted. Farther into the kitchen but close enough to be within eavesdropping range, Annabel and Drew had their heads together in a heated debate.

"I still think we should be there," Annabel hissed. "To make sure they don't ask the wrong people."

"And I still think that's not going to work," Drew countered. "That school has only got, like, a hundred people in it. You think they're not going to notice if a bunch of people show up who don't go to the school?"

I bristled. Obviously Annabel and Drew were talking about the Wilburton High prom, and whether or not we would pick the "wrong" people to bolster our ranks Saturday. The conversation reminded me, unpleasantly, of Ruth: this type of micromanagement was just her style. Still, Annabel had a point. She and her cohorts were far better trained as Seers than Joshua or Jillian; if anyone could recognize netherworld-opening potential in civilians, it was the young New Orleans Seers.

But that didn't mean I had to like it.

Without letting myself go visible, I scooted closer to Annabel and whispered, "What, Annabel, you didn't get enough of prom when you were actually *in* high school?"

I was petty enough to enjoy it when Annabel and Drew jumped a little. Both of them scanned the crowd of their relatives, searching. Finally, Annabel's gaze landed on me. Or, at least, on a spot close to where I stood.

"Funny," she said in a flat tone that told me she didn't think my practical joke was funny at all.

Although she couldn't see me, I smirked. "Almost as funny as a bunch of twentysomethings crashing a small-town prom because they don't trust a ghost to recognize supernatural potential."

"Whatever," Annabel snapped. "What age should *you* be now? Forty?"

"Girls," Drew hissed, using both his hands to do the universal, palms-down gesture of "chill out." Annabel and I both blinked for a moment—I don't think either of us realized that we'd crossed the boundaries of cattiness, until we blew right past them.

"Sorry, Annabel." I unfolded my arms out of the defensive position that they'd taken across my chest. "I guess I was just pissed that you questioned Joshua and me."

"It's a good plan," she offered, in a far lighter tone than earlier. "Getting newbies to help us—that's kind of inspired. Especially since they'll probably end up being targets anyway. But . . . I still think *we* should meet the possible recruits too. Just to be safe."

"Okay," I conceded. "I agree, then. We do like we discussed: lure the non-Seers out of prom for a few minutes, convince them to join us for the fight that night, and then go make our final preparations. Together."

"What about Hayley?" Drew asked. Then, reluctantly, he added, "And Felix?"

His tone made me wonder whether the decision to

threaten Joshua and me with a firearm hadn't been unanimous after all.

"Do they really need to go, or can it just be you guys? I mean, Felix could just hang back, and prep for the battle. . . ."

Annabel shook her head and gave a dismissive wave. "Let's deal with your Felix issues later, okay? What I'd really like to know is how Amelia plans to do it. I mean, to convince Joshua and Jillian's friends that this threat is legit."

I'd just opened my mouth to answer her, when Jeremiah started to call out above all the chatter.

"Everyone? Everyone, it's ten thirty. The limos for the family are here."

He spoke at a professional clip, trying to organize the chaos. But he was clearly trying to keep it together, too—I could see the heavy lines of grief and exhaustion around his eyes and mouth. I resolved to drop the demon talk for the next few hours and focus on what mattered most right now: Ruth Mayhew's memorial.

As the Mayhew family began to file quietly out of the house, I found Joshua and followed him to the limousine. As I approached the long, black car, however, I could see that too many people were piling inside. After a second's hesitation, I stopped and watched the limo fill up and then drive off—probably with Joshua thinking that I sat somewhere inside with him. Finally, the last car pulled out of the driveway. I waited a few more minutes, just to be safe, and then I allowed myself to go visible with a heavy sigh.

Realizing that I had no time to waste, I began to trudge down the Mayhews' driveway. But by the time I'd reached the main road, which would eventually lead me to the highway on which the Mayhews' cemetery was located, I seriously regretted my choice of shoes. Only a few steps on the asphalt of the main road, and I'd decided to go barefoot like I used to.

I'd just paused to slip off my heels when an unfamiliar car with rental plates pulled over in front of me on the shoulder of the road. With my toes still caught in the top of my left shoe, I stumbled backward slightly. I didn't know why, but I suddenly had the instinct to run. When the door opened, however, I relaxed a bit: I recognized the man stepping out of the car, although I wasn't particularly happy to see him.

"Hello, Felix," I said drily, slipping my left foot back into its shoe. "Stopping by to wing me with your forty-five?"

Felix paused halfway between me and the bumper of his car and slipped his hands into the pockets of his funeral blazer. After a beat, he cleared his throat awkwardly.

"It wasn't technically *my* forty-five."

"Oh, well, that makes everything better."

Felix shook his head, cringing at my tone. "Amelia, I really am sorry about that. I didn't want to do it, but . . . but . . ."

"But what?" I snapped. "But you thought threatening us with a machete would have been less effective than a semiautomatic?"

Felix's contrite frown transformed abruptly into a scowl. He jerked his hands from his pockets and threw them into the air angrily.

"God, Amelia, you're a freaking hypocrite, you know that?"

"I'm . . . I'm a *what*?"

At first, I was too stunned to get angry. That moment didn't last long, though—only a few more seconds passed before I was fuming. If I could have touched Felix, I would have stormed over and smacked him right in the face.

"Correct me if I'm wrong, Felix, but *I've* never shot at the person you loved, have I?"

"No, you haven't," he said, suddenly calmer. "But you would do just about anything to keep Joshua out of hell, right?"

That wasn't the response I'd expected.

"Right . . . ?" I answered, unsure where he was taking this.

"So would you kill for him?" Felix asked, leaning forward intently. "Would you *threaten* to kill for him?"

When I didn't answer right away, Felix pressed me further.

"What about for your mother?" he asked. "Or for your *sister*, if you had one? Would you do anything—and I mean anything—to get them out of hell? Including pointing a gun at the one person who might hold the key to their escape?"

Everything clicked into place in my mind, and I slumped out of my defensive stance.

"Felix," I breathed, moving toward him slightly. "I know you miss Gaby. And I'm trying—I'm really trying—to figure out a way to save her. But . . . a gun?"

"I know." He sighed and shook his head. "It was Annabel's idea. But you have to admit: it did get you to use your powers."

"You couldn't have tried a less lethal way?"

Felix lifted one shoulder in a shrug—on him, the movement looked so much like the shrugs Gaby gave me, when she wanted to pretend she didn't care.

"You're right," he said softly. "I shouldn't have said yes. And I'm sorry."

Here, in his remorse, was my opportunity to secure another part of my slowly forming plan for Saturday night. But did I dare take it? I considered him for a moment longer, before making up my mind.

"Where did the gun come from, anyway?" I asked him, keeping my tone blasé.

He gave a bitter little laugh. "I found it stashed in a desk drawer in the actress's apartment in New Orleans, before I left. It's unregistered, as far as I can tell, so I doubt she's going to come looking for it. If and when she ever gets out of rehab, that is."

That's good, I thought. *That's* very *good*.

I flashed Felix my sweetest smile. "Can I see it?"

He hesitated, giving me a wary look. Then he reached into his coat and pulled the gun from his belt. I took it from him carefully, marveling at how heavy it really was. I could feel the coldness of the metal through my gloves. Then I glanced back up at him as innocently as I could and made him an offer.

"Let me keep it for you, in my purse. Just until Sunday morning. You know, in case I get attacked between now and then."

I didn't look up from the gun, but I could sense Felix's reluctance. Finally, he said, "Okay. Just be careful with it, all right? And don't decide to shoot me, either."

"Of course," I said, slipping the handgun into my purse. "*I* would never shoot at *you*, Felix. And I promise: I won't use this unless I have to, to save someone's life."

When I made that promise, he relaxed visibly; he even

smiled. After a beat, he took a step back and gestured to the car.

"Want a ride to the funeral?" he asked.

I gave him another wide, innocent smile. "I thought you'd never ask."

Then, with the gun bumping against my hip through the purse, I followed him to the car.

Chapter
TWENTY-THREE

Ruth's memorial service lasted longer than any other funeral I'd attended. The number of speakers and eulogizers and gnashers of teeth at this thing was *crazy*. Of all the people integrally involved in the memorial, I didn't recognize a single one. Each member of the Mayhew family stayed firmly planted in his or her seat. Even stranger, I caught Jeremiah *grinning* every now and then.

Finally, I couldn't stand the mystery any longer. I tilted my head toward Joshua—who had easily forgiven me for being a few minutes late—and, from the corner of my mouth, whispered, "Any explanation for all this?"

He kept his eyes glued to his grandmother's closed casket, but he smiled just like his father. "Grandma Ruth planned this funeral a long time ago," he explained quietly. "What you're watching now is a carefully orchestrated production. Most of those people are members of Ruth's old coven, and they're reciting lines from a *script* she wrote for them. Think of it as . . . funeral theater."

I shook my head in genuine surprise. Then I started to grin too. It made perfect sense that Ruth's iron fist would reach out from beyond the grave to control her own funeral. But whatever the intended purpose of this spectacle, it also had an inadvertent—but no less positive—effect: the Mayhews themselves were having a great time watching it. One singer hit an off-key high note, and Jillian suppressed a giggle; a eulogizer called Ruth a "fount of mercy and gentleness," and Rebecca fought off a snicker. The other members of the family were no exception.

The first truly somber moment came when the funeral-home director called for all the attendees to file past the grave. I took my dutiful place in line and silently thanked Ruth for instructing that her casket be kept closed. Turning away from the sight of all the white flowers piled atop Ruth's coffin, I focused harder on

Joshua so that I could take his hand in mine. He didn't turn around, but he gave my fingers a firm squeeze. I knew what that squeeze meant: that this part would be far more painful than the actual service. This part would be real.

After paying our respects at the grave, we all returned to our seats but remained standing in front of them. At this point, non–family members came by to give their condolences and their hugs. Then, slowly, they left the cemetery in groups.

While people began wandering toward their cars, I hung back, trying to give Joshua some much-needed alone time with his sister and parents. Soon, Annabel as well as her little sister and parents joined that small gathering, as did Drew and his mother. Together, this group of Ruth's children and grandchildren talked and cried and even laughed, for almost another hour. And I didn't mind the wait at all.

I hardly even noticed when, at some point, Felix, Hayley, and Scott joined me in leaning against Felix's rental car. They all watched with me as the Mayhew family mourned, until Hayley shifted her weight beside me.

"You know, sometimes it's weird," she mused. "Loving a Mayhew."

I arched an eyebrow, surprised at the sentiment—and the insight. "What do you mean, Hayley?"

"It's just kind of intense: this huge family of Seers and the people who love them. A lot of different abilities, and a lot of different opinions on how to use them."

"But you're a Seer, too," Felix pointed out, stretching forward to meet her gaze. She gave him a sweet but close-lipped smile.

"It's different with me and my mom. Jeez, it's different with most Seer families. I mean, do you guys have at least three or four relatives that you can share this burden with?"

I settled further against the car, realizing that I'd been excluded from the question, given that I wasn't technically a Seer. Still, I listened to Felix's and Scott's answers.

"No, man. I don't have anyone." Scott shook his head sadly. "The only other Seer that I know I'm related to is my gran . . . but she's dead now. And *I'm* not even triggered yet."

"Yeah," Felix added. "I didn't even find out until after my sister died. We were around Voodoo a lot as kids, thanks to my grandfather, but the ghost stuff wasn't really front and center."

Hayley and Scott just nodded, obviously reflecting on the perils of being lonely as a Seer. Then, the three of them unexpectedly turned to me.

"What?" I asked, suddenly feeling very self-conscious.

"Is it hard for you, too?" Hayley asked. "Dating a Mayhew?"

"Uh . . . well, I guess *dating* is hard for me."

The three of them chuckled, but not cruelly. For the rest of our wait, we shared a companionable silence and I reflected on the fact that, in a way, I would leave earth knowing that I'd made real friends. Which was definitely not a bad thing.

Of course, it did make me feel sort of guilty about what I had in my purse right now and what I intended to do with it on Saturday night, if I had to.

Finally, the group of Mayhews approached us. Jillian got there first and wrapped her arms around Scott's waist. Next came Drew, who enveloped Hayley in a tight hug. Seeing everyone couple up, Felix rolled his eyes at me with a faint grin and peeled himself off the car so that he could go talk to Annabel a few feet from us. So I craned my neck to find Joshua.

By now, he stood only a few feet from me, talking intently to his aunt Trish. Joshua must have sensed me watching him, because they both glanced over to me at the same time. Trish smiled and gave me a friendly, non-committal little wave; as far as she probably knew, I was just that strange girl who Rebecca and Jeremiah drove home from New Orleans at Christmas. I waved back, thinking of how much I wished I could interact with

Joshua's family in a *normal* way. At least during these last two days.

With deliberate slowness—almost as if they wanted to miss the huge family luncheon that Ruth's old church was holding in her honor—the Mayhews began to pile back into the limo. Instead of joining them, Joshua walked up to me, frowning as though the morning had taken a greater toll on him than he let on. Without saying anything, I concentrated on our touch so that I could slip my arms around his neck and pull him into a hug, which he returned gratefully. We embraced for a few more seconds, before he moved away to take my arm in his.

"This time," he said, "you're riding in the limo, and you're even going to do it visibly. I've already asked my parents."

I smiled, leaning my head on his shoulder as we walked toward the car. "You know I don't need a fifteen-foot-long sedan to be with you."

"That's good," he said, chuckling low. "Especially since they're only, like, ten feet long anyway."

I laughed and then, feeling a little bit intimidated by the sheer size of the limo, ducked into the open door. Joshua guided me to a corner, where he could sit on the only side of my body that might be exposed to one of his relatives. When he wasn't looking, I tucked my purse with its contraband gently between my feet on the floorboards.

When the limo was full and had started to bump down the uneven cemetery road, Joshua laced his fingers with mine and then ran his thumb slowly down the back of my hand. For some reason, the touch ignited a wild reaction within me, and a furious blush burned its way across my cheeks.

What's wrong *with you?* I chastised myself internally. But I already knew the answer. I had, at best, two days left with him. One of those—today—would be mostly occupied with the memory of the grandmother who died defending him; another—Saturday—would be occupied with me . . . doing what I needed to do. Tonight, and only tonight, we had the chance to carve out a few final hours for ourselves. And I couldn't imagine that I would practice much self-restraint with him, given the circumstances.

I fought my blush, trying to focus on the rocking limo and the conversations inside of it. The effort worked . . . sort of.

Later, during the church luncheon and the long hours of coffee and Ruthcentric chatting back at the Mayhews' house that night, I stayed close to Joshua's side—there to support him, if he needed it; there to touch him, if I needed it. I only ducked away for a few brief minutes to hide my purse in a random linen cupboard in the back hallway.

People didn't leave until well after eleven, filtering out in small groups: first, those adults with small children; next, some of the elderly; and, finally, the young Seers. At last, there were only five people left in the kitchen. Jeremiah, Rebecca, Joshua, Jillian. And, of course, me.

At this point I was so worn that I felt somewhat cranky about the fact that I would have to "go home" and shift invisible before I could return. But thankfully, Rebecca solved my problem.

"Amelia, honey, it's so late. Why don't you just stay the night, up in Jillian's room? If that's okay with your parents, of course."

I tried not to groan in relief. "Thank you so much, Mrs. Mayhew. I'll give them a call from Jill's room, to let them know where I am."

I stared meaningfully at Jillian, and she gave me a surprisingly mischievous grin. I frowned back at her, unsure of what her look meant. She shook her head, letting the grin fall away as she innocently faced her mother.

"I'll just go and get the room ready for her," Jillian offered. Rebecca gave her a preoccupied wave, so Jillian turned toward the stairs. Before she crossed through the archway that led out of the kitchen, she flashed me that grin one more time and then darted up the staircase.

I watched her go, confused, until Joshua's arm brushed mine. Sufficiently sidetracked, I smiled warmly up at him.

"Ready?" he whispered, touching the inner crook of my elbow with his fingertips. I had to force myself not to shiver happily as I followed him toward the archway. Once there, I paused and leaned back to thank Jeremiah and Rebecca one more time, if only to reassure them that I would behave myself that night. They both smiled at me, but I could see that they were too distracted by exhaustion and grief to worry about the fact that their son's girlfriend was officially staying the night.

I ducked back through the archway, took Joshua's hand again, and started to climb the stairs with him.

"Are you okay?" I asked quietly. "About today, I mean?"

Joshua shrugged. "I will be. I think it's easier for me, since I know that this was Ruth's choice. And since I know what she's doing with her afterlife. Knowing she's in the light, it—"

His voice caught suddenly, and he stopped short, just a few steps shy of the landing. He looked away from me quickly, but I could tell that his face had darkened. I knew what he was thinking, then; I knew what he couldn't say out loud.

It would be easier for him to accept what might happen tomorrow night, if he knew I would end up in the light. And I wished, so very much, that I could tell him that would be the case.

Instead, I pulled him to me with sudden force and

began to kiss him passionately. He hesitated for a split second and then kissed me back, grabbing ahold of me so forcefully that we accidentally climbed the remaining steps. Before I knew it, my back was pressed against Jillian's bedroom door and my hands were . . . everywhere, it seemed.

But just as quickly as the kissed started, it ended. Joshua used the door to push himself away, until he stood closer to his bedroom door than to me. We stayed that way for a while: both panting, neither moving. Eventually, Joshua had composed himself enough to give me a small, strangely polite bow of his head.

"Good night, Amelia."

And with those words, he was gone, ducking through his bedroom door and shutting it quickly behind him. I stared at it, blinking rapidly for God knew how long. Then, for lack of a better option, I opened the door to Jillian's bedroom and slipped inside.

After I shut Jillian's door behind me, I leaned back against it and closed my eyes. My nerves were still rattling around, mostly because of that kiss: it felt strangely meaningful, as though it was just a prelude.

I was still lost in thought when I heard Jillian sigh dramatically.

"Are you going to sneak into my brother's room tonight and, like, do it?"

With an embarrassed half grin, I stormed over to where Jillian sat on her bed, grabbed one of her ruffled throw pillows, and smacked her playfully with it. Then, without saying a word, I changed into pajama pants and a soft tee and crawled onto the pallet of blankets that she'd made for me on the floor.

Jillian didn't say anything else, either, choosing instead to flop unceremoniously onto her bed. Just before she clicked off her bedside lamp, however, she whispered, "So I guess I'll take your silence as a yes?"

I could make no other reply but to smack her with my pillow again.

D*amn Jillian and her stupid perceptiveness.*

That was the only rational thought I could muster when, around two a.m., I finally gave in to my impulses and snuck from Jillian's room toward Joshua's. I wavered at his door, unsure of how best to enter. Knocking seemed too formal, too unlike *us*. But barging in at two in the morning and demanding that he kiss me again seemed way too crazy.

Fortunately, Joshua solved my dilemma for me. I was still standing outside his room, contemplating my first move, when he swung his door open, grabbed me to pull me inside, and then began kissing me fiercely as he shut the door behind us.

"I heard you coming over," he murmured in between our kisses, by way of an explanation.

"I just wasn't sure about our last night . . . I didn't want to waste . . ."

I couldn't get the thought out, partly because it was so difficult and partly because I couldn't really think straight with him this close to me. Finally, I placed one hand on his chest and pushed him away, just long enough to release a few, painful words.

"If it's my last night on earth," I whispered, "I want it to be with you. No one else but you."

Joshua pressed his forehead to mine and nodded, squeezing my upper arm tightly but not painfully. After taking a few moments to compose himself, Joshua nodded again and whispered, "Let's go outside. To the gazebo."

I blinked back, not sure about the wisdom of that suggestion. After all, the family had only gone to bed a few hours ago, and they might hear us exit the back door. Besides, it was probably cold outside. But, assuming Joshua had his reasons for asking, I slipped my hand into his and let him lead me.

Outside, I discovered that I was right: it *was* chilly. I

began to shiver as we walked from the back porch to the gazebo, and Joshua released my hand so that he could wrap his arm around me for warmth. Then, with his free hand, he pulled back the heavy curtains that covered the gazebo's entrance to reveal the biggest surprise of the night.

Inside, the hanging lanterns glittered like stars— Joshua must have lit them all, because the entire room sparkled with their soft light. I didn't know how he'd done it, but most of the plants within the gazebo were now blooming, too: white petals brightened dark corners, scented the air, fell delicately around the daybed, which Joshua had pushed against the far wall.

In the center of the gazebo, underneath the largest lantern, a wide stretch of wooden floor now lay bare. As Joshua guided me out to its center, I finally recognized the open space for what it was: a makeshift dance floor.

Joshua pulled me to him and, after a few still seconds, began to sway with me at the center of the gazebo. There was no music—we couldn't play anything, unless we wanted to risk waking his family—but that didn't seem to matter. We moved together for a long time, holding each other tightly, not wanting to allow even an inch between us. Eventually, I pressed my hand gently to the nape of his neck to draw his mouth to mine.

When the kiss ended, I leaned back and laughed

slightly, running my fingers along his jawline.

"What's so funny?" he asked, smiling faintly.

"I just had a weird thought."

"And what was that?"

"I wondered whether you missed them," I said softly. "Our sparks."

He turned his head to kiss my fingertips and then gave me a smile that was equal parts tender and playful. "I wouldn't say the sparks are gone, Amelia. At least, not for me."

My laughter was low and rough. I led him to kiss me again and again, until I lost count. I didn't know how long we stayed like that, dancing and kissing under the artificial stars. But after an indeterminate amount of time, I noticed that our circles had grown wider until we stood next to the daybed.

When he noticed this, too, Joshua hesitated. But I didn't. I slipped my hands beneath his shirt, sliding it up over his chest. Despite the chill in the gazebo, Joshua helped me completely remove his shirt. Then he allowed me to pull him gently onto the daybed with me. There, he lay close enough to me that I knew neither of us would feel the cold for much longer.

The sight of him there, on that bed with me, made something wild unleash itself within me. Before I knew what had happened, my kisses grew feverish and I began to guide Joshua's hands to the hem of my shirt. I felt him take the edge of it between his fingers, but then he froze. He pulled his mouth away from mine, frowning heavily.

"Amelia, I can't . . . ," Joshua whispered, shaking his head.

A sliver of ice cut its way through my heart.

"You can't what?" I whispered back, fighting the tears that threatened to spill. "You can't be with me on our last night together?"

He faltered, about to say something different, and then shook his head dejectedly.

"No, I can't."

"You don't want me," I concluded. Now I didn't even try to fight my tears.

"Of course I do." Still shaking his head a little, Joshua pressed his forehead to mine. "I just know that if we do this, we can't take it back. *I* can't take it back. I'd live the rest of my life with this memory of you, with this part of you in my heart, and I can't live with . . . I don't know how I'll . . ."

His voice finally broke, and he turned away from me so that I couldn't see his eyes. I smiled, sad and soft, and then reached up to cup his face in my hands, carefully turning it so that I could look straight into those perfect, midnight-blue eyes.

"I thought you knew the truth about us, Joshua. But I can see now that you don't. So I'll tell you: it's *you* who's been haunting *me*, since the moment I first saw you. No matter what we do or don't do tonight, no matter where I go tomorrow, I won't stop letting you haunt me. And I can't imagine a better fate than that."

"Amelia, I don't mean—," Joshua began, but I cut him off.

"Wait. There's something else I want to say. I . . . I think we both know that I won't be here Sunday. It rips my heart out to do this, but I have to: we both deserve to hear—and say—the truth. And you . . ." I paused, still smiling although I'd started to cry a little again. "You deserve a long life. A *perfect* life. One that you live for the both of us. Because, no matter what, we'll see each other again—I know we will. So when you're a hundred and five and fully satisfied with your life *and* you still love me, you can come find me then, okay?"

While I spoke, Joshua studied me intently. I assumed that he would argue with me when I'd finished, or even fall apart. Instead, he pulled me tightly against him and whispered, "I love you, Amelia. I always will."

I wrapped my fingers in his black hair and closed my eyes, forcing out what tears remained. "I love you, too, Joshua. Always."

And that was how we spent the rest of the night:

wrapped together, no longer speaking. Only once more did we kiss: a soft, tender press of the lips at dawn, before I had to sneak back up to Jillian's room. Lingering there, with my mouth on his, I couldn't shut out my one, brutally insistent thought:

This was the first of our last kisses.

A t breakfast with his family Saturday morning, Joshua and I shared very few words. But beneath the table, we held hands tightly. So tightly that my fingers ached.

Luckily, Rebecca was in too much of a hurry to get to work and fill the florist's orders for prom corsages to notice our odd behavior. Jillian, however, saw right through us; she obviously saw our drawn expressions and the way we desperately clung to each other. So when Joshua announced that he was going to run an errand with his cousins (without revealing that they were actually picking up a beer keg to lure the non-Seer recruits out of their prom tonight), Jillian insisted that she and I hang back and "plan."

Before leaving the table, Joshua flashed me a wary, questioning look. But a barked order from Jillian and a small, reassuring nod from me sent him on his way.

Jillian waited until Rebecca and Jeremiah left the kitchen, too, before turning on me. For a long while, she didn't say anything—just scrutinized my pale features and uncomfortable fidgeting. Then, finally, she cleared her throat as though what she was about to say might bring her pain.

"You know, it wouldn't be so bad."

"What wouldn't be, Jill?" I asked in a jagged, uneven voice.

"Having you as a guardian angel."

The sentiment touched me more than I could possibly tell her. But I also knew that sharing deep emotion wasn't really Jillian's style. Not for very long. So I forced a deliberate smirk.

"Whatever. Like I'm going to waste my valuable harp-strumming time to watch you and Scott make out."

Jillian laughed slightly, but after a long pause, she frowned and shook her head.

"I know, Amelia," she said softly.

I tilted my head to one side and arched my eyebrow. "You know what, Jill?"

"That you aren't planning on joining the light. At least, not right away."

I felt goose bumps crawl their way up my arms. I hadn't admitted that part to anyone—I'd been planning *with* the Seers, and also secretly *around* them, but I hadn't actually said aloud how I really wanted the battle to occur tonight. How I really wanted to end my existence.

"How do you know that?" I breathed.

Jillian's right shoulder rose and fell in a despondent little shrug. "Because that's how you've always operated, especially when it comes to my brother. You've tried to sacrifice yourself multiple times to keep him safe. And I know you won't rest peacefully while that bridge still exists."

I swallowed roughly, once again taken aback by how perceptive Jillian really was sometimes.

"Yeah, and?" I countered, without much conviction.

"And I think you're trying to make a bargain with one, or both, sides: light and dark. I don't really have anything specific to go off of—this is all just speculation. But I think you're going to try and offer the darkness something so that they'll consider leaving us alone."

Her words hung heavy in the air between us, waiting. I supposed my ultimate lack of response was answer enough, because Jillian sighed heavily. She'd figured me out before I'd even fully figured out myself.

And so had Joshua, I realized. That was why he'd rejected me the night before—why he seemed even more dejected this morning. Of *course* he would put all the disparate pieces of the puzzle together. He knew me better than Jillian; better, perhaps, than I knew myself.

"So," Jillian said, interrupting my thoughts, "the real question is, what do I need to do to help you?"

I blinked back, surprised that Jillian wasn't trying to talk me out of my plan, however half-baked and incomplete it still was. But . . . I guess it made a dark sort of sense: Jillian knew I wouldn't change my mind, and she also knew this was the only way that she and Joshua— and her family and friends, for that matter—had a fighting chance of survival. She understood that if I could find a way to outsmart the dark, then her family would be safe.

I folded my hands on the kitchen tabletop between us and stared down at them for a minute before speaking quietly.

"There is one thing you can do for me, Jill."

"Anything, Amelia. Name it."

I closed my eyes and lowered my head.

"Jillian, there's going to come a point tonight when

I might ask you to kill me. I need you to promise that you'll do it."

Jillian stayed silent for far too long. Then she shocked me by taking my hands in hers and giving them a tight squeeze—our first real touch. My eyes shot open to meet hers, which were suddenly filled with tears.

"Okay," she whispered, although we were the only two people in the kitchen. "When the time comes, I'll kill you."

Chapter TWENTY-SIX

A fter she made that promise, Jillian sat there with me for several silent, fraught moments. Finally, I couldn't take the melancholy tension anymore, so I cleared my throat and stretched away from her.

"Mind if I go run a few errands of my own?" I asked with feigned indifference. "Just some unimportant things that I need to get done this morning, before we get ready to crash the prom."

Of course, Jillian wasn't fooled. She narrowed her eyes

and pulled the corner of her mouth up into a suspicious grin.

"Oh?" she asked, in a tone that implied she didn't believe me. "Just some meaningless errands?"

"Yup." I pushed myself out of my chair and moved quickly to the back door. "I'll just . . . I'll see you in a few hours."

Jillian caught my gaze, and her eyes narrowed further. "You better be back here at least one last time. For Joshua's sake."

Frowning, I gave her one heavy nod. "I will," I promised. "Of course I will. I wouldn't leave without saying . . ."

Then, without finishing that thought, I turned on one heel and ran.

By the time I reached my first destination, both my heels and toes ached so badly that they'd almost—but not quite—gone numb; I'd been given a ride to this location for so long, I'd forgotten how long it actually took to *walk* here. Fortunately or not, the walk had also provided me with a lot of time to think, and now I hardly noticed the pain in my feet. Not in comparison to my brutal, panicky heartbeats.

I can do this, I told myself. *I can* do *this*.

Even so, my level of anxiety had reached new heights

and I couldn't help wishing with each step that I was back in the Mayhews' kitchen, eating blueberry muffins and holding hands with Joshua. If nothing else, I wished that he was *here* again, urging me on like he'd done so many times before.

But this morning I faced my mother's house alone.

The sight of it made me ache, like it always did. Today, the dilapidated house seemed prettier, framed by the lush, bright green of an Oklahoma spring. Even still, I stumbled slowly up the gravel driveway, wishing that I were anywhere but there.

I was still throwing the pity party, working myself up to the knock that had eluded me for so long, when the front door flung open and my mother came charging out of house. She was carrying an overstuffed trash bag, and for a moment, all I could think was, *Guess it's trash day.*

I snapped back to reality in time to realize that the trash bag blocked my mother's view of me. I was still safe, if I acted quickly. So I allowed the current of invisibility to run over my skin, just in time to see my mother shift the trash bag and casually glance in my direction. I'd gone invisible by the time the bag slipped from her hands, clattering to the ground and spilling its contents all over the porch. But by then, the damage was done.

Although I knew she couldn't see me now, I didn't

twitch a single muscle. She didn't move either, even as several items from her trash rattled noisily across her porch. When an empty glass bottle rolled off the edge and shattered against a large chunk of rock on her lawn, both of us jumped . . . and *both* of us shrieked.

I slapped my hand over my mouth, but it was too late: if my mother thought, for even a second, that I didn't really exist, I'd just proved her wrong. But even after that slipup, we both remained silent, motionless, for an awfully long time.

Finally, my mother stirred.

"Wherever you went," she called, "you can come out now."

I wavered, still so unsure of what to do or say next. Then, acting mostly on instinct, I ran the current back over my skin. At that moment, I was fully visible to her—no hat or sunglasses to mask my face, no black dress to hide my body. Just me, in clothes and last night's makeup. Looking, for the most part, exactly like I did over a decade ago, on the night that I died.

If I frightened my mother, that reaction certainly didn't show on her face. In fact, her expression remained the same. She continued to frown thoughtfully, clearly taking in each element of my appearance: the pale, drawn face; the abused ballet flats; the designer clothes, now dusty from my walk. Then, inexplicably, she smiled.

"Looks like you've had quite a night."

I blinked back, stunned by how calm she sounded.

"Do you want to come up onto the porch, and talk?" she offered.

Still pretty befuddled, I nodded and began to take slow, unsteady steps toward the house. I stopped before climbing the porch steps and looked up at her.

"How did you know?" I asked softly.

I couldn't be sure, but I thought she flinched slightly— maybe at the sound of my voice. Of course, she'd heard me speak after Serena's funeral, but that was when I *could* have been someone else. Someone who wasn't her long-dead daughter.

Even if she had flinched, I couldn't see any fear in her second smile. All I could see was a sweet, crushing mix of sadness and love.

"Don't you think," she asked kindly, "that I would recognize my own daughter's hands?"

"What . . . what do you mean?" I whispered.

Still smiling, my mother shook her head. "Your hands—when you reached out to put that iris on Serena's casket, I saw your hands. And I knew that it was you; that it *had* to be you."

"Oh."

My one syllable sounded flat and uninspired, but that was the best I could do right then. Without another word, I used a column to pull myself onto the porch—mostly so that I could avoid the steps, to which my mother stood too near. For some reason, I didn't want to come too close to her. Maybe because I didn't want to find out what would happen if she tried to touch me.

"Do you . . . want to sit down?" my mother asked, gesturing to the two plastic lawn chairs that occupied the far corner of the porch.

"Sure," I answered roughly, and then followed her slowly to the chairs, keeping my distance the entire way. I waited for her to sit first before I took my seat, using one hand to sweep the dust off my jeans.

We sat there for another long moment, staring warily at each other. She looked pretty in the early-morning light. Her dark hair, so close in color to mine, lay loose on her shoulders, free of its usual ponytail.

"So," she began, after awkwardly clearing her throat. "Maybe we should start with the basics?"

"Okay. Okay, sure."

"First things first, then. Do you . . . you know about Daddy?" she asked haltingly.

And with that question, I finally burst into tears. A flood of them, actually. They poured out of my eyes, stinging my skin and washing away any remnants of makeup I still wore.

To my surprise, it felt good to cry, especially on a day

like today. Even more surprising, my mother started to cry as well. I didn't try to stop her. Instead, we sat there crying for nearly an hour, mourning my father together.

Not for the first time, it struck me that although my mother had suffered my death with someone who shared her burden—my father—she'd faced *his* death alone. Now, she could finally cry with someone who missed him just as much as she did. And strangely, I felt a weird kind of relief that I could share this grief with her.

After a while, however, my mother and I had both shed enough tears. So we began to talk—a decade's worth of talking, in fact. Initially, the conversation consisted of her asking questions, and me answering them. What happened after I died? Did I know where Daddy was? Did it hurt, to die? I answered her questions as honestly as I could, although some almost caused me more pain than I could stand. Eventually, the conversation turned to her, and her life since my father and I left her. And eventually, the conversation turned to that night.

She asked and, because she was my mother—because I loved her—I told her *everything*.

I told her about Joshua and how I felt about him. I told her about the friends I'd made since my death, including the one I'd lost. I told her about all the things that the demons had done to me, and all that they promised to do. And then I told her about the light and how my father waited for me there; about Melissa's offer to join him straightaway, before the demons had a chance to destroy my soul forever.

Finally, I described my plan—a plan that I hadn't fully shared with anyone until now. When I got to the part that she might play in it, I hesitated, just for a moment. Then I spilled my idea in one breath, running each sentence into the other so that the concept wouldn't sound quite so crazy, or offensive.

Even as I spoke, I questioned whether or not this was the right move. After all, I'd thought about this aspect of my plan since Ruth died, and I still hated it with every cell in my body. Yet I also knew it was the only way I could convince the demons to do what I needed them to. I'd run through the list of candidates for this particular job so many times in my head. Jillian, Scott, Felix, Annabel—I had tried and rejected each one. As much as I fought it, I knew that no one worked quite as well as my mother.

Actually, there *was* another person who the demons would take just as seriously, but I couldn't do it. I'd meant every word I said to him the previous night: that I wanted him to live a full life, full of love and happiness and joy. That wasn't to say that I didn't want the same things for my mother. But then again . . . she was my *mother*; in the end, she was the only person in this world or the next that I could ask to do such a horrible, terrible thing for me.

To her credit, she didn't interrupt me while I talked. She just let me run through my plan—and her place in it—until I had nothing left to say. Then she let me catch my breath from all that hurried, desperate talking.

After a long wait, during which I suspected that she would throw me off her porch, my mother nodded firmly and said, "I'll do it."

I'd already been frowning—so hard my head ached, actually—but my expression only deepened. I *should* have been relieved. Instead, I suddenly didn't think I could go through with my plan anymore.

"Are you sure, Mom? Because this might not work. In fact, I seriously doubt this works."

She snorted lightly and then flashed me a smile, one that looked braver than she probably felt inside. "Lord, Amelia, you're still a pessimist, aren't you?"

One corner of my mouth lifted into an involuntary half grin. "I prefer 'realist,' actually."

"That's what all the pessimists say."

I barked out a laugh, but it sounded small and weak as it echoed off the porch columns. Neither of us said anything else for a while—we just stared out at the trees, listening to their leaves as they sang in the late-morning breeze.

Finally, I broke the silence.

"Mom, you have to understand: there's a pretty good chance that you could end up in . . . in . . ."

"Hell," she finished quietly. "Or worse."

I didn't answer; I couldn't.

"The thing is, Amelia," my mother went on, "I do understand. And I don't care."

I began to shake my head violently. "You can't say that, Mom—you don't know what it's like down there. I've only seen the entrance to it, and that place is bad enough. Plus, Dad won't be there—"

"But *you* will," she interrupted, her voice suddenly fervent. She leaned forward in her chair, so close to me now that I could've touched her, if I'd had the ability.

"Wherever I go," she said, "you'll be there with me."

"No," I whispered. "I mean, I will be, but you won't know that. They'd probably make you a wraith, and as far as I know, the wraiths are mindless shells—just the demons' puppets."

She smiled, this time sadly. "The risk will be worth it."

My mother leaned back and gestured to her peeling, crumbling house. "This isn't any kind of life, Amelia: sitting alone in my pathetic little house, missing my family and waiting to die. If I can do something to help my daughter—if I have a chance to protect her, like I couldn't do so many years ago—then the reward is definitely worth the risk."

"But, Mom—"

"No 'but,' Amelia," she interrupted again, sounding an awful lot like the woman who'd berated me into surviving years of math homework. "I've already made up my mind. Best-case scenario: I'll be dancing with your father by Sunday morning. Worst-case scenario: I spend eternity in the same place that you do. Either way . . . I win."

I brushed furiously at the tears that had abruptly returned to the corners of my eyes. What could I say to that? *Thank you* didn't seem like enough, so I merely sobbed, "I love you, Mom. I'm sorry for all the times we fought when I was, you know, alive."

She laughed softly, looking away from me and staring thoughtfully at the trees. "Honey, I lost those memories a long time ago. Now, all I see is your dad's smile when we danced; all I hear is your laughter. *Those* are things I held on to."

Somehow, her words only made me cry harder. But this time, my mother didn't cry. She didn't look at me, either. She just kept her gaze trained on the tree line and gave a decisive nod.

"I love you, too, Amelia. And I'll see you tonight."

Knowing that was my dismissal, I pressed myself up from my chair, climbed down from the porch, and hurriedly made my way across her lawn. Just before I crossed onto the road in front of her house, though, I thought I heard her call out to me one last time.

I swallowed hard but didn't turn around—just kept walking steadily until, if I *did* turn around, I wouldn't be able to see the house. Mostly because I just couldn't bring myself to take that long, last look at the woman I loved most in the world, sitting near the place where she'd raised me.

Chapter
TWENTY-SEVEN

I dreaded my next errand almost more than my first, probably because of *where* I had to conduct it. I probably could have tried to do this someplace different—a field of daisies perhaps, just for some symmetry. But in the end, I didn't know of any location more supernaturally charged than here, on the riverbank beneath High Bridge.

I paced the bank uncomfortably, avoiding any eye contact with the structure behind me. I'd seen it enough times to know that it still looked menacing in the daylight; and I'd seen it enough times in the past two weeks to know that I'd get my fill of it that night. Instead of looking back, I stared at the mud below me, watching as it squished around the ruined edges of my ballet flats.

"Are you there?" I called softly, with my eyes still trained on the ground. "You said to call if I needed you. And I really need you right now."

Nothing answered but a few springtime crickets and the rushing water of the river. I supposed I wasn't all that surprised by the lack of response; her instructions for calling *had* been pretty specific. So I stopped pacing, closed my eyes, and raised my head.

"Melissa!" I shouted into the air. "Melissa, I need to speak to you. Please."

At first, nothing else happened. Then I heard a soft, whooshing breeze, which brought with it a pleasantly floral scent.

It smelled like heaven.

I opened my eyes, relieved. But I was surprised to find that I was still standing on the riverbank, and it was still empty. No prairie, no Melissa—just that soft, sweet-smelling breeze.

"What's going on?" I whispered, a little afraid of the answer. Was this the light, responding to my call? Or was this the dark, screwing with my mind—breaking down my willpower, before they broke me completely that night?

As if in reply, the breeze blew stronger around me, filling the air with that lovely scent. It was gorgeous, intoxicating, but it was also maddening. Especially when unaccompanied by an explanation.

I straightened my spine, cast a single glance back at High Bridge to make sure nothing waited there to surprise me, and then turned back toward the riverbank.

"Answer me," I demanded. "I called you. Now answer."

Amelia.

The breeze called my name, soft but distinct. After another heartbeat, a faint, translucent form took shape in front of me. Although she was colorless and sheer, I could tell that the form was Melissa.

"Nice of you to come," I said drily.

It's not easy, Melissa replied in that breeze-like whisper, *to appear to you on this plain. I prefer the meadow.*

I couldn't help but snort. "Sorry I didn't have time to pass out so I could talk to you."

When Melissa remained silent, I took that as my cue to speak again.

"So I called you," I began awkwardly, "to give you an answer. Sort of."

Melissa stirred. *You've decided to join us, after all?*

"Yes. And no. Not exactly."

Even though she was sheer, I could still see the outline of Melissa's frown. *I don't understand*, she said, obviously prompting me to clarify.

Here was my chance, then. Everyone's fate hinged on what I asked right now, and what Melissa answered. I stood taller—as tall as I possibly could—and stared directly into what I assumed were her eyes.

"I want to repeat what I asked you the other night: I want you to let me try to save the living people I love, before I join you. And I want you to allow everyone that I save in the netherworld, and even in hell, to join me in heaven too."

Melissa began to whisper a protest, but I cut her off. "Please, just listen to my full request before you deny it. Please?"

Melissa paused and, after another moment's hesitation, nodded. So, like I had done for my mother earlier that morning, I told Melissa about each part of my plan. I described my first line of defense, which included the young Seers and their newly acquired glows, as well as my second, darker plot, which included my mother, Felix's gun, and as much Transfer Powder as I could steal from Annabel's jar before that night's attack. And also like I had done that morning, I admitted each thing that could—and probably would—go wrong.

Melissa listened just as patiently as my mother had,

nodding occasionally without interrupting me. But unlike my mother, Melissa refused to give me a straight answer once I'd finished.

An interesting plan, Melissa whispered. *I look forward to seeing how it plays out.*

"'How it plays out'? What is *that* supposed to mean?"

Melissa didn't really react to my shrill tone. Instead, she shrugged and then whispered, *It means that we'll be watching to see what you can accomplish tonight. Particularly with regard to this bridge and the hell gate.*

"You're . . . you're going to 'watch'?" I gasped. "Without telling me whether or not you'll take the people I try to save? Including myself?"

Melissa tilted her head to the side but said nothing. I saw her gesture for what it was, though. This was her wordless way of telling me that the light intended to adopt the "wait and see" approach to my loved ones. To *me*.

I sputtered, at a loss for what to say next. But I wasn't stunned or even cowed by Melissa's lack of an answer—I was *furious*. I felt so angry, so indignant, that I thought I would ignite right there on the riverbank. I was fairly certain that if I opened my mouth to speak, I might literally choke on my words.

But as quickly as my anger built, it disappeared, as though something had simply drained it out of me.

Where I'd previously felt fire, I now felt only a cold sense of numbness.

Of resignation.

I dropped my gaze from Melissa, back to the riverbank below me, and nodded. "All right," I said softly. "You'll watch."

My desolation must have finally affected Melissa, because the breeze suddenly sounded like a sympathetic sigh. I thought, for a desperate second, that she might actually answer me—at least give me the courtesy of a no. But when the breeze sighed again, it sounded different, like the kind of noise someone makes when they know that the person they are looking at is dying.

I glanced up and saw that Melissa had vanished. Left me with nothing but an empty riverbank and a fading breeze that sounded an awful lot like, *Good luck*.

Of course, that might have just been a trick of the wind.

Chapter
TWENTY-EIGHT

I made it back to the Mayhews' gazebo just in time to smell something delicious wafting out the open windows of the kitchen. Despite everything I'd been through that morning, the thought of lunch still set my mouth to watering.

My knock on the back door was quickly answered by Jeremiah, who looked a little cheerier than he had that morning. "Amelia, hi," he greeted me, holding open the door for me. "Are you joining us for lunch, too?"

"I didn't mean to intrude, Mr. Mayhew. I just . . . um . . .

forgot that I left my shoes up in Jillian's room. My mom will string me up if I don't get her nice black heels back to her." I blushed furiously as I followed him inside, feeling more than a little guilty about the lie.

Jeremiah didn't seem to notice the deception. He nodded distractedly, moving through the back hallway toward the kitchen.

"Understood," he said. "Rebecca wants to string Jillian up on a daily basis. But just so you know, you really are welcome to join us for lunch; I'm already feeding half the family anyway."

He wasn't wrong: inside the kitchen, Joshua and Jillian were once again sitting at the table, digging into a huge, intoxicating-looking bowl of their father's crawfish étoufée. As were Annabel, Hayley, Drew, and Felix; apparently, they'd finished with their keg-fetching errand and were now starving. I didn't see Rebecca any-where—she'd probably already gone to her warehouse, to organize flowers for prom.

"I think I will join them," I told Jeremiah, eyeing the étoufée lustfully. He gave me a distracted wave as he turned his attention to a stack of papers on what I'd come to think of as the business end of the kitchen island.

"No problem." Then he looked briefly up at me. "Are you going with them tonight? To prom?"

I tried very hard not to look surprised. This was our

cover story, then: that the young Mayhews and their dates would attend prom, instead of a diabolical dogfight. In a way, it was perfect. Jeremiah and Rebecca would be too distracted by the endless corsage orders to demand group photos from us before "prom." They also wouldn't be too surprised when their kids stayed out late tonight. I just hoped that the young Seers had thought to tell their older family members that we'd be putting on our formal wear in some other location; otherwise, someone might get suspicious that we were going to prom in jeans and hoodies.

"Of course," I finally replied, flashing Jeremiah my most convincing smile. "Wouldn't miss it for the world."

Then, head down, I hurried to the table. All the seats were taken, but Felix—still trying to make up for the other night, I think—gave me his so that I now faced Joshua. He smiled warmly at me, but the expression was just a shade too brittle, as though Joshua had already started counting the minutes that we had left together. Which, like me, I'm sure he had.

Unaware of our little drama, Felix shifted to one side, waiting until Jeremiah seemed otherwise occupied to lean close to the table.

"Maybe we should all spend the rest of the afternoon preparing?" he whispered. "For prom and the . . . bonfire afterward? And maybe we could do that near 'our' fire pit?"

Judging by everyone else's nods, they also knew what Felix meant—that we should go discuss tonight's game plan. Then, after recruiting at prom this evening, we should go back to Robber's Cave and start doing our Transfer Powder spells. I didn't *disagree*, but I wasn't necessarily ready to leave the Mayhews' house. Not when I only had maybe an hour or two left to spend with Joshua, alone.

"Why don't you guys go on ahead?" I suggested. "Joshua and I will be . . . at the cabins soon."

Annabel shot me a mildly insulting look. "Um . . . Amelia?" she prompted, in a condescending tone. "You're sort of a . . . crucial part of this whole 'prom and bonfire' experience."

To my credit, I didn't scowl or even smirk at her. I just shook my head and smiled lightly.

"I know that, Annabel," I said patiently. "But I need a few minutes to myself. I'm sure you understand."

Again, Annabel's glare told me that she didn't understand, or particularly care. That was just too bad, I supposed; I didn't have enough time left in this day to waste it arguing with her.

"Go on ahead," I repeated, and then made a shooing gesture at the rest of them. "You guys go start prepping. Joshua and I will hang out here for a while to help Jeremiah clean up, and then we'll catch up."

Looping Jeremiah into this conversation proved a smart move. As soon as he heard his name mentioned, Jeremiah agreed that this plan worked perfectly for him, since his mind was clearly on other things than cleaning his kitchen. Now that Annabel would look childish if she continued to argue, she had no choice but to round up her little coven and go.

Which was exactly what she did, albeit with no small amount of muttered grumbling. Eventually, though, the only people left in the kitchen were me, Joshua, and his dad. Joshua opened his mouth—probably about to ask that we be excused—but he shut it when he caught me eyeing the bowl of étoufée in between us.

"Here you go," he said, ladling a few spoonfuls onto one of the clean plates stacked near the center of the table. "You look like you might need this first."

I took the food from him eagerly, and began to dig into it. After a few bites, however, I couldn't help but pause to glance up and share a wistful smile with him. Joshua and I had played this scene before, in the attic bedroom of Annabel's home in New Orleans. That had been my first real meal, and chances were good that this would be my last. Somehow, I didn't think I'd be able to choke down a sandwich tonight when my face-off with the demons was a mere hour away. As far as last meals went, though, this one was spectacular—every bit as delicious as I remembered it.

And for some reason, that reality suddenly washed over me. Before I knew what was happening, I was sobbing silently above my étoufée. Joshua's eyes widened with alarm and, after checking to make sure that his father hadn't seen, he pulled the plate away from me.

"Dad," he said, "do you mind if Amelia and I go upstairs for a while? We'll leave the door open."

Still looking at his stack of papers, Jeremiah shrugged. "Fine by me."

Yet another reason to love dads, I supposed. I breathed a sigh of relief, letting Joshua help me from my chair so that we could walk hand in hand up to his room. Before we crossed through the kitchen archway, however, I threw a final glance over my shoulder at Jeremiah.

Compared to how he'd looked during the last few days, he seemed calmer. Lighter. And I was glad for that: he deserved happiness and safety, just as much as his children did. Watching him now, I realized that although I didn't know him all that well, I cared about him, too, as well as his wife; I wanted to make sure that Jeremiah and Rebecca were safe too.

Which, of course, meant that I would never see them again. Not after tonight.

Hanging my head, I followed Joshua up the stairs. Once we reached his room, he pushed the door almost shut behind us and then drew me into his arms.

"You okay?" he whispered into my hair, after a long silence. I nodded, sniffing a little.

"Yeah, just really weepy today. For obvious reasons, I guess." I paused, and then added, "I . . . I visited my mom this morning."

Once again, Joshua demonstrated why I loved him. Instead of berating me, or feeling hurt that I'd visited her without him, he leaned back and smiled happily at me.

"I'm proud of you for doing that, Amelia. I really am. So . . . how did it go?"

I hesitated again, and then replied, "She's coming to help. Tonight."

Now I'd *really* surprised him. He leaned farther back until he held me at arm's length. He couldn't think I was joking, but he still studied my face, looking for some clue about why I'd invited her.

"I need her, Joshua," I told him quietly. "I need her there . . . for support."

He didn't look like he believed me, probably because I didn't sound very believable. But I'd already decided not to give him all the details. So although I didn't lie, I didn't tell the full truth, either.

Long ago, Joshua and I had agreed that we would fight the demons together—that I would tell him everything that I could. This part of the plan, however . . . I just couldn't share with him. Not only would he fail to support it, but he might also *volunteer* for it. And I couldn't survive everything to come if he did that.

"Okay," Joshua finally said. "If that's what you need."

After a second's more scrutiny, he pulled me to him again. I tilted my head back, gratefully accepting his kiss—partly because it meant that he'd accepted what little I said about the matter, and partly because I just wanted to kiss him.

Although it began sweetly, the kiss soon shifted into something stronger as it continued. The more passionately Joshua kissed me, the harder my pulse raced and the more my breathing sped. And suddenly—possibly even more than the night before—I wanted to experience that fire. That connection. I wanted him, both literally and figuratively, so that I could keep this moment as a memory—lock it inside my heart, to take with me wherever I went that night.

I thought Joshua would eventually close that door and carry me to the bed. But instead he abruptly ended the kiss.

"We can run," he said fervently, bringing our clasped hands between us and clenching tightly. "Amelia, let's just run. We'll call my family, and tell them to stay away from the bridge, and then we'll run away—to California, or Wyoming, or . . . hell, we'll just pick a state with as few rivers as possible and settle there."

Instead of arguing with him—countering his appeals with all the reasons that they were wrong—I shook my head and smiled sadly.

"We can't, Joshua. I can't."

Almost as soon as I said it, his face fell. He nodded dejectedly, released my hands, and dropped into a seated position on the edge of his bed. I stared at him, feeling just as lost and unsure as he looked. Then I dropped as well, falling to my knees in front of him. I lifted both his hands, turned them over, and placed a kiss in each of his palms.

"If it makes you feel any better," I whispered, "I don't want to do this either. But I *have* to. I have to end the fight that started on the night of my eighteenth birthday. If you ask me, this battle has been a long time coming. And the only thing that will keep me going—the only thing that's ever kept me going—is the fact that I love you. That I *will* love you, for as long as I still exist and even after that, if I can."

What more could Joshua say? Like I'd just done, he drew my hands to his lips and kissed both of them. Then he bent forward and pressed his lips to mine one more time.

Chapter
TWENTY-NINE

Despite my patchy memory, I knew I'd always wanted to attend prom while I was alive. But I also knew that I'd never expected to be standing in front of its entrance—half dead, half alive, and dressed in stolen clothes—waiting to go inside and ask a handful of normal teenagers to fight evil with me.

I supposed I should be thankful that I'd had the forethought to change out of this morning's dusty clothes and into my favorite pair of skinny jeans and the soft brown boots Gaby had picked out for me in New

Orleans. Not prom appropriate, but certainly comfortable. At Joshua's suggestion, I'd also thrown on a white cashmere top. Seeing the white threads now, I had to smile; I guessed Joshua would always have a soft spot for that color. Still smiling slightly, I turned to the Seers.

"How exactly are we going to do this? Get inside there, I mean?"

I gestured to the school gym, where crowds of fancily dressed students were now entering. The sun had already started to set, and we all looked too conspicuous milling around the Wilburton High School parking lot in our street clothes. Someone needed to make a decision about how we would accomplish our recruiting mission, and soon.

It didn't surprise me that Annabel had her own overly confident idea.

"We just do it," she said brashly. "Barge in and get as many people to follow us outside as we can."

"Including half the faculty?" I asked, shaking my head. "If we just go ahead and crash the prom like we're a freaking biker gang, we're going to draw way more attention than we want."

Annabel scowled at me, but I could tell that she also saw my point. We were still staring each other down when someone else interjected an idea.

"Why don't we just wait here, and Amelia and Joshua

go inside? They can pretend to attend the dance for a little while and then lure our friends outside to the keg."

Everyone turned to Jillian, who was leaning against Scott's car with her arms folded across her chest. Her suggestion was simple and therefore perfect. Why overwhelm our possible helpers with unfamiliar faces, when we could just give them Joshua? That way, we at least had a shot at recruiting the *girls* of Wilburton High.

Everyone else began to nod agreement. Yet Jillian herself didn't look pleased with her own idea—she frowned heavily, and her eyes occasionally darted to Scott with a clear look of yearning.

"Why don't four of us go?" I suggested with feigned indifference. "Jillian and Scott, me and Joshua? That way we can cover more ground once we're inside."

"Even better," Jillian said quickly, and a little too eagerly. When the rest of the group gave their assent, she flashed me a small, barely concealed smile. I just nodded in response; it was the least I could do, considering what I would ask of her in a few hours.

As Annabel and her crew took their positions between Joshua's truck and their nearby cars, I slipped my arm through Joshua's and then glanced up at him. He smiled down at me, but the expression was tinged with too much sadness for me to return it. So I tugged him onward, looking back every now and then to make sure

Jillian and Scott followed.

Although we made it across the parking lot without incident, we encountered our first problem at the entrance to prom. There, a vaguely familiar woman occupied the gym's ticket booth, allowing those students who had prepaid inside and charging a slightly higher admission to those who hadn't. When Joshua approached her with enough money for four tickets, the woman scowled down at him.

"Mr. Mayhew," she said disdainfully, "I see you've put as much effort into tonight's outfit as you normally put into your homework."

I recognized her then: it was Ms. Wolters, Joshua's surly Calculus teacher. I hadn't seen her in person since I helped him through a differential equation last fall, although I'd seen plenty of her brutal homework assignments.

Joshua was still mumbling an excuse about our clothing when I plucked the money from his hands. Releasing my arm from his, I strolled up to the ticket booth with a saccharine smile.

"Ms. Wolters, is it? Joshua has told me so much about you—particularly about your class, in which he now holds the highest grade."

The old woman eyed me suspiciously. "So far. But graduation is still a month off."

"Well, with your excellent teaching skills, I don't doubt that he'll maintain that grade." Then I leaned forward and lowered my voice so that only she could hear it. "And if he doesn't . . . well, maybe the school board needs to know about that bottle of booze in your desk drawer?"

I had no idea whether or not Ms. Wolters drank on the job—it was just a blind guess. And a lucky one, judging by the stricken look in her eyes. Still wearing a sickly sweet smile, I slid Joshua's money across the counter toward her.

"Four tickets to the prom, please," I said loudly.

Ms. Wolters's hands shook slightly as she took the cash, but I didn't feel the least bit sorry for her. I flashed her one more sugary smile—as a warning—and then rejoined my companions to move toward the prom entrance.

When we were out of earshot, Joshua whispered, "What did you say to her to make her shut up so fast?"

I laughed softly and took his hand in mine. "I just told her that if she needed help counting the bills, you could do it. Since you're so good at math and all."

Joshua laughed like he didn't believe me, but he didn't press the issue. Instead, he pulled me closer and guided me through the double doors into his high school gym.

Although it had started getting darker outside, it still

took my eyes a moment to adjust to the dimmer interior of the building. Once they did, I let out a small gasp of awe.

On some level, I knew that Joshua and I now stood in the Wilburton High gym, staring at a spectacle made mostly out of Mylar and strings of old Christmas bulbs. But if I squinted just right, this place was pure magic— a fairyland of shimmering dresses, twinkling lights, glitter-strewn tabletops, and oversized arrangements of white carnations.

"Wow," I breathed as Joshua and I wove our way through the already-crowded tables near the dance floor, with Jillian and Scott following closely behind. "Is the prom always this pretty?"

"I don't know," he called out above the thumping music. "I've never seen one before."

I glanced quickly at him, surprised. "Really? You didn't go to prom your junior year?"

"Really."

"Why not?"

"Because you and I didn't meet until *this* fall."

I laughed, rolling my eyes and pretending like he didn't just make me go a little gooey-happy inside. Not that it was too hard a task for Joshua to accomplish.

Even knowing what lay in store, I couldn't help but notice how deep the midnight blue of his eyes looked under the sparkling lights that hung in swoops above the gym floor.

With a sigh, I moved closer to him as he led our group toward a long, banquet-style table near the back of the gym, where Kaylen, O'Reilly, and their respective entourages had set up camp. We were still a few feet away but I could see two of the girls I'd met at Kaylen's party, flanking boys who already looked a little drunk. Chelsea, under her layers of pink tulle and sequins, kept leaning forward to share annoyed glances with Mya, who looked lovely in an understated blue silk sheath dress.

Their glances shifted from annoyed to surprised when they caught sight of us approaching the table. I could almost feel their amused appraisal of my top, my jeans, my boots: nothing I wore tonight was prom appropriate, and we all knew it.

Luckily, Joshua's guy friends couldn't have cared less what he wore to prom; they were obviously pleased that he'd actually decided to come. O'Reilly waved to us first, booming loudly across the table.

"Mayhew, dude! And Scott, *and* Jilly-bean! Why don't y'all grab some seats with us?"

Joshua and I exchanged a look, and I shrugged. What could it hurt if we stayed, just for a few minutes?

As if he'd read my thoughts, Joshua pulled out a free chair across from Kaylen and O'Reilly, who apparently had come to prom together. *Good for O'Reilly*, I thought, settling into my seat as Joshua took the one next to me. From the corner of my eye, I saw Jillian rush over to chat with Chelsea and Mya; noticing how happy Jillian looked just to be here, I smiled a little.

While Joshua chatted with his friends, he reached over casually and wrapped his arm around my waist so that he could drag my chair—and me—closer to him. He left his hand at my waist, so I reached for it, entwining my fingers with his. I laid my head on his shoulder, absently listening to his conversation and gazing around the sparkling gym.

After a few minutes, I sighed and lifted my head to stare down the table. Everyone that we could possibly approach for tonight's mission was here, seated at this table. I couldn't ask for a better moment to start recruiting. I knew that we didn't have much time left to do so, either.

Still, I hesitated, not quite ready to end this part of the night yet. And I couldn't even muster up the will to feel guilty about it. I waited for a lull in Joshua's conversation, and then caught his attention.

"It really *is* beautiful in here, isn't it?" I asked him, tilting my head to indicate our surroundings. For a moment, he didn't respond—just stared at me with the same sad smile that he'd worn earlier. Finally, he turned his lips to my ear and whispered, "Yes, it is."

I knew what he meant by that comment—knew *who* he meant. And I suddenly couldn't help myself: I lifted my head from Joshua's shoulder, threw my arms around his neck, and pressed my lips to his. When he kissed me back, a chorus of hoots and cheers from the table interrupted us. I pulled away first, smiling and blushing with equal ferocity.

"Mayhew, dude," O'Reilly called out appreciatively from across the table. "The night is young—save some for the after-party."

I turned my grin on O'Reilly and then, catching sight of his outfit, I burst into laughter. He wore a baby-blue tuxedo with a formal cummerbund stretched tightly over his thick frame.

"I love it, O'Reilly," I said, pointing to his ruffled dress shirt. "It's too bad you shaved off your beard—you would've looked exactly like Barry Gibb."

Immediately, I recognized my mistake. Although O'Reilly had heard of me by now, he and I had never formally met. And judging by his politely confused grin, he didn't feel as familiar with me as I did with him.

"You're . . . Amelia, right?" he asked haltingly. "Mayhew's new girl?"

I tried to keep my voice pleasantly vague as I chirped, "That's right—nice to meet you."

But despite my less intimate tone, O'Reilly's grin remained unsure. "How did you know about my beard, Amelia?"

I blinked back for a second, searching for a plausible explanation. Then I smiled widely. "Who *didn't* know about your beard, O'Reilly? Rumor has it, you had a colony of pygmies living in there."

He boomed a good-natured laugh. "Actually, I think it was just a couple of birds."

"Sexy," Joshua interjected. "And sanitary."

He slipped his hand beneath the table to clutch mine, probably to keep me from tapping my nails nervously on the tabletop. Thankfully, a little more banter with O'Reilly convinced me that I'd averted disaster. He no longer seemed bothered by my earlier slipup.

"Are y'all going to the after-party at Mya's house?" O'Reilly asked me, shouting over the pounding bass line of a new song.

Joshua flashed O'Reilly a bland, if somewhat tense, smile. "No, man. Not really our scene."

Then Joshua looked back at me, silently asking whether it was time to present our bait. I wavered, knowing what I *should* say. Yet somehow, I still couldn't. I began to squirm uncomfortably in my chair, so Joshua placed a steadying hand on the small of my back.

"You all right?" he asked.

"Yeah . . . just, you know, dancing," I offered lamely.

One corner of his mouth quirked upward. "In your chair?"

"Don't knock it. Chair dancing is a valid form of artistic expression in many cultures."

"Such as?"

"Um . . . ours?"

Joshua laughed loudly. Then he jerked his head toward the dance floor. "How about trying those moves on your feet instead?"

I bit my lower lip and peeked over his shoulder at the dance floor. "You think we have time?"

He gave me that sad smile again. "No," he replied softly.

But then, despite his answer, he suddenly pulled me up from my chair and tugged me toward the dance floor, where a shifting, noisy group of his classmates was jumping around like lunatics. When we reached them, Joshua spun me out into the middle of the dance floor.

At first I hesitated, uncertain about whether this was the wisest thing to do. But it didn't take long for me to think, *Why not? And why not* now*?*

The current song was fast and wild, a frenetic mix of synth and drums. I didn't recognize it, but that didn't matter: the song pounded too insistently for me to ignore. The sound of it thrummed through my body, matching the race of my pulse. I began to dance to its beat, letting myself forget about everything that had haunted me since the day I died. Dark, light, love, hate—I let them go. And for a few, ecstatic moments, I was purely happy. Completely free.

Joshua must have sensed the change in me, because he moved in to dance with me. In the brief glimpses I caught of his face, I could see that we both needed this moment of abandon—we needed it desperately.

Of course, those kinds of moments don't last forever. Soon the music shifted into a slower, sweeter song. The new song was pretty enough, but I still felt a twinge of melancholy—of loss, even. I wanted to be free, for just a minute or two longer.

When Joshua drew me closer to him, however, I knew that the moment of freedom hadn't really ended. It had just changed into something softer and more intimate. I slipped one hand around the nape of his neck and then tilted my head back so that I could look into his eyes.

"Thank you," I said, still needing to talk loudly over the music so that he could hear me.

"For what?"

"Bringing me inside tonight."

"I don't think I had much of a choice: Jillian and you kind of demanded it." Despite the teasing words, Joshua's smile was tender.

"Well, thank you for dancing with me, then."

"Always," he replied, so quietly that I read the word on his lips, rather than heard it. And with that one word, my mood darkened. We didn't have "always" to dance together. We had *right now*; I knew that, as well as I knew any other certainty in my bleak future.

But I had to shut those thoughts out, before they ruined what little time I had left. So I laid my head on Joshua's chest and clenched my eyes tightly shut. Although I'd never heard this song before, I hummed along until its melody had anesthetized me enough to meet Joshua's eyes.

When I lifted my head again, however, Joshua was ready. He swooped in before I had a chance to speak and planted a firm kiss on my mouth. I made a small noise of surprise, but then melted into him gratefully.

He knew. He *always* knew.

We stayed like that for a very long time, kissing and dancing slowly no matter what the tempo of the current song. Occasionally, I would catch a glimpse of Kaylen and O'Reilly dancing beside us, or Jillian and Scott holding each other tight. But I couldn't seem to focus on anything except this moment. This kiss. This boy.

Finally, during one of the slow dances, Joshua broke away from my lips to whisper, "Do you realize that we're almost the only people out here right now?"

He was right: the dance floor was starting to clear out as people returned to their seats for the dinner portion of the evening. Back at our table, Jillian and Scott were already waiting, glancing impatiently between us, the tableful of potential recruits, and the doors.

"Crap, Joshua, we've got to go," I cried, taking his hand from my waist and using it to drag him off the dance floor.

Joshua and I were both breathless with urgency when we reached the table. Seeing me collide with my former chair while practically panting, Kaylen smirked.

"Have a good time out there?" she asked, flicking her gaze from me to Joshua. Clearly, I wasn't forgiven for the slumber-party incident. I was about to respond with something extra snarky, but I just didn't have another moment to spare.

"We had a *great* time," I gushed, glancing back at Joshua, who stood a foot behind me with his hand on my hip. Although I truly meant what I'd said, Joshua also knew that that was his cue.

"Such a great time," he added, dropping his voice to a conspiratorial murmur, "that we've decided to share something with all of you guys. I was just going to save it for us, but . . . you all remember that I used to make the beer runs for our parties, right?"

Kaylen looked intrigued, as did everyone who'd heard

him. A few of them even leaned forward over the con-fetti-strewn tablecloth.

"And?" Chelsea prompted as she smoothed down a stray tuft of her princess skirt in annoyance. "You don't just say 'beer' on prom night, and then leave us hanging."

"And . . . I may or may not have come through tonight. Just like the old times."

"Dude!" O'Reilly cheered, already sold on whatever plan we were going to propose. "That's badass."

"Totally," Scott chimed in, right on schedule.

"What about my dinner?" Mya groaned, leaning around one side of Chelsea's enormous skirt.

"You can just move the keg into O'Reilly's truck," Joshua offered. "And then come back in to finish dinner."

When Mya made a petulant noise, Kaylen immediately silenced her.

"Oh, shut it, Mya. All you could come up with for tonight's party was half a bottle of your mom's old peach schnapps. That's hardly going to cut it for all of us."

I released a silent cheer. When we'd been planning this recruitment, Jillian had told the Seers that Kaylen was our linchpin; wherever she went, the mob followed. Clearly, Jillian knew her audience: the other girls quickly agreed with Kaylen, nodding their assent when each of their dates moved to join Joshua and Scott on the keg-moving expedition.

I hung back as Joshua's friends filtered out of the gym in small clusters so that they wouldn't arouse the faculty chaperones' suspicions. While I waited, I allowed myself precisely one minute of utter fear and apprehension. Then I followed the last small group out of the prom, praying that I wouldn't screw this up.

Chapter
THIRTY

Thank God Joshua had parked his truck in a secluded corner of the school lot, where an overgrown blackjack oak tree threw the truck and the surrounding cars into shadows. Otherwise, every faculty member on parking-lot patrol would notice the crowd of teenagers gathered suspiciously in one place.

As planned, I waited on the ground level, watching a few of the boys struggle to position the keg so that they could roll it off the back of the truck. I said a silent prayer of thanks that the Wilburton High students were so excited—and so blinded by the darkness of the night—that they didn't notice the addition of a few unfamiliar prom goers to their ranks. Annabel, Drew, Hayley, and Felix had joined the crowd quietly, and they now stared up at the truck as though they'd been there all along.

"It's so damn dark, I can't see what we're doing up here," one of the boys in the truck bed muttered—possibly Scott, following his preset cues. When a few people murmured in agreement, I cleared my throat.

"I'll help."

Even in the dark, I could feel the derision rolling off of the spectators on the ground as well as the non-Seer boys in the truck bed. But instead of contradicting me, Joshua moved to the edge of the tailgate and took my hand. Jillian and Hayley flanked my sides and, with a few tugs and pushes, I climbed into the bed of the truck.

"Thanks, Amelia," O'Reilly said as I steadied myself. "But I think everything's all—"

"Good?" I finished for him. "Well, let me make it better."

Then, before anyone else could protest, I linked hands with Joshua, closed my eyes, and pictured the worst possible thing I could think of: a swarm of shrieking, birdlike demons, diving toward Joshua with murder in their cold black eyes.

Apparently he'd thought of something similar, because

I heard the soft whoosh that often preceded my glow, coming from his direction. I opened my eyes to find that we'd both ignited—our fires connected and lapped at each other through our clasped hands. As I'd hoped, he could still glow, days after taking the Transfer Powder.

I'd expected gasps from the crowd, or maybe even some screams. But no one around us made a single noise. I guessed that the first sight of spontaneous combustion just had that effect on people.

"We're okay," I whispered to them, taking advantage of their silence and keeping my voice low. "Joshua and I are okay, even though it doesn't look like it. But you all need to listen to me right now."

Since Joshua and I could maintain our respective glows by ourselves, I let go of his hand and positioned myself so that everyone could see me more fully.

"Watch again," I whispered to the crowd. Then I allowed the current of invisibility to run over my skin. I'd never done that while glowing, and the sensation reminded me of Joshua's and my old electricity—warm and tingling, but not unpleasant.

This time, my actions shocked the audience. A few of them cried out, and someone whimpered—perhaps Chelsea. O'Reilly dropped so many f-bombs that I couldn't even keep count. The reaction only got worse when I made myself reappear.

O'Reilly let out another expletive, and I had to give him credit for it: this one was a creative, almost Germanic combination of several curse words into one giant superswear.

Realizing that we'd terrified them into listening, I willed my glow to extinguish itself, and Joshua did the same. He stepped back, symbolically giving me the floor.

"I'm not the bad guy," I said, loud enough so that everyone could hear me. "There are far worse things than me that go bump in the night. And I'm sorry that you all have to see this—to learn all of this. But everyone here is in danger. Some of you more than others. If we don't do something about it—if you all don't help us do something—then the creatures that are chasing us will go after you, too. And you *really* don't want that to happen."

"What . . . what *are* you two?" someone breathed. Kaylen, I thought. I looked down, searching for her in the darkened crowd. But Joshua answered her before I got the chance.

"I'm exactly who you think I am," he said. "I'm the same guy you've known since kindergarten. I'm just a little more . . . enhanced, lately. But Amelia . . . Amelia is . . ."

"I'm dead," I concluded, when he trailed off. "A ghost, to be specific. Because of that fact, I have the ability to glow like that, and the ability to go invisible. I gave some of those powers to Joshua, so that he could help me fight the things that are coming after all of us."

"Nothing's coming after us," O'Reilly scoffed, suddenly capable of saying more than a handful of vulgar words. "Y'all are crazy, and we're all just hallucinating."

I turned back to him again and shook my head. "I wish that were true, O'Reilly. But I think you know, deep in your heart, that it isn't."

"Don't you *wonder*?" another voice added softly, from one corner of the truck bed. "Don't you all wonder why so many people die at High Bridge? Why some of your family members, even, have died there?"

Scott's tone was so sincere, so heartfelt, that it struck me how much all these goings-on must have affected him, too. His gran's superstitions notwithstanding, Scott had been just like these people only a few weeks ago. He'd been a laid-back, baseball-playing, college-bound guy, and now he was dating a possible target of hell. And that meant he might also become a target.

I smiled sadly at him—at all of them. But I shivered at what he said next.

"Some of us have talked about this," Scott went on, more quietly than before. "About the night we can't really remember, when Jillian fell off the bridge. Some of you pretend like it doesn't bother you—like you don't have dreams about shadows that try to kill you—but I know the truth: we didn't imagine them; we didn't hallucinate them. So don't you want to find out what really happened? Don't you want to stop whatever it was that *did* that to you?"

I tried to keep my mouth from falling open and then took a good look into that crowd, which contained so many of the people who'd been there the night that Eli had tried to claim Jillian's soul. Some people didn't register what Scott had just said. But some of them did, staring up at me with frightened, guilty eyes. I knew I had to strike then, before they allowed themselves to forget again.

"Whether or not you remember," I said, "whether or not you believe us, that doesn't make what we're saying any less true. High Bridge is an epicenter of evil in this town. There are demonic forces that live beneath it—forces that sometimes lure, and sometimes outright drag, people to their deaths. The demons have been after me all year. Soon, they'll come after you."

"Why us?" Kaylen asked in a small voice.

"Because the demons know that I care about you—that Joshua cares about you, and that Jillian does, too. That's just how the demons operate. As far as we can tell, it's an ancient cycle . . . and we intend to stop it."

As I finished, Jillian stepped forward and faced her friends squarely. She did so with more conviction than

I'd ever seen her show in front of them and, in that moment, I was pretty proud of her.

"So here's how it's going to go down," she announced, placing her hands on the hips of her cocktail dress. "You guys are going to take this keg, move it into another truck, and go back inside to prom. Some of you will try to forget about what you've seen here tonight and probably use what's inside the keg to do so; I'm guessing that those people will be the ones who stop talking to us in the halls at school. But some of you are going to think about what we've shown you. About what we've said. *Those* people will be the ones who show up tonight, after prom, to help us. Eleven p.m., near the southern entrance of High Bridge. So . . . think about which side you really want to be on."

After that, there wasn't anything else to say. The choice now lay in the hands of the non-Seers. This fact did not bring me much comfort, though, when I considered what happened next.

Acting as though they'd all heard some unspoken cue, the non-Seers began to move. Not to embrace us or attack us, but to leave. Without speaking, the boys in the truck bed went back to work on the keg, tipping it out of its ice-filled trash can so that they could roll it off the edge of the tailgate. I stepped aside for them, feeling defeated when none of them—not one—spared me a second glance.

The non-Seers climbed out of the truck and waited expectantly below the tailgate. After some hesitation, Joshua and Scott lowered the keg down to them. The other boys hefted it over to O'Reilly's truck, which he'd moved over here before my little performance. They loaded the keg quickly, letting it roll noisily to the back of the bed.

With that task completed, everyone seemed to scurry like rats back into the gym. They did so just as silently as before: no good-byes; no screw-yous; no comments of any kind.

Only O'Reilly and Kaylen remained, although she stood with her arms folded across her chest, staunchly refusing to look back at us. O'Reilly just rocked awkwardly on his heels. Like his friends, he didn't say anything for a few long minutes. Finally, with his hands shoved firmly in his pockets, he glanced up at Joshua.

"Sorry, dude," he murmured. Then he jerked his head at Kaylen and the two of them spun around, moving back toward the gym as fast as they could.

Chapter THIRTY-ONE

After my epic failure to get even one non-Seer to leave prom and join us in our fight, we had no choice but to move forward with our final preparations. Now standing near the fire pit at Robber's Cave Park, I couldn't fight the sensation that my clock was winding down, far too fast. It had to be almost ten thirty, and I still hadn't finished transferring my glow to all the young Seers; Felix and Jillian waited for their turns.

On the plus side, I didn't have a difficult time

summoning the glow—credit that to my growing anxiety, I supposed. On the downside, my mouth felt like the Sahara after I'd had to swallow gulp after gulp of Transfer Powder. By now, I did *not* think it had a pleasant aftertaste.

"Just two more times," Joshua murmured, handing me another bottle of water during a quick break. I took a huge gulp of the warm liquid, wishing that someone had thought to bring a cooler. Once finished, I wiped my mouth with the back of my hand.

"Okay, Jill—let's go."

Jillian reached down to the jar of powder at our feet and scooped out two handfuls for us. I held out my palm and, as soon as she'd poured my share of the powder into it, I closed my eyes and called forth my glow. It shined in the dark like a beacon; like a warning.

Soon Jillian had a glow of her own, so I signaled that the Seers should just keep chanting and send Felix forward; why extinguish my glow again, if I didn't have to?

Felix took everyone by surprise, however, when he shook his head. "No, I'm not going to do it. I don't want the glow."

I made a small noise of disbelief. "After everything you put Joshua and me through over this? Why not?"

"Because if I glow," he explained quietly, "then I can't get near her. If we can somehow get Gaby out of there,

I don't want to be able to hurt her—it just isn't worth it, to me."

Some of the other Seers began to object, bemoaning this loss in their already-thin ranks. But I kept silent and watched Felix. He met my gaze squarely, wordlessly asking me to understand. And I did.

I nodded emphatically, folded my arms across my chest, and concentrated until my glow vanished. When Annabel protested further, I held up one hand to silence her.

"Felix can do whatever he thinks will work—we all can."

"What is *that* supposed to mean?" she asked. She cast a glance at Joshua, who in turn frowned at me. He was already suspicious about what I might do tonight, I knew. But I just shrugged defensively, picked up the jar of Transfer Powder, and turned in a direction where the Seer circle had broken by a few feet. For those watching behind me, I made a show of screwing the lid back onto the jar, but not before I'd scooped out as much of the power as I could stuff into both pockets of my jeans. Then I strode over to a rock bench near the edge of the circle and tucked the jar back into Annabel's bag. That performance over, I turned to face the frowning, bemused Seers.

"What I mean, Annabel, is that we all have to be

flexible tonight. We have to keep in mind that we don't know what the glow will *do* to the wraiths, if they get close to it. Mine has scared them off before, but I've never actually touched one. So just be careful, okay? For yourselves, and for them. If you can, try to remember that they were people once, too."

Annabel scowled, but after a moment, she conceded reluctantly. "Okay. We'll be careful."

"So then: should we go?" I asked, changing the subject before the Seers decided to argue Felix's decision further. Without waiting for their answer, I walked over to Joshua and offered him my hand. Still frowning, he took it and let me lead him away from the Seer circle, toward his truck.

"What are you doing?" he whispered, when we were far enough away that his family couldn't hear us.

"Taking over this operation," I replied with a faint laugh. "From here on out, we're going to do things my way."

Joshua seemed troubled by that answer, but he didn't argue with it. He simply followed me to his truck and waited while I opened its passenger door. When he circled to the driver's side, however, I took advantage of the fact that he was out of sight and reached surreptitiously under my seat. I removed the purse that I'd stowed there before we left for the prom, took out the handgun, and tucked it between the small of my back and the waist of my jeans. Then, after quickly rearranging my cashmere top so that it hid the gun, I pulled myself into the truck, shut my door, and flashed Joshua my brightest, most innocent smile.

Although we had so little time left until midnight, the seven of us sat in our respective vehicles and waited by the river, and hoping that a crowd of non-Seers would actually show up to help us. But as the minutes ticked past eleven p.m. and no one else arrived—not even my mother—I knew we were alone in this battle.

Seven kids against the forces of hell. As Jillian had once said, I didn't like our odds.

That didn't mean we could spend all night cowering in our cars, either. With a battalion of helpers or a few scared Mayhews, I intended to end the demonic threats that night.

So I opened my door first, jerked my head quickly at Joshua, and then stepped out of the truck. Clearly trying to appear strong, Joshua followed my lead. As we joined each other in front of his truck, his hand shook as he took mine. That wasn't a show of weakness but of bravery, especially when he moved with me to climb down the dark embankment to the river. Joshua and I waited for the other Seers at the bottom of the hill, still holding hands and standing as close as possible to each other.

"Okay," I said, once they'd all joined us, "I think that all of you should stay down here while you open the netherworld. Jillian and I will go up to High Bridge, to act as bait."

Immediately, everyone but Jillian flashed me suspicious looks.

"Why would we stay down here," Annabel demanded, "if you guys are going to start the fight up there?"

"And why is Jillian going with you?" Joshua asked, frowning heavily. "Why not—"

"Wait," I interrupted, holding up my hand and angling my head slightly over my shoulder. "Does anyone else smell that?"

Joshua opened his mouth, probably to probe my motives further, but then he popped it shut and sniffed the air. "Campfire?" he mused. "Or is that just from our clothes because of this afternoon?"

"No," Felix said, coming up beside us and sniffing the air as well. "That smells like fresh smoke."

"Someone's here," I hissed. I let go of Joshua's hand and, before anyone else had even thought to move, I took off in a sprint down the riverbank. I heard other footsteps pounding into the mud behind me, but I didn't slow down to see who'd followed me.

I'd made it at least a hundred feet along the bank, when

I saw something flickering reddish in the tree line. I faltered, only for a second, before altering my course toward the light of what could only be a fire. When I broke through the trees, I came to a stunned stop.

Two people sat beside a small campfire, laughing and talking until I stumbled into their clearing. Joshua followed behind me, as did Jillian and Scott, but my three friends froze just as quickly as I had. Then everyone—including myself, the three Seers behind me, and our two unexpected guests—stared at one another in surprise.

"*Kaylen?*" Jillian gasped first, addressing the person sitting closest to us on the right. Kaylen Patton, still in her prom dress, gave us all a slight wave.

"Hi, guys," she said, getting to her feet and then brushing off some pine needles that her overcoat must have picked up from the forest floor. Across the fire from her, David O'Reilly did the same, mimicking her wave as he did so.

"What up, yo?" he joked, but his tone belied how nervous he actually felt.

"I thought you guys were . . . where did you guys . . . ?" I paused to amend myself, and then asked, "Where are your *cars*?"

Kaylen laughed and came over to stand closer to us, gesturing for O'Reilly to do the same. With an unmistakable look of adoration, he obeyed.

"I made Chelsea drop us off," Kaylen explained as O'Reilly joined her. "Whatever goes down tonight, I don't want it hurting O'Reilly's truck or my car. I mean, I drive a BMW for God's sake."

O'Reilly snorted derisively but, when he thought we were otherwise distracted, he furtively placed his hand on the small of Kaylen's back. When she didn't brush it away, I wondered whether prom wasn't a total waste for him.

"What about the fire?" Joshua asked.

"The lady was cold," O'Reilly said, giving Kaylen a sly half grin—one that she surprised me by returning.

"Glad you let her make it, then," Joshua teased. O'Reilly socked his friend in the arm in response. While Joshua laughed and rubbed his shoulder, I placed my hands on my hips and frowned at our non-Seer guests.

"Are you guys sure you want to be here?" I asked. "Because earlier tonight—"

"Earlier tonight," Kaylen cut me off, "we were scared. And rightfully so, I might add. But we had a long talk at prom, and we . . . we both remember something happening, that night."

Across from me, I saw Jillian stiffen. Kaylen was referring to the night that the wraiths had possessed her, so that Eli could use her, O'Reilly, and Scott to threaten

Jillian—not one of Jillian's best nights, to say the least.

"Neither of us remembers much," O'Reilly said. "Just feeling weird and then suddenly becoming conscious during some total chaos on the bridge. But . . . still . . ."

When he trailed off, looking unnerved, Kaylen finished the thought for him. "But we both know enough that we don't want it to happen again. And I *definitely* don't want to spend eternity with whatever did that to us."

Everyone fell silent for a moment, some staring up at the stars or glancing awkwardly at their shoes. Then Jillian shocked the group by throwing her arms around Kaylen and pulling her into a big hug.

Kaylen blinked rapidly and then recovered enough to shrug carelessly. "Okay, okay," she said with feigned indifference. "Let's not make a big deal about it."

Even so, we could all see the quick, fierce hug that she gave Jillian back. O'Reilly let them have their small moment of real friendship before clearing his throat loudly.

"So, can we get this show on the road?"

"Fine by me," I said.

I didn't express it aloud, but I felt an enormous wave of gratitude that O'Reilly and Kaylen had joined us. True, their presence only swelled the Seers' ranks by two—but that was still two more people who cared about Joshua and would stand with him, long after I'd disappeared.

"Should we . . . initiate them?" Joshua asked, gesturing to me. I realized that he meant the transfer spell— something we hadn't yet performed on a non-Seer.

"I'm not sure." I caught Kaylen's gaze and then O'Reilly's. "What do you two think about being able to do what I did earlier, outside of prom?"

"You mean the fireball thing?" O'Reilly asked. "Oh, hell yeah. That's pretty much the only reason I'm here tonight."

Kaylen looked less enthusiastic, but she also gave her assent. "I'm cool with it. As long as it doesn't ruin my dress."

"It's silk-friendly," I promised, fighting a smile. Then I turned to Joshua and, taking his hand, nodded. He craned his neck toward the trees and called out, "Annabel, Drew—over here! And bring the Transfer Powder."

Less than a minute later, Annabel broke through the tree line; she and her crew must have been waiting nearby for our signal. Seeing Drew, Hayley, and then Felix step into the light after her, I gave Joshua's hand a quick squeeze and let it go so that I could move closer to what would probably be the center of the Seer circle. I froze, however, when a fifth figure stepped out of the darkness.

"Hello," my mother said quietly. "Sorry I'm late."

I stood motionless, silent. Not finding her car at the entrance to the bridge earlier, I'd experienced a flood of opposing emotions: disappointment; relief; terror that my plan wouldn't work without her. But now that she was really here, I had no idea what to say or do.

Joshua did, though. He held out his hand and introduced himself politely. "Hello, ma'am. I'm Joshua Mayhew."

My mother's eyes darted between him and me, taking in the way that our bodies seemed to angle toward each other—noticing every little detail, like any good mother should. Instead of shaking his hand, however, she actually pulled him in for a *hug*. Then she leaned back to appraise him, recognition dawning on her face. With her hands still clasped to his shoulders, she looked quickly up at me.

"The Bible kid?" she asked. "The one who came to my house this fall?"

I nodded sheepishly. "I was with him that day. I . . . I wanted to see you."

For a moment, I couldn't read her expression. Then I realized that she was trying not to cry.

"It's . . . it's good to see you again," she said roughly, drawing Joshua into another hug before releasing him and wiping at her eyes. Once she'd regained her composure, she turned to the rest of the group. "Nice to meet all of you. I'm Liz Ashley . . . Amelia's mother."

I could tell by all the stunned, open mouths that no one except Joshua had expected this turn of events. Still, the Seers managed to handle it gracefully, welcoming my mother into the Seer circle so that she could wait for her turn to receive the glow.

I let Annabel dump a few servings of Transfer Powder into my hand and then moved to the center of the circle to wait for my first nonsupernatural initiate. O'Reilly stepped forward, accepted his handful of Transfer Powder from Annabel, and came to face me. As the Seers linked hands and began to chant, I could see his eyes widen; they only grew bigger when my glow burst forth. But O'Reilly held strong, standing motionless in front of me until I told him to consume the powder. I took a portion of mine as well and then waited with him, praying that something happened.

A full minute passed before a faint orange light began to spread across O'Reilly's skin. It never grew to that raging brightness that my glow had, nor did it really resemble the glows of the Seers; but still—it was *something*.

"Man," O'Reilly groaned, examining the dim light on his skin, "my fire sucks."

Snickering, Kaylen walked up next to him with her own handful of Transfer Powder. "Step back and watch a pro do it," she boasted.

Kaylen waited until O'Reilly took her former place in the Seer circle before turning to me with a fierce look. "Let's do this," she nearly growled, wearing an intent expression that I imagined she usually saved for beauty pageants—and now, supernatural rituals.

Again, we swallowed the powder simultaneously and, again, the glow took a long time to materialize. When it eventually did appear, Kaylen's glow was no brighter than O'Reilly's. So she trotted back to him sullenly, scowling deeper with each playful taunt that he and Jillian gave her.

Finally, my mother stepped into the center of the circle. Like Kaylen and O'Reilly, she came forward with her own handful of the powder. But unlike the other two, she didn't look confident or afraid. She merely gave me a warm, loving smile and, before I could even ask her to, tipped her palm back to gulp down the powder. I hurried to catch up, wishing that I could hold her hand during this process like I had with Joshua.

Our final gulps must have coincided, because we met each other's gaze with a mirrored kind of anticipation. Her glow didn't immediately appear either. But when it did, the entire group of chanters drew back with a collective gasp.

My mother's glow erupted across her skin like a wildfire, burning kerosene bright. As brightly as mine, in fact. Even better, our respective glows seemed drawn to each other, their flames curling toward each other like magnets.

Like two lines of fire that wanted to join into one destructive blaze.

Immediately the Seers began to speculate about what this meant. It didn't take them more than a few guesses to decide that maybe she and I had Seer blood after all, that some forgotten genetic trait had made us exceptionally, supernaturally flammable.

But my mother and I knew the truth. Her fire-bright glow had nothing to do with our bloodline—it had everything to do with what she had agreed to. It had everything to do with the example Ruth had set and the sacrifice my mother had agreed to make, right along with me.

While everyone else talked excitedly, I leaned close enough that she could hear my whisper.

"What . . . what did you take?"

"Sleeping pills," she hissed back. "Almost half a bottle, as I walked over here. I'd bet we only have thirty minutes, maybe an hour, before I can't stay upright."

Panic crackled throughout my body like lightning. Were it not for the determined look in her eyes, I would have backed out of our plan right then and there, ordering everyone to flee while Joshua and I raced her to the hospital. But who was to say that the demons wouldn't smash all our cars to bits before we could leave, and snatch up my mother's soul anyway?

If we stayed, at least this path would be of our *own* choosing.

Feeling a little light-headed with fear and anticipation, I turned to the Seers, most of whom had started to try and call forth their own glows. One by one, each of them ignited, until a group of living torches stood next to the earthly fire. When they finished, all of them looked expectantly at me, waiting for me to give the order.

So I decided to take a page from Kaylen Patton's book. I repressed my sudden swell of terror, threw back my shoulders, and announced, "Okay. Let's do this."

Chapter
THIRTY-TWO

gainst my vehement protests, everyone insisted that they join me near the entrance to High Bridge instead of waiting on the riverbank below it. This development horrified me. Obviously, I had my reasons for wanting to be up there alone. But I couldn't *stop* everyone from coming with me to the bridge—not without giving myself away too early.

So now Joshua walked bravely by my side, showing a level of trust that both awed and wounded me when I thought about what lay in store for us. As we crossed onto the bridge, I glanced back at Jillian and my mother to make sure they followed us; they were the only two people I actually wanted on this bridge, since my plan just wouldn't work without them.

Of course, there was one positive element to the Seers' and non-Seers' presence: eleven people glowing together like pillars of fire near the demons' earthly fortress couldn't help but draw some attention.

Fortunately or not, the demons didn't wait long to prove me right. No sooner had Joshua and I reached the middle of the bridge than a deep rumble rolled like thunder through the river valley. Although the night had been full of stars only a moment earlier, darkness washed over the sky. Whatever it was, it blotted out all light except for the small patches around the few streetlamps that worked along the road.

The netherworld itself, however, hadn't yet appeared— a fact that, for the first time *ever*, infuriated me.

"Hey!" I roared into the night, my voice echoing off the twisted metal of the bridge. "Did you guys decide to sleep in tonight?"

Joshua yanked me closer to him and hissed, "Seriously, Amelia? What are you *doing*?"

"Picking a fight," I whispered, and then spun back around to face the river.

"Are you listening to me?" I shrieked. "I'm here. Just

like you so graciously requested: I'm here."

And you brought friends.

The words hissed themselves across the bridge, loud enough for everyone to hear. But this wasn't Eli, projecting one of his warnings. This voice belonged to a demon: I could tell by how amused it sounded, how it seemed to slither over my skin.

I didn't have the chance to respond to it before a thousand shrieks, all blended into one horrible sound, pierced the night air.

"Wraiths!" I cried, pointing to the edge of the bridge where the first tendrils of black smoke had already begun to creep over the railing.

Our reinforcements raced to us as fast as they could, making it there just in time to see a huge cloud of inky smoke pour itself onto the pavement. The wraiths broke away from one another quickly, each forming its own pillar of darkness to counter our pillars of fire. Except, of course, there were a *lot* more wraiths.

I threw a glance over my shoulder at the young Seers, expecting to find some of them paralyzed with fear. I was dead wrong: Hayley and Drew both wore savage grins, as did Annabel, Felix, and Scott. *This* was what they'd been preparing for; *this* was their moment. Seeing their faces, I felt adrenaline flood my veins. Without another thought, I released Joshua's hand and dove for the nearest wraith.

With a menacing shriek, the wraith dove for me as well. But the moment it collided with my hands, the black thing hissed and writhed away from me. Instead of counting that a victory, as I had in the past, I clawed for purchase and—unexpectedly—found it. Although the creature looked like some vile mix of liquid and vapor, it actually had substance. And an arm, judging by the limb I now grabbed.

"They're solid!" I yelled to my companions, gripping the wraith harder and pulling it closer to my glow. As it drew nearer, it struggled more frantically and hissed so hard that disgusting gray spittle flew out from where a human mouth might be. Even worse, the portion of the shadow that I now held began to steam. The harder I clawed into it, the more the shadow billowed into the air, releasing an overpowering stench of sulfur. When the steam dissipated, the black beneath it had curled back to reveal an arm.

A *human* arm, reaching out desperately from the ink.

I was so stunned that I accidentally loosened my grip, and the wraith skittered away. But apparently, the damage I'd done was irreparable. As I watched, the black substance began to bubble and peel away from the wraith, falling in nasty blobs to the concrete until all that remained was a bent human figure with faintly luminescent skin.

A ghost.

The figure looked up at me, and I took an involuntary step backward. If anyone had asked me ten minutes earlier what I thought that black shadow contained, my *last* guess would have been this middle-aged woman with a beehive hairdo and cat-eye glasses. But there she sat, huddled and frightened in her pink Jackie O suit. Aside from her ghostly shine, this woman looked like a fifties librarian. Or maybe a mom.

"Help," she gasped, obviously struggling for breath. "Help . . . us."

I stood there, frozen for just another heartbeat. Then I spun back to my friends and yelled, "They're human! But you've got to try to burn them—it will make the shadows peel back."

The Seers flew into action. Hayley snatched at the wraith closest to her, while Drew lunged toward two wraiths at once, pulling them both into a weird embrace. All around me, the others did the same—even Kaylen, who leaped onto a particularly large wraith and managed to wrestle it to the pavement.

Grinning triumphantly, I turned and saw Joshua fighting as well, although he somehow made the effort look more like a rescue. Like his cousins, he also held a wraith but as he did so, I heard him soothing it.

"It's okay," he murmured, crouching with it as it

transformed into a hunched old man in faded denim overalls. "It's going to be okay."

For some reason, the sight of Joshua comforting that broken ghost made my eyes sting. So I rushed to the ghost that I'd felled and knelt beside her.

"Are you okay?" I whispered, tentatively brushing my fingers on the back of her hand. She startled at the touch, staring down at our hands with wide eyes.

"W-what . . . ?" she stuttered.

"I'm a ghost too," I explained gently. "And I'm here to help you. All of you."

"Don't let them go," she replied, jerking her head toward the other wraiths that had started to scatter across the bridge. "Don't let them . . . go back there."

I nodded, fighting another swell of tears, and shoved myself to my feet. I was ready to set another wraith free, when I caught a glimpse of something I didn't like— something that made my stomach flip violently.

One person wasn't fighting the wraiths, or even hiding from them. This person moved through the battle like a glassy-eyed zombie, taking methodic, inescapable steps toward the railing of the bridge. I'd seen a walk like that before; I'd *made* that walk.

"O'Reilly!" I screamed, racing toward him before the possessed boy could plunge himself over the edge. "O'Reilly, stop!"

Unsurprisingly, his relentless march didn't even falter. So I did the only thing I could think of: I dove at him instead of the wraiths. As I struck his midsection and knocked him to the ground, I couldn't help but think, *So that's why I never played contact sports.*

Pain vibrated through my body, from both my blow to O'Reilly and *our* blow to the ground. I groaned as a wave of nausea crashed over me, but O'Reilly pushed himself up, stepping on my wounded shoulder in the process. Like some clockwork automaton, he started to use me as a ladder to climb the guardrail.

"Help," I moaned, but my pain was so strong that my voice barely rose above a whisper. "Someone help us."

My head lolled to one side and, although I could see a number of newly freed ghosts mingling among the Seers, I could also see that we were outnumbered. The wraiths had regrouped and were now diving at the Seers like birds of prey. Worse, Kaylen and Hayley now appeared to be possessed too, since they moved with inexorable slowness toward the guardrail.

"Stop," I whispered, but not to my friends. "Make this stop."

You can stop it anytime, Amelia, the demonic voice whispered back sweetly. *Just make the choice.*

"Okay," I panted. "Okay, I will. I'll join you. Just let them go—all of them."

Swear it, the voice hissed, suddenly vicious. *Swear it, or they'll possess* him *next.*

Joshua—the demons would take Joshua. So it really was time for me to do what I'd feared I would have to, the night I watched Ruth Mayhew die.

"I swear," I whispered, feeling weak as a single tear rolled down my cheek. "I swear I'll turn myself over to you, right now, if you'll let everyone on this bridge go. Including the wraiths we freed."

For a long, brutal minute, the demon didn't respond. Then, in that booming volume that the darkness used for its most serious pronouncements, the voice replied, *It is agreed.*

Suddenly, O'Reilly's foot slipped from my shoulder. He crumpled beside me, as Kaylen and Hayley slumped unconscious to the ground. Although the newly freed ghosts remained, cowering uselessly on the bridge, the surviving wraiths vanished like the puffs of smoke they resembled. All the living people who hadn't been possessed whirled around frantically, clearly unsure of what had just happened.

"Did we . . . win?" Joshua asked hesitantly. But when his gaze fell on me, a look of sheer panic crossed his face. He bolted toward me, practically sliding across the road like the star baseball player he was. I was so weak, both physically and spiritually, that I let him pull me gently to my feet. Just before he folded me into his arms, I caught Jillian's eye and gave her the slowest, most unwilling nod of my existence. The nod signaled that she should now enact her part in my plan.

Joshua didn't see her move furtively toward us; all he could see was me. Whispering my name feverishly, he sought my lips and then gave me a desperate, frightened kiss. I stiffened, not wanting this to be the last time our lips touched.

But knowing that it was, I relented, kissing him with more passion, more love, than I ever had. I wanted to do this forever: to hold him close, to breath him in as if he were mine for all eternity.

The kiss was too short. Too painful. Too perfect, as always.

With a violent sob, I broke away from him and darted for Jillian, ducking behind her as she threw herself between me and Joshua.

"Grab him!" she shrieked at Scott. "Do it!"

Scott blinked in confusion, but did as he was told. He dove for Joshua, pinning his arms behind him and signaling to Drew and Felix for help. Within seconds, they had Joshua immobilized.

"Amelia?" he cried, struggling in their grip. "What . . . what the hell?"

"I'm sorry," I said. "I'm so, so sorry. And I love you. Always."

Then I pulled the gun out from beneath the back of my shirt. Everyone must have seen it at the same time, because they froze all at once.

"No," someone whispered, although I couldn't be sure who.

"I have to," I said quietly. "I can't let them have me as a Risen ghost. Whatever they do to me—it will be too painful."

And I need the demons to think I'm desperate, I added in my head.

Annabel and Felix understood what I was saying first; they both nodded their grim assent. My mother and Jillian already knew, as did Scott, judging by the way he held more tightly to Joshua.

Joshua, however, began to scream. Deep, guttural sounds that wrenched through me.

The darkness must have enjoyed those screams— relished them, in fact. Almost as if it wanted to set the scene, the netherworld began to appear around us, plunging the bridge into abject darkness. Everything frosted over, and the temperature dropped so dramatically that Joshua's screams started to puff visible in the air.

Still standing behind Jillian, I took a few steps closer

to the edge of the bridge. Peering over the railing, I could just see it below: the horrible, swirling maelstrom of the hellpit.

It *waited* for me.

"Help me up," I croaked at Jillian, jerking my head toward the guardrail. She simply winced and then shook her head vehemently. Instead of arguing with her, I gripped the gun by its barrel and held it out to her.

After a long pause, she took the gun and tucked it into her belt, her hands trembling badly as she did so.

Trying not to tremble as well, I turned around so that my back pressed against the guardrail. Then I placed my hand on Jillian's shoulder and began to climb, backward, up the railing. However unwillingly, Jillian boosted me and steadied me whenever I needed help. My movements tore through my shoulder like a gunshot, but I kept going until I could grab a girder and balance upright on the edge of the rail.

From that vantage point, I had a clear view of my companions. Kaylen, Hayley, and O'Reilly still lay motionless on the bridge; Annabel held tightly to my mother, who'd already started to sag under the weight of the chemicals in her system; and the boys . . . the second my eyes flitted toward the boys, I started tearing up so badly that all four figures seemed to blur together.

I squeezed my eyes shut, whispered, "I love you," and

prayed that Joshua heard my last words to him.

When I opened my eyes, I was startled to find that Jillian had already pointed the gun at me. But her hands shook so badly that I couldn't tell exactly where she intended to shoot.

"You okay?" I asked her.

At first, she blanched. Then Jillian released a short, incredulous laugh.

"Are you kidding me, Amelia?"

Through all that horrific pain, I felt my lips lift into a faint smile. But it faded so quickly, I doubt Jillian even saw it.

"Do it," I urged. "Please."

Hearing me, Jillian took one shuddering breath. In the split second before the gun went off, I thought I heard her sob. But then the bullet pierced my chest, and I didn't hear anything anymore.

The pain was so vivid, so hot *and* cold, that I stopped breathing altogether. I reeled backward, letting go of the girder. As I fell through the air, a single memory flitted through my mind: Gaby, clutching the gunshot wound in her abdomen and telling me that it didn't hurt.

She lied, I had time to think. Then utter darkness enveloped me.

Chapter
THIRTY-THREE

B y the time I woke up somewhere cool and dark, all
my pain had vanished. No throbbing, no burning,
no searing. No physical sensations at all, actually.

I rolled over and pressed myself into a seated position,
blinking as my eyes adjusted to the darkness. While they
did, I patted my jeans pocket, relieved to find that the
Transfer Powder had stayed with me. Then I performed
a quick self-assessment. I was surprised to find that my
glow had returned. Not the protective fire glow, but the
one I'd had as a ghost—the one that Joshua used to tease

me about, when I shined faintly in the dark.

It was done, then. I was truly, fully dead again, like Gaby had been after Kade shot her. And this place was hell.

I was surprised by how . . . *ordinary* it looked. No fiery cavern full of torture devices and gleeful devils. Just a tall, seemingly endless corridor, painted dark gray and lit overhead by a similarly endless line of metal light fixtures.

The only things that disturbed the monotony were the long rows of black metal doors that lined each wall, extending on into the distant horizon as though a million different rooms led off the same hallway.

"Where does this place *end*?" I asked aloud.

"It doesn't."

My head whipped toward the quaking, unfamiliar voice, which came from somewhere behind me. As I peered into the darkness, another figure emerged on the floor a few feet away from me. It gazed up at me with flame-blue eyes, and pulled back in horror. Although this thing wasn't Eli or Gaby, it resembled their projected forms so closely that I knew it had to be some *shadow* of a ghost.

"Who are you?" I breathed, leaning away from the creature.

"A former reaper," he replied. "I once gathered souls for this place. I trained an assistant as well. . . . You may have met him?"

I stared at him blankly, and then it hit me. "You're Eli's former master. The one he replaced."

The old reaper gave a laugh that sounded more like a cough. "For all the good it did him."

"Why are you here?" I demanded. "With me?"

"I'm here to guide you, obviously." Despite his decrepit state, he managed to sound petulant.

"Where?"

"To your room," he answered flatly, as if that was supposed to make sense. Seeing my confused frown, he waved at the endless row of black doors. "Everyone has their own room."

I glanced around, feeling a slow chill creep over me. *That* was hell, then. Each soul confined to its own room, its own torture.

"Show me," I whispered.

The old reaper bowed his head slightly and then began to move. But instead of standing up to guide me, he crawled along the floor, dragging himself inch by inch with his hands. Trying not to gag, I followed him down the hallway until he paused outside a door that was indistinguishable from all the others.

"Try this one," he offered.

My hand shook as I reached for the doorknob. It felt an awful lot like that gunshot—hot and cold at the same time against my palm. Still shaking, I turned the knob and opened the door on a plain room that looked much like the outer hallway: simple, dark, and painted gray. But in its center, a middle-aged man in a suit sat in a straight-backed chair. He was crying and staring so intently forward that I couldn't help but follow his gaze. There, hanging on the wall in front of him, was a picture of a woman. She wasn't pretty nor was she smiling. But he still sobbed, watching her picture with that trauma-tized, wide-eyed stare.

I turned back to the former reaper, frowning. "I don't understand."

"You wouldn't—it's all very personal. Try another door, if you don't believe me."

So I did, closing that door and opening the one to the very next room. This room was far more interesting: it looked like the inside of a circus tent, with brightly colored silks hanging from the walls. Again, a person occupied the middle of the room, except this time it was a teenage girl in a pink tutu, sitting cross-legged on the floor. In her lap lay what looked like a wounded white rabbit. The poor animal continued to whimper and squirm . . . with no discernible change. Although I watched it for a long time, the rabbit never recovered or died; it just went on in that perpetual agonized state. At first, I thought that the rabbit was being punished, but when I saw the girl's face—red and cracked from all the tears she'd shed—I thought otherwise.

For some reason, this room disturbed me more than the first. I shut the door quickly, moving on to view room after room in the hope that I'd find something better. But of course I didn't.

There was the wrinkled old woman drinking from a bottle of whiskey that kept refilling itself after each swig; the man suspended midair, in what looked like a vat of water; the little boy who couldn't seem to stop digging in a patch of foul-smelling mud; the gorgeous young woman applying and reapplying the same garish shade of red lipstick in front of a cracked mirror; the elderly man watching a single hanging lightbulb swing back and forth.

On and on the rooms went, each containing a person who seemed to be locked in some inexplicable moment, staring at the same scenery or repeating the same relentless tasks over and over for all eternity—scenes and tasks chosen especially for them, from some cruel place in their psyche.

Hell isn't other people, I thought, recalling something Melissa had said in the prairie. *Hell is yourself.*

Finally, I'd had enough of this tortured voyeurism. And anyway, I had no idea how much time I'd passed down here—no idea how much time my mother had left.

"Can you show me my friends' rooms?" I asked roughly.

For some reason, the old reaper grinned. "Of course."

He dragged himself onward for a long stretch of hallway, until he stopped outside another nondescript black door. "Here you go," he grunted, slapping one palm against the metal. "Eli Rowland."

I approached the door slowly, hesitantly. I held the doorknob for so long that, when the reaper cleared his throat impatiently, I simply had to yank it open, almost like ripping off a Band-Aid.

This room was one of the largest I'd seen, and the most occupied. It appeared as though an enormous concert venue stretched out in front of me, full of a teeming mass of laughing, dancing, singing people. All of them faced a stage, upon which an outrageously dressed band played a catchy rock song. Everyone in this room seemed happy; joyous, even. Everyone except one person, who stood close to the stage. I almost didn't recognize Eli, he looked so dorky in his plain khaki bell-bottoms, burgundy sweater, and horn-rimmed glasses. I would have laughed, were it not for the look on his face. He stared up at that stage with such misery, such longing, that it actually *hurt* me to see him like this.

So this was Eli's real prison: exclusion and anonymity.

I slammed Eli's door shut, closed my eyes, and leaned against it. Once I'd somewhat recovered my breath, I opened my eyes and whispered, "Gaby, please."

My guide pointed at the door to my right. "She's his neighbor. . . . Go ahead and have a peek."

Trying to glare at him, I turned to Gaby's door and then yanked it open like I had Eli's.

I wasn't too surprised by what I found inside. The entire room looked like it was underwater. In fact, when I brushed my fingertips along the shimmering wall in front of me, they drew away wet. Inside, buried beneath all that water, a car floated nose downward. And inside the car, I could see three figures, frozen with permanent screams plastered to their faces: an attractive older couple in the front seat, Gaby in the back. Gaby was staring wide-eyed at an empty seat beside her, as though there was an invisible person there, drawing her attention.

Was that where Kade once sat?

Gaby and her parents had died after crashing into a river because Kade had forced their car off a bridge. And now Gaby had to relive that moment for all eternity. There was no worse fate—I would know.

I slammed this door shut even harder than I had Eli's, glancing back at the old reaper without even attempting to hide my tears. He watched hungrily as I cried, like he enjoyed it. So I wiped the tears away, as fast as I could.

"Why wasn't Kade LaLaurie in there with Gaby?" I

demanded, glancing up and down the hall. "Where's *his* room?"

Finally, my guide looked less smug—he even trembled a little. "Doesn't have one."

I frowned, trying not to let myself show hope, or excitement. "Why not? Too important to the cause?"

"Because," my guide spat, "you *ended* him. There is no Kade LaLaurie anymore."

I couldn't stop my small gasp of relief. My salvation—Gaby's and Eli's and Serena's salvation—might happen as I'd planned. Assuming that Gaby, Eli, and Serena agreed to it, and that my tactics worked.

I straightened my mouth into a hard line, praying that my face gave nothing away. Luckily, the old reaper didn't seem very observant. So I asked my final question.

"Serena's room? Where is it?"

He made that laugh-cough sound again. "She doesn't have one yet. The masters have . . . another purpose in mind for her, first."

The reaper thought he was being so clever. So cryptic. But I already suspected what the demons wanted Serena to do: kill me all over again, once I'd arrived at my room; end my existence for good like I'd done to Kade. Only the demons could decide when that event would occur—tonight or a millennium from now, after I'd received some sufficient torture.

I took one shuddering breath, and then I turned back to the old reaper. "Well, why wait, then?" I asked. "Show me to my room, please."

With an ugly smirk, the reaper bowed his head. "Whatever you say."

I kept my steps steady as I followed him, even though we seemed to walk for hours down that monotonous hallway. Not for the first time, I wondered whether this was part of the torture too: knowing that you weren't some special victim, escorted in grand fashion to your eternal punishment; you were just one door, out of countless millions.

But when we finally reached it, I took a shocked backward step. Unlike the hundreds—maybe thousands—of doors we'd already passed, mine lay open. Waiting for me to walk inside.

So I did just that, without a single glance over my shoulder at the nasty creature who'd obviously enjoyed his former job, even more than Eli.

My room was so dark, I couldn't see anything in the instant after the door slammed shut behind me. But before the slam stopped ringing, a row of auditorium lights came on at the other end of the room. I blinked, momentarily blinded by their shine. When my eyes adjusted, however, I saw what I'd expected I would: a tribunal of demons were sitting in what resembled a jury box. My room even looked like a courtroom with its high ceilings and paneled walls—all in gray, of course.

The second I saw the demons, my glow flared bright; I doubted it would disappear the entire time I was in their presence. This was both lucky and unfortunate, since it made me appear far more rebellious than I would have liked.

The male demon with whom I was familiar—Belial— sat in the middle. Once he'd made eye contact with me, he stood to open his arms benevolently.

"Amelia Elizabeth Ashley," he said. "Welcome home."

Inexplicably, I laughed. Then I reminded myself of what I'd come here to do and composed my expression into something more serious. More reverent, even.

"Thank you," I whispered, in my most respectful tone. "I'm sorry that it took me so long to make this decision."

Judging by their frowns and whispers, the demons had expected defiance—not submission. I took advantage of the moment, falling to my knees and bowing low to the floor.

"What is the meaning of this?" Belial demanded. "Why do you bow?"

"Because I *am* sorry," I said, my voice muffled. "I thought I could fight you, but tonight, I came to realize that you truly are more powerful. And . . . and I don't want you to destroy me."

When the demons began to chuckle, I allowed myself a glance upward. Belial caught my gaze, flashed me that sharp-toothed smile, and waved his hand at an empty corner of the room. There, a black shadow solidified into Serena Taylor, looking very much like the puppet I'd seen the week before.

"I know that Serena is part of your plan for me," I said hurriedly. "And I beg you to reconsider."

Belial grinned again, but this time I could see a trace of respect in the smile. "You are a clever one, aren't you?"

"Maybe," I said, bowing my head so that I didn't seem prideful. "But don't you think I could be useful too? That I could serve you, far better than Kade or Eli or that thing out there in the hallway? I've outsmarted two out of three of them—don't you think that counts for something?"

Now the murmurs flew so wildly between the demons that they sounded like buzzing bees. After a long, obviously contentious pause—during which Belial conferred with his hive-mind companions—he turned back to me and smirked.

"Perhaps you would be useful, in the position we originally chose for you. But we cannot trust you; just remember what you did to poor Kade."

My heart wrenched inside my chest, but I kept my face impassive. Earnest.

"Let me prove myself to you," I offered. "Let me kill someone and then drag their soul here, to you."

Now, *that* intrigued the demon. He raised one eyebrow, grinning. But then he shook his head with feigned sadness. "How could one soul matter, Amelia? What would some stranger who you pluck off the street prove?"

"What if it wasn't a stranger?" I countered, barely speaking above a whisper now. "What if I killed my own mother?"

Chapter THIRTY-FOUR

I don't believe that you would do such a thing," Belial said, sneering down at me. "That you even could."

But despite the demon's words, he didn't look convinced one way or the other. In fact, he seemed to appraise me with a mixture of doubt and . . . maybe respect?

"Make me a wraith," I suggested. "Just for the killing. That way I won't have any choice—I'll have to do what I promised. Then, if I don't deliver, you can make me stay a wraith."

"Or destroy you anyway," another demon hissed from the jury box. I gulped but said nothing. Belial considered these options for a moment and then smiled.

"What have we got to lose?" He laughed, turning slightly to his companions so that they could share his amusement. "This sounds like an interesting night's entertainment—one we haven't had in a long time. So shall we agree to it?"

"Wait!" I called, holding up my hand like a child in school. "I do have *one* condition."

Now, Belial looked *less* entertained. I could tell that he was about to deny whatever I said, so I spilled my request in a rush of words.

"All I ask is that you bring Gabrielle Callioux, Eli Rowland, and the *real* Serena Taylor here, so that if you decide to destroy me, then you destroy them and my mother as well. If I go, they all go."

Each of the demons balked for a moment and then began to laugh uproariously.

"What an inspired suggestion!" Belial crowed. "How on earth did you come up with it?"

I shrugged as best I could in my groveling position. "If I can't survive in some form, why should they?"

I could tell from the demons' subsequent laughs that I'd just spoken a language they understood well: the language of callousness; of selfishness; of cruelty for sport. If I told the demons the truth—that I wanted to spare the people I loved an eternity of torture in this place—then my appeal would surely have been denied. But stating the request as I had, I'd captured their interest further.

After a few more seconds of amused deliberation with his companions, Belial faced me again.

"All right, Amelia Ashley—we will make you a wraith for the sole purpose of killing your own mother and bringing her soul to us here, in this room. Then, when you return, we'll decide what to do with you."

Once again, I lowered my gaze to the floor. "Thank you. Thank you for this chance."

I heard them laughing, mocking my decision. So I spared another glance upward, just in time to see Belial flap his hand at me dismissively.

Abruptly, my ears began to ring. I sat upright and tried to clap my hands over my ears but found that I'd lost control of my arms. They wouldn't move, no matter how much I ordered them to. Suddenly, I couldn't move my legs, either. Or my mouth or my eyes or anything else.

I'd lost control of my own body.

That wasn't to say that I'd stopped moving. On the contrary, some outside force had animated me into standing, turning around, and walking like some wooden soldier into the hallway. Evidently, a mere wave of the demon's hand had turned *me* into an automaton.

As I crossed into the hall, I could see the old reaper waiting for me with a condescending sneer. His expression shifted into one of astonishment, however, when I stopped just a few inches past him and then rose several feet into the air.

While I hovered there, immobile, a black shadow crawled across one wall of the hallway to envelop me. Although I could tell that it had obscured my entire body, I could see out of the shadow as clearly as if it were glass. Of course, that didn't mean that I'd regained even an ounce of control. I was still the puppet of whatever force was manipulating my body right now: fully aware of my actions, but unable to stop them.

The shadow held me in the air, floating inertly for a few more seconds. Then, without warning, it rocketed me down the hallway. I flew so fast that I wanted to scream in terror. I even tried, but the sound died in my throat.

I had no idea how fast or far I'd flown when the shadow jerked me to an abrupt stop and then my body shot upward, toward the ceiling. I thought that I would slam into it—the butt of some demonic joke, after all. But just before I crashed into it, the ceiling parted like a storm cloud, allowing me to pass through without harm.

I continued to shoot upward through an utter, impenetrable blackness. I wanted to look down, to see how far below me the hallway was, but I couldn't; my eyes stayed fixed on some unseen target, high above me.

I didn't have to wait long to find out where I was headed. Without warning, I burst through the darkness and into a glittering, purplish space that could only be the netherworld. In my peripheral vision, I could just make out the edge of High Bridge, looming to my right.

Of its own volition, my wraith body continued to swoop high into the night sky, shrieking as it did so. I couldn't help but marvel at the sound that tore out of me—it was so plaintive, so desperate, that I wondered how I'd missed the agonized quality of the wraiths' shrieks before now.

Finally, my wraith body reached the peak of its ascent and then arced back around to dive. On the surface of the bridge, I could just make out a group of figures: still-glowing Seers and their friends, as well as a handful of luminescent ghosts. I didn't have to tell the shadow which figure to target; it was already making a sharp beeline for my mother, who looked as though she could hardly stay on her feet any longer.

I was less than a hundred feet from her when I had a sudden thought—one that I desperately hoped would work, if only for a few seconds. As I continued to dive, I repeated the same word over and over in my mind, like a prayer.

Possess, possess, possess.

Finally, the shadow collided with my mother's body, and I spent an endless, terrified moment thinking that I'd crushed her. But when the shadow pulled me into her like a vacuum, I felt light-headed with relief. Within seconds, my vision shifted from staring at her horrified face, to staring out *from* it at my horrified friends. At Joshua.

I had almost as little control over my mother's body as I did over my own, especially since the shadow, tricked into this possession, had already started to push me back out of her. Worse, her body felt lethargic and almost unresponsive—very near the peaceful, sleeping death that I would have preferred for her, rather than a forced drowning in the netherworld river. So I focused all my energy on making my mother do one last thing before the end.

"Run," I gasped with my mother's captive vocal chords. "Off . . . the bridge. Run."

Then, before I could warn my friends further, the shadow ripped me out of my mother.

Immediately after I left her body, she doubled over and began gasping for breath. But the shadow had no mercy. It ducked down, wrapping its tendrils underneath her arms and hauling her to her feet.

As it dragged her to the edge of the bridge, I expected

her to scream and struggle. But instead, my mother closed her eyes and extinguished her protective glow. When she opened her eyes, she looked directly at the shadow's face and smiled as if she'd managed to find me beneath all that evil.

"Amelia," she whispered, her words already slurring, "I know it's you. And I'm ready."

I could hear her heart, hammering loudly but sluggishly in her chest, slowing down under the influence of all those sleeping pills. I started to cry, and the shadow made no attempt to stanch my tears; I supposed that was another nasty twist to being a wraith—the darkness controlled your body, but allowed you to feel as miserable as you wanted.

I continued to sob as the shadow-me pulled my mother up onto the railing, tugging her away from the hands of my friends, all of whom had started to scream her name. Even then, my mother surprised me: as the shadow wrapped more tightly around her, she wrapped her arms around it, too.

"I love you, honey," she whispered. "Now, let's go."

And then, without further delay, the two of us plummeted backward off the railing and into the abyss below.

Chapter
THIRTY·FIVE

W hen I woke, no longer a wraith, I was once
again lying on the floor of the menacing
hallway. And I had more company.

"Amelia?" my mother croaked, rolling to her side and
reaching out to me. I reached out, too, and clasped her
ghostly, faintly shining hand in mine. Only one other
time had I been so grateful to feel another person's touch.

"Mom!" I cried, using her hand to drag myself next
to her. Lying there on the cold floor of hell, my mother
and I pulled each other into a tearful embrace. "I'm so,

so sorry," I sobbed. "That was way more awful that I thought it would be. Did you feel it? Please, please tell me that you didn't *feel* the drowning part."

"Shhh," she breathed into my hair. "I didn't feel anything. I was unconscious before we even hit the water. And anyway, as long as I was with you, I knew it would be okay."

"Oh my God, Mom," I moaned, "I'm sorry. For everything. I didn't want this for you, I really didn't."

A derisive snort interrupted my apology. "How touching," the intruder spat.

With no small amount of resentment, I turned away from my mother to face the old reaper. He hunched nearby, watching my mother and me with a combination of hatred and longing. Holding his gaze, I gave my mother a last, fierce hug, and then helped her to rise from the floor. Once we both stood, I gestured between my mother and the reaper.

"Person of No Consequence—meet my mother."

The reaper snickered, as if my insult pleased him. Still laughing, he gave me a low, sarcastic bow of his head. "Madam, I've been asked to escort you and your mother to the masters. It seems that you all have much to discuss."

A wave of nervous nausea washed over me. I repressed it as best I could, drawing a few deep breaths. Then I threw back my shoulders, took my mother's hand again, and put on my bravest face.

"We're ready," I told him.

He gave me another ironic bow and then began dragging himself in the direction of my room. Seeing this macabre creature move, my mother froze, wide-eyed and frightened. But she soon regained her composure and marched just as bravely as I did down the hallway.

This walk seemed much shorter than it did earlier, probably because I now knew what waited at the end of it: a long-shot chance at redemption, or a lingering, certain demise.

My mother must have sensed my fear because she gave my hand a firm squeeze, just as we paused outside the open door to my room.

"I love you, Amelia," she whispered again. "No matter what happens next."

With tears in my eyes, I yanked her back into a hug. Pressed close to her again, I slipped my hand into my pocket and then forced her to take what I offered: a handful of Transfer Powder.

"At the right moment," I whispered into her ear. "Just like we talked about this morning."

When she nodded her understanding, I gave her a quick peck on the cheek and, aloud, said, "I love you, too, Mom."

"And she loves you, and you love her for loving you, and we all love each other," the old reaper snarled. "Now, quit stalling and go inside."

As we crossed the threshold of my room, I gave the pathetic, broken creature a final glare. From the corner of my eye, however, I noticed my mother hide her powder-filled hand behind her back. Now that we were as ready as we could be, I took her free hand and we stepped more fully into the room.

As before, my room remained in total darkness until the demons were good and ready to reveal themselves. When the lights finally popped back on, and my eyes adjusted to the sudden brightness, it took everything within me not to drop my mother's hand and run toward the jury box.

Gaby, Serena, and Eli crouched in front of it, looking very much like themselves instead of projections or puppets. Yet I wouldn't say that any of them looked *well*, either. Even Serena, who'd been dead for the shortest amount of time, seemed more gaunt and broken. She bore the same bruises and cuts that Gaby and Eli did—fresh wounds that might have been inflicted right before my mother and I arrived.

"As you requested, Amelia," Belial said grandly, stepping forward to sweep his hand above their heads, as if he'd brought them here as presents for me.

"May I . . . Can they come over here?" I asked haltingly. "To be with me, when you all make your decision about my future?"

"You're making another demand of us?"

"No," I said, shaking my head quickly. "Not at all. I'm asking that you show just a little mercy—that you allow me the comfort of my loved ones if you decide to end me."

After a pause, Belial shrugged, chuckling. "Oh, I don't see why not. After all, you *did* perform the task that you promised you would."

I didn't like the way he leered at my mother as he said the word "task." But I couldn't chastise him for it; not when I was so *close* to victory. I looked down at the other ghosts—Gaby, Serena, Eli—and, without a word, held my arms open to them.

Immediately, all three scrambled toward my mother and me like we were the last drop of water in the desert. First, Serena collided with my mother, wrapping her in such a ferocious hug that we had to drop our linked hands. That wasn't necessarily a bad thing, since Gaby drew me into a similarly all-encompassing embrace. Eli just fell at my feet, touching the toe of my boot as if he felt that was all he really deserved.

"It's you," Gaby breathed, already sniffling back tears. "You *found* me."

"Shhh, I'm here," I said loudly. But as we held each other, I spun us around so that her back faced the demons. I ran one hand across her shoulders in a comforting motion. Then, *very* carefully, I used my other hand to pull some Transfer Powder from my pocket and fold a portion of it into Gaby's palm.

"When I tell you to," I whispered, "swallow this and then try to do whatever it is that I'm doing, okay?"

She nodded imperceptibly and then released me so that I could crouch down next to Eli. Before I touched him, I glanced back up at my mother. I could see that she was holding a similar conversation with Serena, slipping her the powder as subtly as possible.

Knowing that it was now or never, I gently placed my empty palm on Eli's shoulder. He flinched under my touch, cowering so badly that he shook. The demons noticed his behavior and laughed, which only made him drop lower to the ground.

"Eli," I murmured, still touching him, "Eli, look at me. Please."

When he finally peered up, I was stunned to see that the rims of his eyes were so red, they looked raw. If those eyes were any indication, he'd been crying nonstop for *months.*

"I'm sorry," he moaned, tearing up once again. "Amelia, I'm so sorry. For you—for everyone I trapped in here."

Slipping my powder-free hand beneath his elbow, I hefted him upward so that we were both on our knees, facing each other. Now that his body blocked mine from the demons' view, I cupped his hand and meted out about half the powder I still had in my palm. This meant that I had very little left for myself—just enough for one last gulp.

Eli frowned in obvious confusion, but he took the powder without comment.

"I forgive you," I said loudly. "I hope you can swallow that forgiveness. Internalize it, you know?"

Understanding dawned on Eli's face and he rose with me so that we both stood now. I opened my arms, signaling that we should all come together for a kind of group hug. After they'd done so, I hissed, "When I glow—you do it, too."

Then I stepped forward from the pack and faced the demons.

"Thank you for letting them stand here," I said, using a far more commanding voice than I had earlier. "Now, have you made a decision about me?"

Belial did not miss my new, insolent tone. He arched one eyebrow questioningly.

"I'll have to confer with my fellow judges first."

"No," I said firmly. "I want to know now."

In the jury box, the demons began to murmur angrily.

Belial peered back at them before turning his black eyes upon me.

"What gives you the right to make a demand of us?" he asked.

"You bargained with me," I insisted. "My mom's soul, for my future."

The demon let out a shrill, skin-crawling laugh, as did his companions. "I said we would *consider* your future. The option of destruction is still very much on the table."

"That's not fair!" I shrieked, forcing my voice into a higher octave than it had ever reached.

My glow erupted across my skin—dim at first, but gaining intensity as I grew genuinely angry. I'd expected the demons to double-cross me; in fact, their treachery was integral to my plan. But that didn't mean I had to *like* it.

Seeing my glow, hearing my shriek, Belial actually winced but he soon recovered, giving me a glare that could have melted titanium.

"*Silence*," he boomed, seeming to double in size. He suddenly towered over me, casting sinister shadows across the room. "Return to your companions while we confer."

I started to shudder uncontrollably. Although I'd been trying to fool them earlier, I certainly didn't need to feign terror now. I hurried to rejoin my mother and my friends, trying to not shiver as I stood closer to them.

"Now. Swallow now," I hissed. Each of my fellow ghosts ducked down, hiding their heads as they ingested the Transfer Powder I'd given them; I did the same. When we'd finished, I motioned that we should spread out, take one another's hands, and stand in a unified line: Serena, my mother, me, Gaby, and, lastly, Eli.

Standing there with my small crew, I began to pray to whoever might listen. *Please,* I whispered in my mind, *please give them your holy fire. Just once. And just enough.*

When Belial turned back around, wearing a beatific smile, I could see my companions stiffen in anticipation. "Wait," I whispered when I sensed their restless tension. "Wait."

Each of these ghosts had suffered, but none of them had ever faced *anything* like this. Still, they couldn't act without ruining everything. Not yet.

As Belial continued to smile silently, I felt an electric frisson of worry. If the demonic tribunal really did decide to make me a soul reaper or—worse—a wraith, then all was lost; everything I'd had to do to Joshua, my mother, my living friends and my dead ones . . . all of it would be wasted.

But when the rest of the demons stood, too, rising like a real jury, triumph surged within me.

"Amelia Elizabeth Ashley," Belial pronounced. "We

have decided. We have hereby determined that you are too great a threat to be allowed to roam free as a reaper. Moreover, we do not relish the idea of you occupying your own corner of *our* world. So we will grant the request you did not actually make: we will end your soul, as you ended Kade LaLaurie's. And, as you *did* ask, we will also end the souls of those who stand beside you now."

"No," I pleaded, faking my tone but not my tears. "You can't do this to us—not after I killed my mother for you."

"That was your mistake," he taunted softly. "Not ours."

"H-how?" I stuttered, willing my glow to burn just a watt or two brighter. "How will you end all of us?"

The demons appraised me for a moment, and then their leader grinned. Obviously, Belial had received a clear message from the demonic hive mind—a message that I hoped to God worked in my favor.

"Fire," he breathed. "Your existence will burn out in the very fire of which you're so fond."

I tried not to smile. I also tried not to cry, especially when five purple-hued trees appeared, standing tall behind each of us ghosts. Still gripping tightly to Gaby's and my mother's hands, I spun around and saw that a small pile of kindling lay beneath each tree. Five wraiths waited next to the trees, each holding a weirdly blue-flamed torch.

I knew instantly what the trees and torches signified: the demons intended to burn us at the stake, like witches.

"N-no," I stuttered again, partly in genuine horror. "Please, anything but this."

"This grows tiresome," a female demon called out from the jury box. "Let the entertainment begin."

Belial wasted no time: he jerked his head at my wraith and it immediately obeyed, snaking an inky tendril around my shoulders and wrenching me backward, away from my mother and Gaby. Before I could fake another struggle or protest, the wraith pinned me to the tree, which then came to life as it wrapped two branches across my arms and abdomen. Within a matter of seconds, I could no longer move.

This new element of confinement frightened me, almost beyond thought. My entire plan hinged on my companions and me being able to hold hands so that our glows would connect. I had no idea how this might work, otherwise. I writhed and twisted inside my bonds, all the while watching the same imprisonment happen to my mother, Gaby, Serena, and Eli. Eventually, we were all pinned to our hellish stakes.

After trapping us, the wraiths waited until Belial signaled to them again. Then, moving in unison, the wraiths stood behind us with their torches. Without further signal, mine set the kindling beneath me afire.

I could see my companions craning desperately toward me, wordlessly begging me to give the order—to make whatever attempt we could, right now, before any of us suffered unspeakable pain.

But I couldn't give that order yet. Not until I saw how the bluish hellfire reacted to my glow.

"Wait," I screamed to my companions as the fire crawled up my boots and jeans, searing my flesh beneath them. "Wait!"

I could hear my mother screaming—I could hear them all screaming. I was almost past the point of rational thought myself when I saw the two flames join. At that second they began to boil and bubble like liquid, doubling in size and brightness, shifting until they'd both turned almost white in color. Combined, the two flames became something new—something incendiary that resembled pictures I'd seen of exploding atom bombs. Together these flames were terrible. Unstoppable.

Perfect.

"Do it!" I sobbed. "Do it now!"

Even over the growing roar of our pyres, I heard the distinct sounds of supernatural glows as they ignited. I also heard the collective gasp of the demons, as five separate glows united with the hellfire. It had started to spread across the floor, becoming one enormous, super-natural bonfire.

Soon, the flames were licking at my neck. I'd never felt anything like this—anything so painful, wretched, *evil*. But I still had the strength for one more plea.

"Please!" I screamed, crying out over the roar of the fire and the demons' panicked shouts. Crying to the light, to the Highest Powers.

"Please, take us. *Please.*"

I ended my begging with one broken sob as the pain overwhelmed me. Blessedly, I began to lose conscious-ness. But not before I thought I heard Belial shout, "Divert it! Direct it toward the High Bridge hell gate before it incinerates us all!"

"Please," I mumbled, forcing my charred neck to lift so that I could stare upward, toward whatever or who-ever waited high above this evil place. A name rang in my mind, so, in a final, desperate attempt, I called out. Not to the Highest Powers or even to Melissa.

I cried out for my father.

And suddenly, an earsplitting boom echoed throughout the room—possibly throughout all of hell. Immediately thereafter, I went deaf.

Through the white flames, I could see the demons scrambling and running. I could see chunks of the ceil-ing cracking and falling to the floor. And I could still feel the fire, searing into my skin.

I lost, I thought. *I'm lost.*

But suddenly, I *remembered*. Memories from my life, and my afterlife—they came flooding back into my mind, slowly at first but then gaining in speed.

My favorite stuffed animal—a bunny with an orange ribbon for a necktie, worn ragged by too much love. My first bicycle, a purple one with pink ribbons on the handles. The smell of my grandmother's perfume. The way my dad's hands felt when he held mine; the happy wrinkle just along the right corner of my mother's mouth. How much Serena laughed when she couldn't climb a rope in gym class, how bright the stars shined through my telescope, how excited I was when I solved a calculus problem. How I died, how I awoke from the fog. The taste of beignets the smell of salt water the silky lining of Gaby's cape the slight chip in Jillian's left canine the way a good song could run through my body like electricity Joshua's smile Joshua's kiss Joshua Joshua Joshua. . . .

And then, with his name still ringing in my mind, my world ended in a bright, beautiful flash of light.

EPILOGUE

Just after dawn, an enormous, earthquaking boom echoed throughout the river valley. And just after *that*, High Bridge exploded into a thousand little pieces.

Immediately, everyone took cover. Everyone except Joshua Mayhew.

He watched his friends and family run, diving for the tree line as fast as they could. But he couldn't bring himself to move from this spot on the riverbank—the place where she'd told him to run. Or at least, he *thought* that wraith had been her. It was hard to tell, through all of its murky black shadows.

But whether or not Joshua knew the identity of the wraith, he certainly knew what the explosion meant. Especially with regard to *her*.

The last time she'd tried to destroy the bridge, it had rebuilt itself within minutes. But this time, when the chunks of concrete and threads of wire landed with sickening thuds on the riverbank, they stayed put—no screeching shadows or smirking demons appeared to reclaim them.

Even better, when the bridge fell, the darkness fell with it. As the remnants of High Bridge rained down, the netherworld melted away like paint that had been splashed with turpentine. Purple and red stains, gnarled trees, icy splinters—they all slid into puddles and then retracted in upon themselves, as though they were evaporating. Slowly, branch by branch and eddy by eddy, the riverbank of the living world began to reappear.

Eventually the rain of pavement and metal ended, and Joshua could better assess the damage. First, he glanced up to where the bridge used to stretch above the river. Now, two jagged ends of a rarely used road faced each other across the empty expanse. On the portion of the bank closest to the part of the road where the cars were parked, huge slabs of concrete had piled on top of one another. Almost as though they'd organized themselves for easier cleanup.

Looking at these ruins, Joshua experienced a strange rush of both triumph and misery. He had hated that bridge as a child, and his hate only grew after he fell in love with . . . her.

He still couldn't make himself think her name. Because he knew that the final destruction of the bridge didn't just mean the end of this portal into the netherworld.

It meant the end of *her*.

Joshua didn't know how, but she'd obviously done it: pulled down one of the entrances to hell, when no one else could. He'd never doubted that she was capable of it, but he'd hoped—God, he'd hoped—that she wouldn't be willing to pay the price it required.

While he continued to stare at the wreckage, he heard the sound of voices moving closer to him. One by one, his friends and family rejoined him on the bank. Wisely, though, none of them spoke to him as they arrived. Not until his sister walked up to him.

At first, she didn't speak either—just wrapped one arm around him and pulled him into a half hug.

Jillian waved vaguely to the river. "This is . . . ?"

"Impressive?" Joshua offered. "Horrifying?"

"Both," she said softly, tightening their hug.

She didn't ask to be forgiven for the role she'd played

in all of this, and she didn't have to. Joshua knew why she did it and, in a way, he agreed. They were safe—their entire *town* was safe—because the girl he loved made a sacrifice, and because his sister made one too. Joshua knew that, despite her uncaring façade, Jillian hadn't wanted to pull that trigger.

After a long pause, she asked, "Do you think it's over?"

Joshua hesitated, looking around the littered riverbed, and then nodded. "Yeah, it's over. She did it."

"You know, I kind of didn't think she had it in her."

"I did," he said quietly.

The rest of their bedraggled little crew must have been listening to this entire exchange, because they all moved in unison, grouping more tightly together around the Mayhew siblings. Only now did Joshua notice that some of them were sobbing. He couldn't say that he blamed them, after what they'd seen.

Joshua raked his fingers through his hair and then rested his palm on the back of his neck. He knew he should say something comforting to everyone—tell them that he would be okay. That they would all be okay, from now on. But he just couldn't gather the strength. In fact, he suddenly didn't think he had the strength to be around anyone, anymore.

So he turned abruptly on one heel and began trudging down the riverbank, toward the embankment. He ignored the calls of his friends and family members; he ignored the pleas of his little sister, who'd started to tag halfheartedly behind him.

Joshua let his mind go dark and angry, let each step tear into him like a knife. By the time he reached his truck, he wanted to punch something. Or maybe jump off of something tall. He wasn't really sure which option sounded best right now.

He yanked open his truck door so hard that it squealed in protest. He'd almost dived inside, ready to drive off at a ridiculous speed to some unknown location, when a faint scent made him stop.

This wasn't the trace of the campfire that he'd noticed the night before. Nor was it the tangy, metallic smell of the ruined bridge, or even the muddy odor of the river. Instead, this scent was sweet—a strange mix of nectarines and flowers.

Joshua jerked away from the truck, searching. Nectarine was *her* scent, he knew. Before she Rose, he would catch it every now and then when they were close to each other. But no matter how hard he searched, he didn't see her; didn't see anything but a destroyed bridge, a broad river, and an empty forest.

And Joshua didn't want to see *any* of those things right now. In fact, he'd nearly decided that he never wanted to see those things again, for as long as he lived, when something white in the nearby tree line caught his eye.

Tiny white dots, scattered throughout the forest. They were sparse at first, but as he watched, they began to spread fast, taking over the tree line near the road and then moving along on both sides of the riverbank like sudden, inexplicable flurries of snow. Defying natural law, the tiny, fragrant white flowers consumed the river valley.

The vines on which they grew wound their way up tree trunks and across branches, over rubble and wreckage, spilling a gorgeous scent into the air. Within a matter of minutes, the valley was full of exquisite, sweet-smelling flowers.

Honeysuckle.

Joshua didn't know he'd started laughing until he heard people calling to him from the riverbank below. They sounded alarmed, as if they thought he'd finally cracked up. So he wiped his eyes (since he'd apparently started crying, too) and yelled down to his family and friends.

"I'm all right. I'll be all right."

And to his utter amazement, he realized that what he'd just said was true. Or it would be, someday.

Because he knew who sent those flowers to him, and he knew what they meant. They were a sign that her soul had survived. Seeing those flowers, Joshua knew that she'd made it someplace good, with her family. That she still loved him, and one day, after he'd lived a long, full life, he might get to see her again.

That he might get to love her again.

And so, on the morning of what should have been Amelia Ashley's birthday, the river valley that had once housed High Bridge changed for Joshua Mayhew. For the first time in many years, it seemed beautiful to him.

For the first time in many years, it *was* beautiful.

ACKNOWLEDGMENTS

To my editors, Barbara Lalicki and Andrew Harwell: you have cheered, guided, and watched over me. I've become a better writer because of you, and I will be eternally grateful. The same goes for the entire team at HarperTeen and EpicReads. How is it possible that so many rock stars work in one place?

To my agent, Catherine Drayton, who I can always trust to be honest but also encouraging. I know I'm in good hands with you! And to foreign rights agent extraordinaire, Lyndsey Blessing—thank you for keeping an eye on my books across many borders.

To the most beautiful child and loving husband a woman could ever want. Wyatt and Robert, you are my angels, and I will love you both forever. In the immortal words of Bryan Adams, everything I do, I do it for you.

To my mother, Karen Stine, who is simultaneously my guardian angel, Jiminy Cricket, and best friend. I love you so very much.

To my father, Dennis Stine, thank you for every fairy tale, fantasy, horror story, and fable you read to me, from the crib days until the night that I insisted I read them myself. Without them, I wouldn't be the well-adjusted weirdo I am today.

To Jinx Hudson, thank you for making me one of your own.

To Melissa Allgood and Kris Beery, the sisters I met as an adult but will keep for the rest of my life.

To Amy Plum, Josephine Angelini, Tessa Gratton, Natalie Parker, and Anna Carey: oh how I love my Wenches of Wereboar. Duck in a Can for you all!

To Beth Prykryl, Andi Newby, Jason Brown, Krissy Carlson, Tony Andre, and so many more: your support and friendship mean more to me than you can know. To Matt Berery, thanks for giving me one job that allows me time to do another. To Dave Luke, because he asked.

And finally, to my brilliant, kind, enthusiastic readers—thank you, thank you, thank you! I'm so glad you're on this journey with me.